BOURBON STREET BURN

SOMMERVILLE SUSPENSE

ANASTASIA AMOR

BRODT PUBLISHING

Brodt Publishing
AnastasiaAmor.com
Anastasia.Amor@hotmail.com

By ANASTASIA AMOR

ADIE STURM MYSTERIES:

A Corpse for Cozumel
Days of the Dead
The Curse of the Carnaval
Dead Delicious

SOMMERVILLE SUSPENSE:

PARANORMAL FANTASY SERIES
Havana Heat
Bourbon Street Burn

EROTIC ROMANCE

Exploring Irresistible

Praise for ANASTASIA AMOR
ADIE STURM MYSTERIES

A CORPSE FOR COZUMEL
"The suspense starts in the first few pages and continues until the very end. The strong, sexy characters and intense sexual tension keep you wanting more…great read that's hard to put down." —*Two Lips Reviews*

DAYS OF THE DEAD
"Funny – or maybe just weird situations abound. This is a fun read, and will be very welcomed by fans of the series." —*Long And Short Reviews*

THE CURSE OF THE CARNAVAL: *Epic Award Nominee*
"*Sensual…an excellent suspense read … "—Readers' Favorite*

DEAD DELICIOUS: *Global Nominee*
"A great book for a day on the beach or a night in front of the fire – any time you are ready for some hot action and steamy sex." —*Readers' Favorite*
"Highly Recommended! Anastasia Amor is truly the queen of steamy mysteries." — Natalie G. Owens, *An Eternity of Roses.*
"Entertaining!""—*ChrisChatReviews*

SOMMERVILLE SUSPENSE SERIES
HAVANA HEAT
"…a one of a kind tale that will immediately draw you in with its enchanting allure. There is quite a lot going on in the story, but Anastasia Amor seamlessly blends it all into one thrilling tale and keeps it feeling authentic. Anastasia perfectly captures the essence of Cuba and it is evident that she has a deep understanding of the region she chose as the background to this amazing tale. Through her words, you can perfectly picture the setting and feel the genuine spirit of Cuba. Once you pick this book up, you will not put it down. It is original and very well delivered." —*Readers' Favorite*

"Fast paced and drop dead sexy, Amor's writing style hits all the right spots for me. You're going to love this, and trust me, the romance on these pages queen of steamy mysteries." — Natalie G. Owens, *An Eternity of Roses.*
"Entertaining!""—*ChrisChatReviews*

BOURBON STREET BURN: Suspense, spirits and romance in haunted New Orleans.

Chapter 1: THE FOOL

Shimmering vintage bourbon enhanced with Peychaud's bitters, a dash of quality French Absinthe and the pièce de résistance—a squeeze of lime. With one slight change it was his concept. Rene sniffed, tossing a strand of black hair back from his forehead. He knew his version was more popular than Antoine's. So what if he was a fraud for using their recipe. Stealing paid off. The wealthiest citizen of New Orleans, Jean Lafitte, was the most notorious pirate of them all. Lafitte gave them what they wanted, just like Rene Renard.

Tilting his glass to the light, the restaurateur admired the sparkling shades of bronze before bringing the Sazerac to his lips and throwing it back. The liquor burned his throat, searing its way down and finally punching his gut like exploding dynamite. Rene coughed, quickly reaching for the white linen handkerchief tucked in his breast pocket. After wiping his mouth he examined the red-stained cloth before tossing it on the table in disgust. Pushing the dinner plate loaded with steamed oysters away, he jiggled the table to steady himself and stood to his full height of six feet.

Staggering to the stairway Rene gripped the wooden railing tightly, teetering up the winding staircase, his tall frame casting a wobbly shadow on the creamy wall. At the landing he paused to stare at an oil painting in an elaborate gilded frame. In a high-waisted lacy peach gown, a silk wrap over one tawny shoulder, the blonde exuded a deliberate air of sexuality. The artist had painted her so that no matter where the viewer stood, her eyes would follow. They were bewitching eyes, a brilliant azure as blue as the Gulf.

Like a bloom on the verge of opening, she waited for a single glimmer of sunlight, a ray to pierce through the clouds. He would never be that ray. She had made sure of that.

On the upper floor he paused to catch his breath and gaze at the excessively decorated room he admired. The larger than life Egyptian statue at the entrance stood proudly, arms crossed, ebony eyes glimmering with ancient wisdom. The pharaoh wore a shoulder-length headdress, made of tiny rivulets of black embedded in gold, and a floor-length robe, blue triangles scattered down to a round base.

Inside the lounge, tasseled Moroccan pillows in turquoise and bronze silk were artfully scattered on red velvet couches and a leopard print settee. Above the furniture hung a row of oil paintings, pretty ladies cheeks dotted brightly with rouge, wearing cap-sleeved gowns in the post-French revolutionary style.

Rene grimaced at the irony. The fashionable women on these walls were whores rounded up in Paris, shipped as cargo to New Orleans and put to work in brothels, yet their squalid lives were far better than the guillotined aristocrats, their heads impaled on pikes, eyes blindly staring over the entrance of the royal palace.

The blood bath in France caused a domino effect all the way to the colony of Santo Domingo. Revolution wrought havoc on the island. When the slaves set fire to the family plantation, Rene's father abandoned his wife but took her jewels and little Rene to safety.

In a small ship, along with other free men and merchants, they sailed to New Orleans, a city of opportunity for enterprising individuals. It wasn't long afterwards, Rene Senior married and little Rene's life became a living hell.

His stepmother whipped him into obedience for minor infractions before she ended the marriage and headed north up the Mississippi with an American steamboat captain. Deserted, Rene Senior's fascination with bourbon grew as did his negligence of his son.

Celisse, his father's mistress, invariably locked him in a closet while her lover, a brawny blacksmith built like a bull and hung like a horse, came to visit. Their raunchy couplings progressed from wall to bed and ended on the cold, marble floor. Through the crack in the door Rene learned about sex as Celisse made the bull her beast, whipping him on the buttocks before throwing the belt away to tear off her dress. When Celisse shrieked like a banshee, claws embedded in the big man's back, the rutting would come to an abrupt end. Yet young Rene had to wait, wondering anxiously if she would let him out before he wet himself.

Rene grew to be suavely attractive to the ladies, but that was on the outside. Inside, a river of rage coursed through his veins. He hated women. Most of all he despised Marie Laveau, the Voodoo Queen with her superior airs. When he recklessly voiced his thoughts, a chicken head, grave dust and the guts of an animal were left in a cloth bag on his doorstep.

Rene knew he was going down. Phlegm gathered in his mouth. He spat on the floor as if to rid himself of the Voodoo curse.

Rene was Creole, his ancestors French and Spanish, and somewhere in his Dominican roots there was a black grandmother. None of that mattered for a majority of New Orleans' citizens. Mixed blood was the norm but high society intermarried to maintain a pure lineage. Rene found that out when he became interested in a French landowner's daughter, the pretty Chanel de Jardin, a minx who was definitely not as virginal as she pretended. Her family thought he wasn't good enough but Chanel had a mind of her own. She teased him relentlessly in her provocative gowns. One day, Rene cornered the fake virgin and gave her what she wanted.

Chanel cried rape. The community believed the lady. Rene was a restaurateur with a dubious pedigree. He was promptly arrested. His only chance to escape jail was to hire the woman whom he hated. In return, Marie Laveau wanted the deed for a house on Rampart Street.

The next morning gris-gris was left on the judge's chair. Chanel recanted and fell head-over-heels in love with Rene. Their nuptials were the event of the season. Within a year Chanel gave birth to a son they called Robert.

Shortly afterwards, Chanel caught the dreaded yellow fever and died. Rene pretended he was grief-stricken but deep down he was relieved. He had Chanel's wealth to squander at the tables or so he thought, until Marie Laveau told Rene he owed her. Chanel's death was Marie Laveau's doing and now she wanted the restaurant. Stupidly, Rene ignored her. He had ideas that would make him rich that didn't include a partner.

Although fine dining was a pastime New Orleans' residents enjoyed, it didn't pay nearly enough. Rene supplemented his income with prostitution and drugs. The lounge in which he stood, resplendent in rich reds accented with gold, was the place where men chose a girl and smoked the hookah. The other rooms were for gambling, or buying stolen goods.

From a shelf Rene reached for a decanter of bourbon and poured three fingers of the deep brown liquor into a glass. Out of his jacket pocket he pulled a flask of laudanum, brought it to his thick lips, and slurped noisily. Rene followed that with a bourbon chaser.

Like bullets from a firing squad, stomach acid drilled his gut. In seconds the chemicals compounded, numbing him as smoothly as creamy rich butter spread on a fresh baguette. His mind detached from his body and he floated on a fluffy cloud, slipping into a state of euphoria. Like the Negroes singing at Congo Square, screeching at the top of their lungs, he felt *good*. He would miss the dancing, drugs and debauchery. A man guffawed grotesquely as a crystal highball glass vaulted in the air, crashing into the wall, shattering on the marble floor in a million clear fragments. Inside Rene's foggy brain he realized it was his own voice he heard.

From a burgundy curtain he wrenched a braided sash and laid it flat on a high table, forming an "S". He attempted to circle the rope, fumbling several times in frustration and ended up repeating the process, this time keeping his work tight. Knotting the end of the corded section, Rene let it hang loose while he tugged the opposite end into a sizeable loop.

With one hand he pulled a chair out and climbed up, holding the rope. Swaying slightly as the drugs numbed his body, Rene tossed the cord around the wooden beam above and tightened it before lowering the noose.

For a moment he considered a fresh start in Baton Rouge away from Marie Laveau's power. But deep down he knew his life was shattered like a wooden shack after a category four hurricane. A friendly game of bourré had turned out not so friendly—the cheater took his fortune as easily as he slit throats. There was no other option. Head through the noose he kicked the chair away, his last thought for vengeance. He was after all, *Renard, the fox!*

Legs dancing wildly, Rene's throat jammed. Like a bullfrog singing a sunset serenade, his eyes bulged out of their sockets, blood vessels erupting in rivers of red. A brown stain originating at the seat of his pants widened and streaked irregularly down his dangling legs to the top of his expensive gray-patterned alligator boots. Rene hung lifeless. Dead as a rattler snapped up in a gator turtle's jaws.

***

The clatter of hooves grew louder. Outfitted in a fancy, red leather harness, a feathered plume on its head, a gray mule trotted slowly forward, pulling a carriage, loaded with passengers. The driver wearing an old-fashioned buttoned-up white shirt tucked into breeches held up by suspenders was also the tour guide.

Coming to a stop, he shouted out, "We are in the French Quarter, folks, called the Vieux Carré. Rebuilt after the fire in the eighteenth century, the wooden houses were replaced with eighty-five square blocks of Spanish buildings."

The guide swept his hand in a grandiose gesture at the white L-shaped structure on Chartres Street. "Y'all is lookin' at the oldest survivin' buildin' of the Great Fire, the Ursuline Convent. Worth a visit, folks."

He shouted over his shoulder, "Y'all heard of Bourbon Street? Anyone been to Lafitte's Blacksmith Shop?" There was a rumbling reply from one of the passengers. "Yup, nothing like Nola tap beer or try the New O'leans' Hurricane cocktail, ladies."

The tour guide's voice took on that sing-songy tone that guides have from repeating the same story day after day. "Lafitte's Blacksmith Shop on Bourbon was owned by our most respected pirate, Jean Lafitte. He was a hero in the war against the Brits. No one knows how he died but his spirit has been seen at the Blacksmith Shop." The rest of his commentary was lost as the mule clipped away.

Bourbon Street attracted tourists like flies to a praline. A Mecca of strip clubs and bars. They flocked there for a buzz or to scam a loser who had one. Drugs, murder and crooked politics in New Orleans was the reason for the Big Sleazy handle. With each horrifying death a ghost took up residence.

I was standing on Ursulines Avenue where the taxi had dropped me at the corner across from the convent. Its high white walls towered majestically over the formal manicured gardens. The right wing of the convent had long rectangular glass windows edged with fully-operational shutters on the first floor matching those on the second floor. Higher up the brown-shingled roof held six tightly closed casements.

The opposite wing had a series of arched stained-glass windows and most likely contained a chapel. I could imagine the pews filled with nuns in black habits kneeling in prayer, in search of answers.

Like them, I needed a solution. Each night my brain burned as if attacked by a swarm of Louisiana fire ants. The nightmares were slowly eating away my life. Inevitably, I had to go to New Orleans.

The Hotel Memoire, the lettering in scripted gold on a green awning, billowed in the breeze over the doorway of the red brick building weathered with age. Inside, through the glass doors, the lobby was situated to the left. A chunky girl who would have looked more comfortable behind the wheel of a Massey-Ferguson tractor stood behind an antique desk, her head bowed over a ledger. The cropped fuchsia tank, distressed low-cut jeans, along with rows of blue tattooed skeletons on her forearm reminded me the "Q" in Quarter stood for quirky. Pushing back a strand of candy floss hair from her silver eyebrow ring, she directed me to the bakery across the street while she arranged for my room to be readied.

The early Toronto flight, blah airport food, and a long boring wait at O'Hare browsing shops geared to Cubs fans, made the trip to New Orleans about as enjoyable as a root canal. Once I left my suitcase with the desk clerk, I didn't exactly bolt across the street but I managed an enthusiastic trudge towards the fragrant baking scents wafting in the air.

At a window table I sank into a retro plastic chair, the plush aqua seat held up by a metal frame. Stirring two packets of sweetener into my coffee, I revisited the dream which haunted my nights.

As an experienced bartender I recognized the sparkling bronze of the Sazerac cocktail in the man's hand. It was found exclusively in New Orleans. Now I had to find the hotel where he killed himself.

Reflectively, I tipped my cup and sipped the bitter brew. Caffeine jolted the spark plugs in my motor, revving all the way to my starter, but I needed more. As I picked up the freshly baked chocolate beignet I told myself how stupid I was to be eating it. The gluten in the wheat would do a number on my gut. But that would be later and right now I needed the chocolate.

Silky cocoa wrapped in a delightful doughnut slowly melted from the heat of my mouth. I held it in as long as I could before reluctantly swallowing what could only be described as the nectar of the gods. I am a chocoholic. Restraint is not part of my MO, modus operandi, or in plain English, method of operation.

"Stop, fool! They won't let you into karate with a muffin top!" My Logical Voice barked in my brain like Tommy the Trainer.

Really? Ripped power machines—in karate? More like toothpicks or big boys with beer guts. Good luck making the cover of "Men's Health", guys.

There was another female in the club, a slim brunette training to take down her ex. She had a snowball's chance in hell. Women lacked the upper body strength. Her best defense was to scream and run. If she lucked out, a strike to the junk would take the three hundred pound SOB to his knees, sniveling like a baby, and give her a chance to get away and stay alive.

I'm petite. Pushups, squats and kicks gave me muscle but didn't alter the fact I'm a light-weight. It also did nothing for my love life. Men are wild about pencil-thin girls with sky-high legs to their armpits poured into tiny spandex dresses.

My Hormone Voice sighed. "A real man appreciates a woman like you. And what about passion? Those bulimic super models haven't got a clue about that."

Hormone was right. I had passion and more importantly attitude. Logical could chug-a-lug protein shakes loaded with kale and berries. I had *the* super antioxidant—chocolate. My brain released a pleasure bomb as I swallowed with more gusto than a starving bag lady camped out behind a McDonalds' dumpster. A lethal tweak of white powder had nothing on this cocoa explosion. My psychic senses flew into a state of heightened awareness. Flinging the door open like Wonder Woman on Red Bull, I powered across the road.

Ursulines Avenue was an urban sauna, moist heat seeping through the crumbling sidewalk cracks like steam rising from an overboiling kettle. I was a mess. My sweat-coated arms shone like Gulf water after a major oil spill.

Once inside, the Hotel Memoire was considerably cooler, a trace of air conditioning escaping from the lobby. The hallway had vintage décor. A worn Oriental rug carpeted the corridor where a small antique wooden table partnered with French Provincial chairs.

The spacious hallway gave me a start until I realized it was an optical illusion created by a mirror on the wall. Glancing at my reflection, I could see the hairspray had failed. My hair had the limp look of overcooked spaghetti. As I wiped a speck of mascara away from my cheek a woman appeared behind me.

Piercing onyx eyes, a short broad nose and plump lips, made for an attractive face until her upper lip curled into a snarl. When her long tapered fingers reached out to grab my shoulder, I backed off and then remembering my karate training, raised my arm to block her. There was no need. The woman swept down the hall, as if propelled by a silent motor. She disappeared around the bend, leaving the passageway frigidly cold like the inside of a meat freezer, a musky smell of over-ripe peaches lingering in the air.

I had that gut ache I get when I'm super nervous but Anabelle Sommerville is not a coward. Mr. Alligator Boots from my nightmare might be connected to Peaches the ghost. Nasty as she was, I had to confront her. For protection I gripped the turquoise stone on the silver chain around my neck, gave it a quick squeeze and rushed after her, down the corridor to a light airy room opening onto an inner courtyard scented with Bougainvillea.

Golden light filtered through the trees onto the balconies and into the garden, a magical hidden patch of rain forest in a concrete city. A stone cupid spotted with green algae spouted water in a high arch into a pool surrounded by hibiscus trees, moisture wetly coating the broad leaves and open orange flowers. The unpleasant smell of rotting peaches was gone and to my inward relief so was the ghost.

When I retraced my steps to the lobby, a blonde cherub had replaced the farm girl at the desk. She wore a sleeveless blue print sundress scattered with daisies, one bare bicep notched with a detailed brown yin-yang tattoo.

By the window two thirtyish brunettes sat at a table. One looked like a young Sly Stallone, heavy-lidded brown eyes and a boxer build, broad shoulders encased in a "Who Dat" sweatshirt. Her head was shaved to a fuzz with the exception of the bangs fringing her eyes. Across from her, an ebony-haired beauty with the delicate features of a Russian gymnast sipped coffee, a pinky tilting upwards.

When I set my bag down the desk clerk gave me a gap-toothed smile.

"Where y'at?" she said. "I'm Sandra."

"Hey. I'm Anabelle Sommerville."

"You phoned?"

I nodded.

8

The cherub glanced down, muttering to herself distractedly, a look of consternation as if the ledger was written in Klingon. She flipped pages forward and back as she sang in a squeaky off-key voice, a pop song about a tiger.

I cleared my throat, hoping to draw her attention back to me without appearing rude.

Her dark brown eyes flicked up and she said, "There might be something."

I was worried. "I reserved a room weeks ago. When I came here earlier the girl told me to go to the bakery while she arranged it."

"Jenny Ellen?"

"Pink hair?"

"Um-hm." Sandra glanced back at the ledger, a pearly fingertip trailing to the middle of the page. "You have the courtyard room." She stared off into space a moment before she began to write a notation in the ledger.

"Wait. I need to ask you something."

Sandra perused my face.

"What I'm about to say may seem odd but I had a premonition to come here." At this point I was sure I sounded like a nutjob but I continued, conscious of the brunettes from the window table listening in. "I envisioned a white clawed bathtub with a pedestal sink, a shower and toilet in the corner. The walls were a deep purple with white trim. Would that be the courtyard room?"

"No-oo. Sounds like the balcony bathroom, described to a 't'." She smiled broadly. "Say, ya must be psychic."

"I'm a witch," I blurted out. It was meant to be a joke, but from the silence in the room I got the distinct impression the women took me seriously.

Sandra chirped happily, "How awesome. You know I've met Voodoo priestesses before but a witch right here?" She shook her head in wonder. "I am so into it. Voodoo, Wicca, you name it." Leaning her elbows down on the desk, she said confidentially, "I've had my aura read."

Auras surround people in soft colors extending from their body to several feet beyond. I was lucky. Sometimes I saw them.

"The priestess said my aura was olive green." Sandra's lips twisted in a frown. Her forefinger tapped the book with what I took to be displeasure.

I focused on Sandra. Light filmed her body and a yellow haze extended from her figure. My words came out in one breath. "I see yellow—a bright daffodil yellow."

Sandra grinned. "Aw-ww, cool. What does that mean?"

"You are in a joyful space in your life."

"That's so much better. I'll give ya an upgrade to the balcony room suite. Same price." She handed me a plastic key card.

"Thank you. Wonderful."

Avoiding my eyes she glanced nervously back at the ledger, her lips pressed together.

Chapter 2: TEMPERANCE

My suitcase barely fit into the small tapestry-upholstered elevator. From its appearance, I guessed the narrow chamber was built in the early part of the nineteenth century. I pressed the button labeled "4" and waited. The elevator groaned dangerously as it lurched up to the fourth floor. A sign inside read: "Treat her as you would your grandmother. She is old".

With a thud the lift shuddered to a halt. The door opened to narrow carpeted steps leading to a landing. At the top the metal door plates read "400" and "401". I stuck the plastic key card into the left slot and pushed the door ajar.

Sunlight filtered in from the balcony door window. The room was furnished with a lace-covered daybed, two green and gold brocade chairs and a wooden table, the legs carved in curves, feet ending in claws. A black and white family portrait dated to a by-gone era hung above the day bed in a wooden frame, the print worn and peeling.

A solid white door opened to another room painted ivory, embellished with an Egyptian print wall-paper border but what caught my attention was the king-sized bed, high like a "Princess and the Pea" bed done up in fluffy green pillows, emerald sheets and a matching duvet. The suite was much larger than a single room and must have cost considerably more.

Fronting the bed, two wing chairs upholstered in gold brocade stood on either side of a round wooden table. A copy of the Times-Picayune lay on the tabletop beside the hotel phone.

French doors opened to another balcony, between a row of high windows, all curtained by heavy red brocade. On the opposite wall, a flat-screen television sat alongside a mirror on a long dresser. I walked past a high chest of drawers and entered the bathroom.

It was exactly the way I'd pictured it. A pedestal mirrored sink, a toilet and a shower took up the corner. A white porcelain bathtub on lion-clawed feet was situated in the center of the room, a jar of sea salts and a bar of soap perched on the bathtub ledge. If I wasn't so anxious to eat, I would have filled up the tub and taken a leisurely bath.

About to slip off my dress and pop into the shower, I heard a knock. I traced my way back into the outer room and swung the door open.

With a grin, Sandra said, "Ya mind me visitin'?"

"Come on in." I was surprised but shouldn't have been since I blurted out I was a witch. I waved her to the wing chair.

Sandra made herself comfortable. From her skirt pocket she pulled out a small silver case. "Okay for me to smoke?"

"Cigarette?" I didn't particularly want my room reeking of tobacco but I owed her one.

Sandra dug into her pocket and flipped out a doobie. "No, weed," she said, sweeping the joint from side to side.

This was getting more and more like a trip down the rabbit hole. I opened the balcony door in anticipation of the sweet odor and plopped into the other chair, prepared to go with the flow.

My guest was not a first-timer. She withdrew a pink-floral Bic lighter and brought the thickly rolled reefer in brown cigar paper to her lips, lighting it in that efficient way users acquire over a period of time. After puffing rapidly to get the joint going, she hesitantly started her story.

"My daughter and I lived with mom west of Canal on the upper floor of a restaurant. It wasn't fancy but suited us. One night I was working late so I stayed here with my daughter. Dana was four." Lines etched her forehead as she exhaled slowly.

She passed me the joint. I inhaled and waited for her to continue.

"This calms me and takes the pain away. After the divorce, my ex gained custody."

"You don't ever see her?"

"He's from a prominent Louisiana family." She blew a smoke ring. "He won't allow it."

"I'm so sorry. Have you seen a lawyer?"

"He has money. Enough to make my life hell if I fight him." Sandra leaned back, her expression wistful.

"Put positive thoughts out there. It will help."

With a deep drag, Sandra exhaled, her face losing the tense lines between her brows. "Thanks, Anabelle. It's a charming name by the way." She passed the blunt. "I've been thinking about changing my name. Do ya think I should call myself Sandra or Sandie?"

"You don't like Sandra?" I inhaled and handed the joint back.

"Ya think Sandie is too much?"

12

I examined her fresh, youthful face. "No, you make a good Sandie."

Sandra leaned back against the chair, the cherry-tip glowing brightly. "I'll be Sandie from now on." Holding up the reefer, she said, "Say, Anabelle, those women downstairs wanted ya to give them a reading."

I shook my head. Even though I could sense things, I was hardly ready for actual readings.

Sandra nodded, her lids half-mast, smoke escaping her lips. "That's okay. Told them to leave you alone."

A sense of peace came over me much like a soldier on leave but with the realization that the enemy was out there in the form of Peaches and Mr. Alligator Boots. Eventually, I would have to battle them or go crazy from lack of sleep. "Why did you give me this suite, Sandie?"

She regarded me intently. "To tell the truth, Anabelle, ya kind of blew me away, being a witch and all."

I raised an eyebrow.

"I feel a connection like you're a sista from anotha mista. And you are gorgeous."

"Oh-hh," I said, taken aback by the compliment. "Thank you."

Abruptly, the room chilled and a haze of white formed by the window. The stench of over-ripe peaches filled the air. A woman appeared, in a flimsy, long white dress, her lightly tanned shoulders bare.

"Who are you?" I whispered, trying to keep the fear at bay.

Her coal black eyes pierced me like a knife. "My name is Delphine."

"Why are you here?" I managed.

"Because of you!" The apparition picked up the ashtray from the table and threw it against the wall. Miraculously, the glass landed in one piece on the floor.

Chills ran through me.

"Anabelle!" Sandie's voice was faint as if she was far away.

Delphine's hazy form filtered into sunlight pixelating like a badly coded download.

Sandy squeezed my shoulder. "You okay?"

I was surprised to find myself standing beside Sandie looking down at the ashtray, intact but for a hairline crack. "Just now I saw a spirit woman wearing a long white gown."

Sandie's eyes widened. "She's a poltergeist. Do you think you're in danger?"

My fingertips were so cold I warmed them in my palms. "I can handle her," I whispered. There was a reason I was here or I wouldn't have visualized this very suite.

My eyes flicked to Sandie. A putrid green crept like a snake into her yellow aura. I had the distinct feeling Sandie was keeping something from me. I was picking up a ton of anxiety. "Talk to me."

Crushing the tip of the joint into the ashtray on the floor, Sandie tilted her head up. "Why did you come to the Quarter?"

"Something in my past life is reaching out for me. I'm convinced I can find the answers here."

"So ya came alone?"

"You mean without a man?" My stomach twisted in a knot, thinking about him. The breakup had been bad and if I didn't solve this mystery I'd have a financial nightmare to return to, maybe even lose my share in the restaurant. "There was one."

"I get it." She muttered, "Dicks," under her breath.

I met her eyes. "Your turn."

Sandie's eyes flicked around the room nervously. "Maybe as a witch ya can deal with them better than I could." She stared at her fingertips.

"The spirits?"

"I don't like coming into this room alone, especially at night. Scares the crap out of me." Her eyes averted to the door between the master bedroom and the sitting room, "They slam that door over and over." She shuddered. "Could be a logical explanation like a draft 'cept Dana saw them." Her eyes nervously flit to the master bedroom. "I should go." Sandie took the pen from the table and scribbled on the pad. "My cell number." Making a quick exit, she clicked the door shut behind her.

A gusty breeze shook the balcony door, flinging it wide open against the wall. I left it that way and started towards the other room. As I came to the heavy wooden door between the rooms it slammed shut inches from my face. A twist of the knob and a push did nothing. Putting my body weight behind it all the way, I forced my way into the master bedroom. Curious as to why it was so difficult, I stared at a row of nails at the top of the frame pointing downwards as if someone wanted to keep something out.

Inside the master bedroom the balcony doors were open. Sunlight filtered on the green cover of the bed in a cloudy haze. Before my eyes a man's form appeared. He was stretched out the full length of the bed, his hands clasped behind his neck, long muscular legs encased in tan pants, tucked into high boots. That part looked great. The rest of him was perfect. Dark hair curled onto his forehead from under a blue bi-corne hat. A loose long-sleeved cotton shirt open to his broad chest covered a pair of wide shoulders. When I stared his eyes verdant as forest foliage looked curious as if he was not sure of what he saw.

Shapely lips curled into a smile. "Bonjour, cher," he said in a deep voice. "I thought you'd never come."

"What the heck!"

His laugh was as charming as his low voice was sexy. "Come sit with me." He patted the duvet.

I was speechless.

"You haven't changed much. A little blonder but just as beautiful. Those turquoise earrings bring out that unusual blue of your eyes."

I sank down on the edge of the bed and glanced up. He had a strong face, a significant chin, and a slightly crooked nose, handsome in an interesting way. "Tell me why you are here."

"To see you." With a quick tug he pulled his hat off. "Such pink cheeks. Are you blushing, cher?" He added something in another language.

"What language are you speaking? It sounds strange."

"Perfectionist," he said, with a teasing grin. "Truthfully, no one speaks proper French here." He shrugged his shoulders. "It's New O'leans. We're criminals from France, slaves from Santo Domingo, free blacks, deported Acadians from Canada—" He trailed off and gave me a direct look. "I entirely understand how you must be conscious of our faulty French being Parisian."

This was news to me. "How did you ever get that idea?"

Suddenly, he jumped off the bed, bowed deeply, sweeping the air with his hat. "My apologies, cher. You obviously don't remember a thing. Let me introduce myself. Alain Ducoeur, at your service."

My first impression was this was not a regular sort of guy,

besides the fact that he spoke with an odd accent. On the dresser I spotted a pistol and at his waist there was a knife. Major clues. I looked around again for a sword but didn't see one. Besides being a ghost, he most certainly was a pirate.

My second impression was that he was tall. No surprise there. Men, and I might also add most women, have a few inches on me. My glance swept over the debonair pirate ghost. "I am Anabelle Sommerville." I held out my hand.

"A pleasure." He took my hand and kissed my wrist. He motioned to the bed. "With your permission?" Not waiting for my reply he sat down beside me. "Chocolate?" From his pocket he pulled out a bonbon, unwrapped it, and presented it to my lips. "You will love this."

My resistance is nonexistent when it comes to chocolate. The sinfully-rich chocolate melted slowly, trickling dark delight down my throat. As the elixir kicked in, my mouth reluctantly released it and I mumbled, "That was wonderful. Thank you. But why chocolate?"

He grinned widely. "I know your addiction and what it does to you, cher. Frankly, I want to kiss those beautiful lips." And with that his lips caressed mine as softly as the touch of butterfly wings.

Astonished, I pulled away. "Shouldn't you be on the other side?"

He turned his head towards the doorway, displaying a handsome Hollywood profile. "You mean in there?" he said with a grin, motioning to the other room. "No, definitely not. I paid Delphine plenty. Besides, I like this bed."

"Tell me about Delphine."

"The angry vixen who owns this establishment?"

Delphine had appeared to me twice. I had a feeling Ducoeur knew all about her and why she was presenting herself to me. Grabbing his sleeve, I pulled his arm down forcing him to gaze into my eyes. "Please, Alain, she bothers me."

He laughed. "Never mind that troublesome female." A forefinger stroked the area between my brows." She's not worth causing frown lines." He took my hand and drew it up to his lips. "You know me," he said, before caressing my wrist tenderly, "very well indeed. And now that you're back here in New O'leans I want you to get to know me all over again."

Suddenly, the middle door banged shut. I nearly jumped out of my skin. Sandie had warned me a draft could cause the doors to slam or were there more spirits? My thoughts trailed off. I looked back at the devastatingly handsome Alain Ducoeur or what was left of him—an orange haze. An impression was left on the duvet and the air inside was warm and balmy, a hint of sea breeze lingering.

Chapter 3: THE MAGICIAN

I left. It was not because Alain Ducoeur scared the bejesus out of me. Really, it wasn't. History intrigues me. Who was I kidding? The pirate spirit was sexy as all get out. There's nothing like a man of mystery to charge my battery. But this was creepy. Alain Ducoeur was dead.

When the elevator shuddered to a stop on the main floor, I heaved a sigh of relief. I was almost free and clear. My fingers smoothed over the turquoise stone pendant. Turquoise is protection for the wearer, especially for a Sagittarius and from the looks of fierce dark-eyed Delphine and her drama I might need it.

The front door opened to oppressive humidity. Concrete sidewalks aligned with the street joined up with more concrete and only touches of green trees broke the gray. Hell couldn't be hotter than this.

Instinct pushed me towards Chartres Street. A block down, I turned onto Governor Nicholls Street. The houses here were soothing shades of neutral and earth. When I passed a doorway with messages to Angelina scrawled in red felt pen it dawned on me the gray building was the Angelina Jolie condo. As awesome as this was I needed to forget about a-listers and find out where the man in my nightmare had hung himself.

At the corner, a metal plaque on a residence explained the cross street was once called "Real". The three-story building, windows draped, had such an eerie vibe I wondered if this was it. Scooting across the street I approached the two dusky-skinned men in T-shirts and jeans sitting on a stoop.

"Excuse me. Can you tell me anything about that house?" I pointed to the gloomy mansion.

They stared up. At first I thought they didn't speak English but then the small man resembling a rodent, hair mottled like a squirrel's summer fur, wrung his hands together as if he were squeezing a walnut and said, "It's haunted."

Well that summed it up. I gritted my teeth and stared at the other guy hoping he could share a little more.

Sadly obese, haunches spread over most of the stoop, leaving the tiniest portion for his little buddy, his doughy cheeks quivered as he whispered, "Evil place that. Madam Lalaurie and her hubby tortured slaves. Firefighters found bodies and mutilated folks on the third floor. They wanted to lynch the Lalauries but the police let them escape. No one kin live there no more." He slowly rubbed the cross strung on a row of black and white beads around his neck between his thumb and forefinger and closed his eyes as if in silent prayer.

Squirrel muttered, "The dude who bought it got cursed. Even after he moved away to run his dead daddy's restaurant the black magic stayed. He lost everything."

My eyes flicked to the house flowing with dark energy. "There's more, isn't there?"

Squirrel crossed himself. "Dude hung himself."

I knew it! "Do you know where that restaurant was?"

He shivered as if talking about it would bring a curse down on him. "Still is, but that dude is long dead and gone."

I looked at Jabba the Hut.

"Ain't no good come out of you goin' there, girlie." His eyes sank back into their sockets, pupils like tiny black pin-heads.

"Thanks," I said.

Crossing back, I passed the Lalaurie House walking briskly, trying to make as much space between me and the negative force radiating from the gray walls as soon as possible. I didn't need any of that energy on me.

The encounter with the men threw me off so much I almost missed him. In a red borg-lined basket on a window ledge, a cat, gray stripes on his back, white legs and chest, and a white-tipped tail was stretched out. The massive cat was incredibly long. I was compelled to go in.

The bell on the door jingled as I swung it open. A slim young man in a lab coat, his hair styled in a military cut came forward to greet me. "Hello, I'm Doctor Rou. May I help you?"

"Hi. I couldn't help but notice your cat. Would it be all right to pet him?"

If the vet thought the request was strange, he didn't let on. "I'm sure he would enjoy that." He glanced over at the tabby and the feline nodded as if in assent.

As I scratched the big guy's chin and looked into a pair of

hypnotic slanted eyes, I understood why medieval people feared cats. Felines can be daunting. When my cat Minnie stares unblinkingly, her vibrant green eyes message telepathically, warning me of danger. Her instincts are right on and I felt this large feline had the same intuitive ability, yet Minnie's noble brown-tipped nose was nothing like this boy's mystical wine-red triangle. Together with his gigantic size and demeanor, this feline was almost alien in appearance.

Lightly stroking the jungle cat's head my thoughts turned to Zee, my newly rescued tuxedo cat, golden eyes, round as globes and a pitiful meow that begs attention. What Zee lacked in brains he made up with affection, a rumbling purr relieving my stress in seconds. If ever I found a man who was a combo of those two, I'd be head over heels.

"You don't need men," Logical said stoically. "Stick to your mission and you'll know why that idiot killed himself and then you can go home and find a nice Canadian boyfriend to settle down with. No, wait," she snickered, "you had one of those and you know how that worked out."

Hormone smirked. "The girl's single and open to possibilities."

Logical scoffed. "One night stands, you mean."

"Sh-hh," I muttered to the voices bickering in my brain when I noticed the brass name tag attached to the leather collar around the cat's neck. I turned to the vet busy scribbling notes at the desk. "This kitty's name is Morpheus?"

"The Greek God of Dreams."

This had to be a sign. My bet was Morpheus was channeling into my dream. I rubbed the cat's head and let my hand trail down his back. When I picked off a loose tuft of fur, Morpheus gave me the evil eye. Quickly, I withdrew my hand. That was definitely a cautionary warning. "Thanks for allowing me a visit," I said to the vet.

He stared intently. "You're psychic, aren't you?"

"I've been told so."

The vet's coal black eyes narrowed as if seeing something disquieting. "Good vibes to you."

"Thank you." As I left, I wondered if that's all I needed.

A couple arm in arm passed me in the street. I envied those

people walking through life in pairs doing everything with their soulmate. But if I was lonely for an instant all that was forgotten as I strolled down Royal Street.

Whimsical could only describe the parade of Spanish homes, balconies entertaining American flags mounted between black wrought iron railings, glittery Mardi Gras mannequins in gold lamé dresses, pirates in elaborate red wide-brimmed hats and ivory angel statues, wings spread ready for flight.

At the corner I came to a cross street where a forest green bungalow headed a myriad of colored homes from orange on one end of the spectrum to a gorgeous robin's egg blue. A click of my camera later I found myself stepping back as a woman of indeterminate age wearing a pale blue tank and a mid-calf denim cotton skirt pulled up on a bicycle.

"Oh, I'm so sorry," I said.

"That's quite all right," the woman said, stepping down and parking before swinging around to face me, taking me in through round wire-framed glasses. Her curly, auburn hair was windblown around a fresh rosy face, splattered with freckles. Off the bike, she stood tall and stocky. "I've been expecting you."

"You have?"

"I sensed a significant visitor."

Not knowing what to make of this I glanced back at the bright green house, bungalow style with green cement steps, black iron railing and a low-pitched black roof.

Through the front window I could see into a room furnished with a couch above which a green lace cross was fixed on the wall. A narrow purple candle was situated on a white tile floor where a pentagon within a circle was drawn in black.

"Nice house."

The woman smiled, her pert nose crinkling, and gestured to the row of houses. "You're not from here, are you?"

I shook my head.

"This is a camelback shotgun house. The frontage is narrow to avoid high taxes. The back's two-story. They say if you shoot a shotgun from the front it exits the back."

I nodded, hoping she'd tell me about the altar and the candle, but she parked her bike at the side of the steps and said, "They call me

Shotgun Sue."

I took her hand and shook it. "Anabelle. Why Shotgun?"

"Because of the house." She laughed. "Luckily, they didn't decide to nickname me Camelback. Sightseeing?"

"On my way to see Marie Laveau's tomb."

Sue scratched her chin thoughtfully. "Not a good place to go alone."

"Oh?"

"Not long ago, a woman was shot point blank in the face for the amount of money the kids could have pried out of a parking meter." She reached into her pocket and brought out a cell phone. When she started texting, I took that as a cue to leave.

As I started down the street Sue called out, "Wait, darlin'. Got a bodyguard for you. You'll love this man. Amusing and a talented photographer. He's keen to take pics. He'll meet you at the cafe on Royal. Cell number? "

A second later a text came in. *c u in 5. Markus*

The cynical side of me was wary, yet the way this happened made me believe it was fate. "Thank you, Sue. Appreciate it."

"Thank Markus."

"And I will know him how?"

"By the expensive camera." From the top step, Sue pointed to the cross street. "Go a block past St. Ann Street. It's on your right," she added, before clicking the screen door shut behind her.

On Royal Street, I saw a cafe similar to a popular Canadian standby. Timmy's is a tradition. The board above the counter was the menu but there the similarity ended. Grits, chili, Po Boys, and beignets were the headliners, followed by coffee and tea, presumably iced. A young cashier, a blue lion tattooed on his shaved head wore a brown apron over baggy shorts and a plaid shirt. He was making a latte and paid no attention to me.

At a table near the counter a pony-tailed Asian, sporting a black shirt and jeans hunched over a coffee. Across the table from him a woman with the dead eyes of a meth addict jiggled her chair up and down like a see-saw. Her torn Mickey-Mouse tank top hung loosely over torn jeans. She smelled like sour sweat and cheap perfume.

The couple glanced in my direction. "Where y'at?" the woman

said, her red lipsticked mouth parted to an orifice of black stubs. Her aura came in dark, almost black.

"Good, thanks," I said, backing away from the sketchy couple. I was ready to hit the street alone when something caught my eye. At the counter a brunette wavy hair to her waist, was making a T-shirt purchase—a cartoon dog in a NOPD police uniform arresting a cat in a burglar's mask. It looked cute.

"Buy one. It's for charity," a husky voice drawled over my shoulder.

"But it's for a guy," I said, to the trim tall man with beard stubble and black aviator sunglasses beside me. He was wearing an olive T-shirt, and khaki shorts. His hair was hidden under a charcoal toque tight to his head, a few dark curls escaping onto his neck. A heavy camera hung around his neck.

"No guy to buy for?"

I was about to cut him off when I clued in. "Hey, are you Markus?"

He grinned. "Anabelle?"

"Nice to meet you."

"Same here. Sue told me you needed an escort to the cemetery."

"Are you okay with that?"

"Sure." He grinned, his smile charismatic. "I don't mind at all. We could go now," he looked around, "unless you'd like a coffee first?"

"No, I'm good." I checked him out. Over six feet tall Markus had the build of a professional athlete and a smile that brightened a room. If this was a musical I'd be breaking out into a corny rendition of a "girl meets boy" Broadway tune. Luckily for everyone, I avoided embarrassing myself and followed Markus out the door.

Thick with locals and tourists, we maneuvered around posts and people. "I appreciate this," I said over the din.

"I wanted to take some photos of Louis No.1 anyway. Kind of a coincidence that Suzy texted me, isn't it?"

"You think it's dangerous?"

"New O'leans is. There was a shooting on Bourbon a while ago. Nine people hurt." His full lips curled into a smile. "Don't worry. You're with me."

"And if they have guns?"

Markus smiled, patting his jean pocket. "I have a device they don't sell in most places." He took out a silver pen from his pocket. "It's powerful chemical spray that could kill a bear. Got it in Montana."

When I made brown belt in karate the master said I was good. I could hold my own out in the street but I definitely felt better with an armed male in my corner.

Markus held up his elbow for me and I latched on. Walking together felt comfortable.

"You'll find this interesting. A couple of blocks from here there's a priest who keeps a record of killings."

I raised an eyebrow.

"Someone shoots someone from the Seventh Ward and the next day it's a random shooting in the Ninth."

"A war zone attitude."

His chin clenched. "Not much different than what I saw in Iraq. These kids have bad parenting. Discipline is a good whoopin'."

I got the distinct impression we were talking about his life. Mine wasn't as brutal, just lonely. After my father left, my mom got sick and died of cancer. I had sisters but we grew up with different foster parents and lost touch. But with every "yang" I believe there is a "yin". Even the worst experiences give something back.

At the corner perched on a stoop in front of a gift shop, an old black man, a felt hat on his head, wearing a red shirt under overalls strummed a guitar, singing a bluesy melody about his baby and how she'd left him. I had bills in my bra but no change. "You have anything for him?"

From his jean pocket Markus dug up coins and threw a handful into the open guitar case on the sidewalk. He jerked his chin to the cross street. "This is where we head north."

We hadn't gone more than a hundred feet when the rain started. A bar on the right advertised Bloody Marys, two for six dollars.

When the drops pelted down and the wind whipped up, Markus said, "Let's pop in here."

We settled on wooden low-back stools at a long round bar. It was a typical pub, dark inside with square tables, the patrons drinking beer. Right now we were the only ones at the bar. A teenage boy, scraggly brown hair falling over his face was washing glasses. A tall brunette with lengthy extensions came over.

"Two Bloody Marys," Markus said to Josie, the brunette bartender. I knew her name from the plastic name tag pinned just above the neckline of her tangerine lace top. She winked in answer.

At the back of the room a band made up of a white accordion player, black guitarist and mulatto drummer were warming up. A slim attractive girl with flaming orange hair, a board hanging from her neck, joined them.

"This band is different. What is that thing the girl has? It looks like something pioneer women used for scrubbing clothes."

"It's a *frottoir*. He flicked his eyes to the accordion player. "When the Germans came to New O'leans the accordion became part of the La La. The black Creoles added the blues. It's like gumbo soup. Itty bitty music bits mixed together."

The girl jumped around like a yo-yo on a string, hitting the spoons on the washboard while the old bearded white guy in a checked shirt and overalls sang the lyrics.

"La La, eh?"

"Called Zydeco, now."

A hefty blonde appeared carrying a violin. She joined in as a backup singer when she wasn't fiddling.

Outside a tropical storm poured buckets of rain. It cooled the street, but inside the atmosphere was hot. Patrons left their beers on the tables and partnered up to swing on the hardwood floor, dancing a two-step. I'd never seen anything like it.

Our drinks arrived. Gigantic red cocktails loaded with string beans soaked in tomato juice and vodka. The Bloody Mary hit me hard. I had questions for Markus but before I could speak he grabbed my hand.

"Let's dance."

A step to the left, a shake, and then a foot back. Sashaying back and forth, I caught on fast and negotiated a one-handed swing without falling flat on my face. Two songs later we returned to the bar breathless and laughing.

Leprechauns, green hats and a poster of "Brad Pitt for Mayor" decorated the bar. I pointed to the poster on the pillar next to me.

"What's this about?"

Markus' tone was serious. "Brad's a hero for the work he did after Katrina. The Quarter survived unlike the ninth ward. Just a swamp of dead people, animals and sewage there." He gazed at me steadily. "Where are you staying?"

I grinned. "Near Brad. A street down."

With his sunglasses now on the counter, a fine pair of dark-lashed hazel eyes met mine. The light from the lamp above reminded me of the sun as it disappears into the ocean with a flash of green. They say the green ray is lucky but scientists explain it away as an illusion. I didn't think Markus' eyes were anything but magical.

"What hotel?"

"Hotel Memoir" was barely out of my mouth when my jaw dropped. Markus pulled off his wool cap. It was like tearing the wrapping off a gift. Beats me why I thought he'd be bald. Touchable, dark waves tumbled onto his forehead. Drop dead edible.

Josie's eyes glazed over. She muttered "Doggone!" and glared resentfully at me before serving another customer.

I took another look at Markus over the rim of my glass. "So tell me about you."

Markus speared a bean and held it in his mouth the way I savor chocolate. "Well, I'm from Louisiana originally but lived out west the last few years. Came back two years ago. I'm interested in my family's French roots. The last few months I've searched the area. My last name is Cadeaux with an 'x'. Not the usual French spelling I was told."

"Oh, but it is." I felt myself blush. "In French it means presents."

Markus frowned. "I wish I knew more French." He leaned in. "Maybe you can teach me?"

"I'm not an expert." His eyes threw me off. I felt like a nervous teenager. I had forgotten how exciting it was to flirt.

Markus took his paper coaster and started folding it. "How is it you know French?"

"High school."

"Where?'

"The English part of Canada. My mom had German roots."

26

"And your dad?"

"Spanish. He left when I was two." I tipped back my glass, the spice nipping my lips. "I've forgotten a lot of the German I learned and even more French."

"I admire your abilities. I wish I could speak another language."

Feeling the kick of the cocktail, my words came out slowly. "Did you like it out west?"

"Louisiana is home." He contemplated his drink. "What do you do there in Canada?"

"Mostly I'm a chef in a restaurant."

"Interesting?"

"Not like here."

He nodded, his eyes far away.

I wondered what he was thinking. He was too hard to read.

Glancing outside, Markus said, "Rain's stopped, Anabelle. Let's see No. 1 before it closes."

The brunette bartender peered over at us. "Y'all want another?"

"No, thanks." As delicately as I could I dug into my bra and tugged out a ten. "Drinks are on me."

Markus lifted an eyebrow.

"No purse, no robbery."

His eyes swept to my cleavage and winked. "I wouldn't be so sure of that."

The sun climbed out from behind fluffy clouds, rays of gold streaming into a rainbow of red and violet in the distance. There were only a few blocks left to walk. As we headed to the edge of the Quarter, the sidewalk crowd thinned and we came to the wide street running parallel to Louis No. 1. When the traffic cleared, we crossed.

White stone gates rose high on either side of the entrance. Creamy rectangular mausoleums, roofs pitched forty-five degrees were next to shabby rippled upright cement boxes, gray walls exposed underneath. Chocolate and russet brick structures, crumbling with neglect, the size of garden sheds, were further along. Random cement paths, dotted with metal drainage grates every few feet, connected the tombs.

I craned my head to see a white towering monument, an angel perched on the roof in the distance. Thinking that could be it, I started out with Markus behind me. Just ahead a group of tourists led by a wiry, bearded guide suddenly stopped in front of a small white structure. His voice carried as he recounted the story of Marie Laveau, the Voodoo Queen of New Orleans.

"Many folks have come here to ax fer things. See those rows of x's? A hundred years ago, lots of folks couldn't write their name so they put them x's there. People have sighted her. Her spirit remains here in Louis No. 1." He added sternly, "Don't be stayin' here after them gates git locked. She can be angry when people invade her privacy and ya wouldn't like how she punishes those who anger her."

He gestured to a pile of coins, lipstick and roses lying in front of the mausoleum, silver and green glass and plastic Mardi Gras beads mingling with purple and gold ribbons strung from a ledge where silver keys and jewelry perched. "Those are gifts from people axing for love, money or whatnot. Knock three times on the tomb if you want to make a wish. Many have come back to leave a present after it's granted. Now, let's move on, folks."

The guide motioned for them to proceed and I was left alone in front of the tomb. X's in groups of threes were scattered in red and blue, randomly marking every side of the mausoleum along with hearts and happy faces.

"You came to make a wish, didn't you?" Markus' voice from over my shoulder was soft, in a dialect I couldn't readily identify, more noticeable when I was tuned to his voice, no longer distracted by his remarkable eyes.

When I turned he was adjusting his complex Nikon unlike my simple point and click Canon.

"I'm thinking about it," I said, taking a photo of the front of the ancient stone structure with the words "Marie Laveau", engraved in capital letters.

Markus kneeled on the scruffy grass aiming his Nikon towards the sky. "Well, what's the verdict?"

"Don't laugh. I think I will."

Markus looked fleetingly at the tomb. "I would be in trouble if I did."

At the side of the structure, focusing on the white clouds shifting in the clear blue canopy of sky, mystical reminders of all those indefinable unknowns, I asked for love and for an end to the nightmares before lightly knocking three times on the mausoleum wall.

When I looked around, Markus was gone. From above there was a sharp cry of a bird. A cluster of palm fronds trembled as a crow shot out into the air. Could the priestess have heard my request or was the crow a warning to leave?

A hot breeze wetly caressed my face with humidity and suddenly I realized I was no longer alone. A woman appeared her, lithe body in a long white dress, red turban wrapped around her hair, and a green shawl over her shoulders. From where I stood her face was the color of brown honey.

Dark eyes met mine. "Belle," she drawled. "I am Marie. Different now as a spirit but still the same friend you had. Don't be afraid. Come here."

I hesitated.

"I have something for you."

Now I was curious. Taking no time to reconsider I crept nearer. "What is it?" Before I could run, I saw the green shawl warming her shoulders was actually a gigantic living snake. The enormous python reared up, undulating back and forth.

"Do not fear. Zombie is my friend. He helps me speak for the great loas. Papa LaBas has told me your story and of the forces against you." From her pocket she pulled out a small cotton bag tied with a pink ribbon. "This will help on the river to truth." She snatched my hand, forcing my fingers apart. The bag was shoved into my palm and she pressed my hand tightly shut. "Place the gris-gris under your pillow. The magic will protect you."

In the distance a bell clanged and a voice shouted something incomprehensible. As I turned to speak to the Voodoo Queen, her wispy figure turned away and swept down a path. I tucked the tiny bag in the pocket of my dress.

From behind a mausoleum, I caught sight of Markus, camera in hand, coming toward me. "Hey, cher. We need to leave."

I glanced back at the passage between the tombs. A haze surrounded the alley.

"You okay?"

I nodded.

"They're locking up." Markus put his hand on my back to guide me to the gate. I don't know if it was the empty cemetery abandoned by tourists or seeing Marie's spirit that made me suddenly glad for his company, feeling not so alone in this struggle to unveil the forces in my past life.

At the entrance, the guard, a brawny black man, a sullen expression on his face had started to secure the gates with heavy iron chains. He glanced over and growled, "Yer late."

"Sorry, bra." Markus called out over his shoulder as we started out. "Enjoy your day."

Traffic rushed rapidly in both directions on Basin Street.

"Let's go." Markus kept protectively close to my side, his hand coming up to stop me when I failed to notice a car. Once on the other side, we headed back to the Quarter. He glanced at me sidelong. "What was your wish?"

I shook my head. "If I tell, it will never come true."

Markus pulled his sunglasses perched on the top of his head down over his eyes. "Something is still bothering you. If you don't mind me saying so, you're pale. Almost as if you've seen—"

"A ghost?" I feigned a laugh. Not wanting to talk about the spirit I'd just encountered, I said, "I haven't been sleeping well. I have nightmares about a man who killed himself back in the 1800's."

"So you dream about the past." Markus brushed a strand of hair away from his eyes. "Have you ever seen a psychic for help?"

"I did. She was exceptional maybe because she's aboriginal."

"I have a touch of that in my roots." His eyes sparkled green as he spoke. "Natives can be very perceptive. I often pick up on emotions."

The direct look that Markus gave me brought heat to my cheeks. I wanted to reach up and run my fingers through his thick wavy locks. "I thought you said you were French."

"Mostly. That part knows how to keep a woman guessing."

"And you're trying to do that?"

He smirked. "How about a photo here against the building?" The sign straight ahead was for a restaurant called "Six Sisters". I leaned against the railing, throwing my head back in what I hoped was a model's pose.

Markus adjusted his camera after each shot. "You're a natural."

"Let's see it," I said, squeezing in closer against his arm.

"Later." Markus clicked the lens closed. "Let's get you to a psychic."

He leaned in. His lips touched mine so softly my heart raced and warmth flowed through my body. Markus' smile dazzled but it was his eyes which drew me in like a moth to a flame.

"Anabelle, I know this restaurant on the river. Will you join me tonight?"

Chapter 4: JUPITER

The priest called on Papa LaBas, the crossroads saint, the go-to loa for those who were lost or in doubt of what course they should take. Papa LaBas, much like St Peter, guarded the gates to heaven, but he was the Voodoo version. He needed to be appeased, given his due, so to speak—something like life insurance. Payments were made on a regular basis. Every few days Philippe gave a dollar to the homeless because he knew the saint would get riled up if he didn't.

As a Voodoo priest he believed he had the ability to communicate with saints and they, in turn, could speak to him. He was usually full of self-confidence but this thing was driving him insane. His past life was beckoning like the Death card in the center of his readings. It meant change in tarot not death, but still the energy coming forward was evil like Katrina, growing larger and stronger every day until it crushed the levee and flooded New Orleans, changing it forever. That's what he was afraid of. His protective shield was losing power and forces from his past life were pushing into his present. He had to find out what happened back then and come to terms with it before it destroyed him.

He took comfort from the display of the rum bottle, cigars, and candies arranged neatly on the table. Doctor Philippe lit a candle and made a wish for help. Lightly stroking the python hanging from his shoulders, he felt the saint's presence.

The candles flickered as if Papa LaBas was blowing in answer to his silent wish. Satisfied, the priest took the albino snake and placed him gently in a woven basket behind the chair. The snake reared up, a pale eye steadily watching before he sunk down deep into his bamboo house to sleep for another few hours.

From a gap between the curtains, Doctor Philippe saw Jacqueline at the cashier's desk—shoe-black hair to her shoulders, a green tattoo next to her left eye shaped in the sign of Pisces, two fish swimming in opposite directions, and brown Magnolia tattoos sketched on her creamy arms. The girl sported a cropped black top and was squeezed into a pair of skinny blue jeans. Doctor Philippe knew that Jacqueline loved drama. Under the thick Cleopatra wig she wore to the shop, Jacqueline was a pretty blonde.

The clients loved Jacqueline. She explained the charms in a way the non-believers understood. On the other hand, the two male clerks in preppy designer shirts and narrow jeans treated the customers with disdain. Doctor Philippe made a mental note to give them a warning to wise up.

The Voodoo priest's attention swung back to Jacqueline speaking to the visitor. Her hands gestured animatedly as she explained in her perky voice, "Cats are like familiars for a witch. They make spells happen."

"I met an unusual cat at a vet's clinic on Royal. He had the unusual name of Morpheus."

"Really?" Jacqui's eyes widened. "He's my boyfriend's cat."

The customer's reply was barely audible, her whispery voice suggesting a soft sea breeze ruffling the Gulf on a clear windless day. He caught a glimpse of her when she turned towards him. This was the woman he had been waiting for. From the strong blue outer aura and a fiery inner orange, he knew she was an intuitive, greatly blessed. Was she good or evil, and would she journey with him to return to the past?

A flash of foreboding spurred his sixth sense. Doctor Philippe's head ached like a pressure cooker threatening to explode. Pain shot from the nerves at the base of his neck to his throbbing temples. The headaches came much too frequently lately. Doctor Philippe knew it was a build-up of negative energy.

He had to cleanse the room. The ashtray heaped with dry sage and sweet grass was ready. Drawing it in closer, the priest lit a match and blew on the flame to keep it going. When smoke rose from the herbs he picked up a large green feather and fanned it to each corner of the chamber. Satisfied he had cleared the energy he sat down.

When a bell tone signaled an incoming text he clicked it open.
Is she there?
Doctor Philippe tapped out: *yes.*

The priest stood and opened the curtain. He took the petite blonde's right hand as she came in, not to shake in greeting but to read her palm.

***

An arresting man with a shaved head and steely gray eyes

wearing a pale blue denim shirt and jeans stood to greet me. He had an indescribable strong energy, unlike anything I had ever encountered. Jacqueline had told me Doctor Philippe was a Voodoo-Wiccan priest from Haiti.

"Have you seen a psychic before?" Doctor Philippe asked as he pulled me forward.

I took a seat in front of him, our knees inches apart. "I have, Doctor Philippe."

"Call me Philippe," he said, studying my palm. I was getting strange vibes from him. His aura was a deep mauve with a fiery red centre—mystical yet infused with passion.

"There are two life lines. The second one is long," the words streamed from his lips as if from some inner force.

I was apprehensive, knowing he could be the key to deciphering my dreams.

"You had two break-ups."

I pursed my lips. He was a fake babbling a trumped up story. "I've only had one serious relationship."

Doctor Philippe went on patiently as if I hadn't caught him in a lie. "The other liaison was a long time ago. You were in love but something blocked your path." His forehead crinkled in consternation. "I see swords drawn. Blood spilled. You're a warrior. Watch out for enemies." He closed his eyes a moment before he added, "Your Orisha is the Queen of the Seas. Water is good for you. And to answer your question, you could be happy here in New O'leans."

"You know why I'm here?"

"I sense confusion."

I stared at him. "I'm afraid to sleep."

Doctor Philippe got up quickly. "I break in half an hour. We could go meet up down the street at the Hotel Belfoire for lunch. I could tell you more."

I nodded. What harm could it do?

Chapter 5: THE WORLD

The gold shield on the bartender's lapel read "Chuckie". He was a living breathing potato, thick spouts bagged in black dress pants and a white golf shirt. Skin the color of coffee dosed heavily with cream, he was a Creole—a black mixed with white or Hispanic. Calling him homely was being kind. In this case the mixture was an experiment gone horribly wrong. Tiny eyes like raisins squinted at me from a pudgy face before he took hold of the oyster and shucked it.

A pile of shells was heaped high in the sink. He selected one and opened it. His disfigured hands caught my attention. Deep scars the color of pink worms marred his skin. My guess was he'd made a living on a fishing boat shucking oysters long before he worked at the Hotel Belfoire.

"What kin I git you?" he drawled, the easy Southern hospitality missing from his tone.

"A Sazerac, please."

Chuckie grunted, dropping the oyster in a large bowl filled with shells before shuffling over to the shelf lined with rows of standard bottles of liquor. He selected Canadian rye whiskey and brought it to the counter. His squinty eyes ogled the skin revealed by the scooped neckline of my dress.

Someone needed to teach potato man manners but it wouldn't be me. I wanted to pry open this clam. "Worked here long?"

"A while." Chuckie swung around, picked a bottle of a pale liquid off the shelf, the label written in a fancy script I couldn't make out, and set it on the counter.

"Bartending?"

From a shelf he tugged out a glossy menu and slid it across the counter. "And cookin'."

I looked around. Elegant old New Orleans. Mirrors and paintings hung on ivory walls, ceiling-high windows filtered sunlight in from outside, and a dozen square tables covered in red linen were scattered throughout. It was high end. The hardwood floor in warm oak extended from the bar to the dining room. Through the open doors I could see tables set in white linen, the cutlery and plates ready for dinner.

The bar room was almost empty but then again it was midway

between lunch and dinner. An older couple more interested in food than conversation, shared oysters at one of the tables in the rectangular room.

At the end of the semi-circular bar, a couple of college girls, one with straight auburn hair to her shoulders and the other a curly bobbed brunette, both in tight tube tops and shorts held Pimm's Cups in perfectly manicured coral tipped fingers. Feigning sophistication they exchanged quips with Chuckie, tossing their bangs back in synchronicity.

From the menu I gathered the Belfoire specialized in oysters but I didn't like eating anything raw. Reluctantly, Chuckie shuffled back to my end of the bar, credit cards in hand.

"Are there steamed oysters?" I asked.

"Yup," Chuckie grunted, his attention once again diverted to the girls like a cat watching two juicy mice wondering which one to torture first. He headed to the cash to complete the transaction and gave the girls a receipt before going over to the bar to pack ice into an Old-Fashioned glass. His eyes narrowed, watching their mile-high legs as they sauntered off, pink flip-flops slapping the steamy street.

Getting back to business, Chuckie dropped a sugar cube in a second glass, splashed Peychaud's bitters on top, and crushed the sugar. Then he added bourbon and Legendre Herbsaint.

"Herbsaint not absinthe?"

"Has the same anise taste," he muttered.

Pouring the contents through a strainer into the glass, he added a twist of lemon before serving the Sazerac.

This is it, I thought, examining the sparkling bronze cocktail. The same drink the man in my dream had before he killed himself. I tipped the glass back. "I heard certain restaurants started the Sazerac tradition.

He shrugged.

"You know any place where they use lime?"

"Renard's on Bourbon at St. Ann."

So Jabba the Hut was right. I had to go there.

Chuckie reached over and picked up an empty glass from the counter and wiped the spot it left with a cloth. "You want anything from the menu?"

"When my friend gets here. You know Doctor Philippe?"

"He your friend?"

"Mm-mm."

Chuckie turned away quickly but not before I saw him cross himself. "Conjure man," he muttered.

I wanted to talk but Chuckie made for the far side of the bar where a pretty light-skinned black bartender tended a customer. A plastic name tag with "Dee" was pinned to the pocket of the black vest she wore over a white cap-sleeved collared blouse. Straight ebony hair in a blunt cut brushed her cheeks as she leaned forward to the barrel-chested man sitting on the bar stool across from her. The tiny black skirt and three inch pumps gave her a sleek look which she used to full advantage.

The man's brown linen trousers were held up by suspenders over a long-sleeved striped shirt, and a hat covered his balloon head which I suspected was hairless under the straw fedora. Fluttering her eyelashes and smiling, Dee enticed the old geezer to add a few bills to the pile of tip money on the counter.

Chuckie came up behind Dee. "See her at the bar?" His eyes flicked to the blonde sitting further down the bar. "She a witch." He squeezed Dee's arm. "Take over fo' me, girlie."

Paying less attention to Chuckie than the fly buzzing around the cash register, Dee thought: Shucker Bateau should hustle his nasty ass right back and tend to the white gal, witch or not and stay the hell away from her. He was uglier than homemade sin but it was more than that. He gave her the skivvies the way he huddled up close to her. She swore she could feel his woody.

"What you goin' on about? If you hexed, there be nothin' fer you to do nohow." Dee jerked her chin towards the blonde and said, "Go, she's waitin'."

***

Distractedly, I mulled over the menu wondering if I'd made a terrible mistake to meet up with Doctor Philippe. Chuckie had that caught-in-the-headlights look a fox gets on a dark stretch of highway when a car jets past, inches away from killing him.

Before I could text, Doctor Philippe slung himself in the seat next to me.

"Hey," I said slowly, momentarily taken aback by the man's icy gray eyes. I was not a fan of shaved heads—there was nothing like a good handful of hair to run my fingers through, but I had to admit combined with the hawk nose and full lips he was interesting.

"Jacqui said you are busy." With dark shadows under his eyes, Doctor Philippe was not just tired, he was not sleeping any better than I was. Something was eating at him in a bad way. It suddenly occurred to me he needed my help even more than I needed his.

"It's good to take a break." He smiled slightly. Doctor Philippe signaled Chuckie. "A Dixie and half a dozen oysters for me and for this lovely lady..." he paused, raising an eyebrow.

"Oysters Bienville, please."

Nobody looked more anxious to leave than Chuckie but he reluctantly returned bringing a long neck and a glass before disappearing into the kitchen.

Doctor Philippe took my hand and closed his eyes. When he opened them his gaze was direct. "I see a book."

"What kind of book?"

"A diary."

"I can't see how this is relevant."

Doctor Philippe shook his head, his eyes glazed and far away. He hesitated as if he was working hard to find the words to describe something incomprehensible. "That journal was tucked away."

"And if I find it would I understand why I'm having these dreams?"

He nodded.

I sensed he was hiding something. "Why are you so interested in my past life?"

Doctor Philippe hesitated and then said, "My past is linked to yours.'

"How?"

Before he could answer Chuckie appeared with oysters. He glanced furtively at Doctor Philippe before placing the plates on the counter along with paper napkins and forks.

When he shifted away to the fridge out of hearing range, I asked, "Have you worked as a psychic long?" A whiff of woodsy aroma as I leaned towards him was unexpectedly enticing. I wasn't sure if it had to do with his psychic ability or the Voodoo he practiced. Psychics have the ability to attract the opposite sex. I set up a barrier. At this point his influence could be just as much negative as positive.

Casually, Doctor Philippe picked up a shell and sucked out an oyster drawing my attention to his full lips. "For the last ten years I've had a TV show but decided to center on the store. The employees do most of the work, anyway, making the items and ordering books."

"What was the TV show about?" I forked up an oyster baked in a thick sauce, a blend of parmesan cheese, mushrooms and bacon, a gourmet's delight.

"The first season was about hauntings and past lives." Shoving the glass away Doctor Philippe drank his beer straight from the bottle and then setting it down he wiped a thin edge of foam off his upper lip. He sat back in the high bar stool. "On a day like this nothing goes down better." He turned to me. "You enjoyin' New O'leans?"

Doctor Philippe was quite charming when he relaxed. "The French Quarter is good."

"Where you stayin'?"

"Hotel Memoire."

Doctor Philippe shot me a look.

"You know it?"

"Nice area. Close to some exceptional restaurants and of course, music." His forehead furrowed as his eyes studied my wrist.

I glanced down aware of the heat coming from the small white scar I'd had all my life. It was raised and pink.

Doctor Philippe ran a finger over the inflamed scar. A chill raced down my spine.

I withdrew from his touch.

"What's it from?" The Voodoo priest sucked up an oyster from its shell while keeping his eyes on me.

"A scratch I think."

Doctor Philippe's eyes narrowed. "You don't know?"

I shook my head. "I asked my foster parents but no one knew anything about it." I remembered the crow calling out at the cemetery. "Do you believe in totem animals?" I asked.

His cool eyes stared into mine. "Definitely, I'm French, Choctaw and black. My training is all over the map."

I examined his face for his mixed heritage but saw only the French part.

He ran his finger over the jagged scar. A tremor shot down my

39

arms. Doctor Philippe's voice faded and I entered a white haze much like a cloud. I heard voices.

A dark-hued man built like a tank, a bandana tied on his square head, wide khaki pants fluttering in the breeze, brought his fist into a man with skin the red tone of a Native American. From his pocket waistband Tank pulled a knife. The steel tip glinted in the sunlight filtering through the clouds. The Native grabbed the knife and twisted it away. They struggled. Somehow I knew the Native was the one to help. Picking up a bucket, I brought it down on Tank, hard enough to give the other man a chance. A gun fired. Tank fell back on the deck, a crimson puddle spreading over his chest.

A chain reaction followed—clashing swords, shouting and gunshot fire. A hand pushed me away from the men. The voice belonging to the hand yelled, "Take this, cher". Green eyes sparkling with excitement met mine.

My eyes swept over his powerfully built body. A loose long-sleeved cotton shirt, open at the neck, fell over breeches tucked into long black boots. He was armed with a sword in one hand and a revolver in his belt. Unruly dark curls flew about in the wind as he handed me the sword. "Use it if you must."

It was Alain Ducoeur and he definitely was a pirate.

The rocking vessel heaved from side to side, along with my stomach and its contents. Waves struck the deck hard, spraying a fine mist over my body, my clothes and hair clinging to my skin.

"Go hide before they kill you!" my inner voice screamed.

Even if I could find a place to hide, the boat was rocking so hard it was too difficult to walk. The sword tucked into my belt, I gripped the railing to support myself. No longer able to control the cramping, I grabbed a metal pail and gagged, emptying my breakfast into the bucket.

I looked up. Scruffy men with wild feverish eyes of jackals on a hunt, were battling it out. Bone-chilling screams filled the air as blood painted the deck red. Blood splattered my face. With my sleeve I wiped it clean but in doing so loosened my grip on the sword. It didn't take much to knock it away.

The man's head had the shape of the back of a thumb, wrinkled and concave. A black patch covered one eye. His scarred nose minus a nostril, twitched like a dog getting the scent of steak on a grill.

From the deck I grabbed an oar and deflecting his punch, I twirled the oar around, clipping his ear. He shook his head as if to rid himself of the pain, and moved rapidly forward, his sword held high. I backed into the railing. Thin lips curled into a triumphant grin under a pencil moustache.

With all my strength I brought the oar up and struck down but he sidestepped as deftly as a tango dancer. I wasn't prepared for a sharp kick to my ribs. A split second too late to break the fall, my hand smacked the deck. The pain jolted through my arm.

He took full advantage. Snatching a handful of my hair, he pinned me to the deck and mounted my inert body, imprisoning me with his thick thighs. He pulled me close, rank body odor a mixture of sweat and booze so strong I struggled not to gag. He growled, "Where is it?"

His weight was suffocating. When I wiggled my hips he pulled over enough for me to snake my hand to his lapel. Locating his hand, I held it close to my chest, and shot my left hand straight up, spearing his throat. He jerked back.

Another jerk of my hips unbalanced him enough to swing a leg over his thigh and roll off. Springing to my feet I brought my leg up in a side kick, making contact to his temple.

He drew back but came at me again firmly cuffing my cheek. Tears welled up in my eyes but there was no way I would give in. Seizing an opening I brought a foot up and kicked his groin. My foot connected but like a crack addict he was oblivious to the pain. I was picked up like a sack of potatoes and thrown against the cabin wall. As I lay stunned he pulled out a knife and dug the edge into my throat.

"Where has he hidden it?" he hissed, between clenched teeth.

At that moment I thought I was done. No matter how much I struggled he would kill me even if I knew the answer. Belle must have died here.

But I was wrong. A gunshot deafened my ears. Clumps of brain matter splattered on my face and clothes as the man slumped over, his knees crumbling beneath him. He dropped limply to the deck.

"Cher, are you all right?" A pistol still gripped in one hand, Alain Ducoeur pulled me up. With a handkerchief he wiped my face. "I think I'll need to bathe you," he said, with a grin. "Go down to the cabin and wait for me."

"What's this all about? What's he after?"

"Lafitte's treasure. They think I have it." He patted my butt. "Go quickly woman."

I glanced around before heading down the steps. Ducoeur's men were dumping the dead into the bayou. The fight was over.

Downstairs, the open cabin door revealed a dark-haired man at the desk rifling through the contents of the drawers.

I was instantly suspicious. "Who are you?"

Springing up, he came towards me, eyes narrowed into dark burning embers. From his belt he pulled out a gun and pointed it at my chest. "Where is it?"

"Anabelle!" A low voice tugged me out of the white haze. I was back at the Hotel Belfoire, Doctor Philippe squeezing my hand. The memory faded into a steamy mist.

Doctor Philippe lifted his head, his eyes far away. "I could smell it."

"What?"

"Swamp." Doctor Philippe shut his eyes. His face lost color.

"What did you see?"

"A ship."

I nodded. "Anything else?"

Doctor Philippe's expression was serious. "I saw you but not as you are now. Your hair was a golden blonde and your features were similar but different. Do you know how you got the scar?"

Strange how he thought the scar was so important. I glanced down and focused on the jagged line. A flame shot up from the scar, startling me. And then as quickly as it ignited it fizzed out.

"What is it?"

The priest grabbed my trembling hands. This was not me. A helpless woman caught in a net from a past life, flopping around like a fish out of water, gasping for air.

"Tell me," he urged.

Uncomfortable with the physical contact, I pushed him away. From my purse I took out a twenty and threw it on the counter. "Thanks, but I have to go."

"Wait," he said, grabbing my elbow. With his other hand he flipped open the catch on my purse and dropped in a business card. "My cell number. You will need my help. Believe me you can't deal with this alone."

I didn't look around but I could feel his eyes drilling a hole in my back as I closed the glass door behind me.

***

Shucker watched the blonde until she disappeared into a flood of tourists. She was far too tiny for his sort of bedroom romp. He preferred a tall girl's long legs hooked tightly over his shoulders.

It was no coincidence she sat with Doctor Philippe. The priest's eyes were cold enough to freeze a brother's soul, like a black vulture settling on Chuckie's body to feed on his entrails. Nervously, he rubbed his cheeks upwards to his shiny shaved head and squeezed as if to prompt his brain for answers. Sweat dripped off his brow. There was only one thing to do. He had to see Auntie Ruthie.

"I'm goin'," he yelled out to Dee. The uppity bitch grimaced and went back to flirting with the old coot.

Known as Toad to the locals, he was the unfortunate owner of saggy jowls which by some quirk of nature adhered to his scrawny neck. Some thought Chuckie was ugly but in the bartender's opinion, a white or black man with a waddle jiggling, was beyond gross.

Dee needed a real man and Chuckie would see that he was that man. This time he wouldn't take no for an answer. With a glance at Doctor Philippe, Chuckie flung his apron behind the counter and slamming the door in his hurry, hit the street. He had to get to Auntie Ruthie's shop on St Ann before closing.

Arms flung wide, wild-eyed as a bull pierced by a matador's sword, Chuckie shoved a wizened gray-haired lady back, barreling down Royal. She swung her cane in the air in retaliation narrowly missing his broad backside. Chuckie didn't care.

Nobody was spared the tree-trunk body as he careened through. A young couple collided into a display of modern art in their hurry to avoid him. Chuckie didn't care. He was in a panic and only Auntie Ruthie could help.

As a Hoodoo woman, the old lady supplied people with herbs and animal powders. A month ago he'd asked for gris-gris to use on a college girl. Auntie Ruthie's potion was so strong the beotch's brain shifted into cruise control, doing everything he asked with a

43

big grin plastered on her face. Luckily, no one reported her missing for the two days she spent in his bed. Chuckie ended up dumping her on the Tulane campus. Security found the co-ed naked, rolling in the grass laughing insanely, having no recollection of where she'd been or what she'd done.

He had to be careful this time. The composition of the potion could have been lethal and he would have gone down for it had the girl reported her story to the police. They'd charge him with possession or worse. Luckily, the gris-gris was more powerful than roofies. Chuckie thanked the loas no one came after him.

The heat was beginning to slow him down to a steady trudge as he turned north on St Ann towards Rampart. When he spotted the shotgun house, he stopped and wiped his brow. The outer room facing the street connected to a room in the back where the old lady sold gris-gris and charms.

Chuckie stepped inside slamming the screen door lightly behind him. He wandered down the hallway where a black pit bull was penned in a small sunken room, a lounge area furnished with couches and table, and a fireplace off to the side. The dog barked in warning.

"Shuddup, Big Daddy," he said, as he always did before going further. He was filled with apprehension, dead sure he had been singled out by the Voodoo priest.

Auntie Ruthie's store was the room at the end of the hallway. She sold charms and amulets, made up potions for a few dollars and told fortunes. When he poked his head in, Auntie Ruthie's frizzled gray head was hunched over a gris-gris bag, loading it up with who knows what. Her shriveled coal face looked up, the raisin eyes receding in shadowy sockets identical to his but hers had misty-gray veils from the cataracts creeping over.

"Where y'at, Shucker?" From the dark corner of the room a plump black girl stopped her beading to examine Chuckie's sweaty face. "You runnin' from the po-lice?"

"Shaddup, Eurma. And don't be callin' me Shucker, if ya knows what's good for ya." He was born Charles Bateau but with Bateau meaning boat and working an oyster boat for seven years, he'd acquired the Shucker handle from the speed he could shuck oysters, which was right quick. He hadn't won any contests but his skill with the oyster knife was phenomenal at thirty-three shucks per minute. Not quite a competition winner but he came darn near close. He was proud he was good even if he had missed and wounded himself. It was the way women said "Shucker" that made him feel like a cockroach. They always looked at his hands, disgust in their eyes and then back at his face as if he was one big scab. All of them, white or black, thought he was a freak.

Eurma smirked. "Well, you sure as dung have a boner about somethin'."

"Yer mouth is flappin' louder than a barn door in a storm. I need to speak private. Wait outside, Eurma."

"Dumb as a bag full of hammers, ya are, Chuckie Shucker," Eurma shot back.

Chuckie's eyes flattened like a shark's. "I'll knock you so hard you'll see tomorrow today if you speak like that ta me agin."

Feisty Eurma was not stupid. She hurriedly jiggled to the door.

Auntie Ruthie peered up over her reading glasses. "Hush, baby."

"Like two possums in a tow sack," Chuckie said, eyes glued on Eurma's booty.

At the doorway Eurma turned about and hissed, "You is sick."

Chuckie's cheek twitched like a panicked moth trapped in a jar before he lunged forward. Eurma ran, making it half way down the hallway before Chuckie's foot connected to her substantial behind. The girl struggled to keep from falling, righted herself with a grunt and took off to the bedroom. He heard the door click.

"No need to hurt her, Chuckie," Auntie Ruthie said quietly. "Eurma works hard doin' God's business."

"Thinks you mean loa business, Auntie Ruthie."

"Voodoo gods or t'other. Same thing. Now sit, boy, and tell me why you here."

Chapter 6: *THE CHARIOT*

On Bourbon Street the going was slow. Tourists strolled three abreast holding plastic go-cups filled with Pat O'Brien Hurricanes. The crowd overflowed from the cracked sidewalk to the narrow street, squeezing between Southern Comfort delivery trucks and cars crawling at a snail's pace through the Quarter.

An empty NOPD car was parked in front of a corner store. The cop sat at the counter drinking coffee and munching a beignet. It wouldn't be long before the clubs filled up and trouble began.

Just past Dumaine Street, a cozy, quiet piano bar strained to compete with a blues band warming up in the bar across the street. Walking at a brisk pace it was hot and I was feeling it.

At Ursulines Avenue I turned right. A lean black man in overalls, a short-sleeved shirt and a straw hat swept the sidewalk in front of an art shop. I nodded a hello.

"You are lookin' mighty fine in your dress, ma'am," he said, with a toothy grin.

"Thank you." That made my day. I went on trying to forget Doctor Philippe, Voodoo and the pirate ship.

When my cell beeped, I saw two messages: *Get ready for a night out. M*

An evening with a hottie. *Sweet.* I clicked again.

There's more to M. Text me the latest. Sue

A warning? Did she mean he was hiding something or was she looking for gossip?

At Ursulines Avenue I saw a sign for rental apartments. Wouldn't I just love to live in this quaint part of New Orleans with a sexy man. I was tempted to go in and inquire but then I thought of what I was really here for. I had to find Renard's tonight.

Inside my hotel, I passed the door to the front desk where a dark-haired young man was busy talking on the phone. A massive bearded man walked in from outside and joined me at the elevator doors.

He was tall and trim and from the size of his biceps, worked out regularly. He wore a taupe felt hat, the type Blues singers wear and a muscle shirt with "Black Angels" printed in white on a black background, tucked into a pair of black jeans. When the doors opened, he motioned for me to enter first.

"Which floor?"

"Four."

He pressed the "4" and the elevator began its ascent. Inside the tapestry covered elevator it was airless.

"Creepy, ain't it," the man remarked, glancing at the carpeted walls, "makes you wonder how long anyone could survive in the elevator if it got stuck." He scratched his chin thoughtfully.

"I'm sure there's a panic button behind you on the panel. The desk would know if the elevator got stuck."

The man glanced behind his shoulder. "I suppose, eventually."

I shot him a look and didn't like what I saw.

With a last rumble, the ancient elevator trembled to a halt and the doors creaked ajar.

"Place is haunted." He cracked a smile that didn't reach his eyes. "People gettin' decapitated in their sleep," the man added, as I stepped out. I glanced back at the stranger just as the doors closed. He was one big bad ass with attitude. It was a relief to see the elevator heading back down.

More than ready to retreat to the safety of my room after that encounter I shoved my card into the door slot. The key card flashed red. I tried again but when it still didn't work, I took a ride down the elevator.

The doors opened to the main hallway. Thankfully it was empty. No ghostly figures or threatening Goodfellas.

At the front desk the lean young man I had seen on my way in, was still there.

"Hello, I'm Warren."

"Hey. I'm Anabelle. I'm having a bit of a dilemma. My door won't open. Room 400."

"Oh-hh, I see," he said, a faint smile on his lips. "No problem, I'll get you another. You likin' the room?"

His Southern accent was charming. I could listen to him all day long.

"It's beautiful. I couldn't ask for a better suite," I said.

Warren raised an eyebrow and gave me a second look. "Really?"

"I told Sandra I had a vision of a purple room with a clawed bathtub. It's exactly what I pictured but I had no idea about the rest of it."

He grinned. "Activity happens."

"You mean spirits." I wasn't sure if he'd ever seen what I had, nor was I sure I should tell him about Ducoeur or Delphine. "So that's why my key card was demagnetized."

"Most likely." Warren handed me a plastic key. "This one should work fine. Enjoy your stay."

Once inside the suite I sat on one of the brocade upholstered French provincial chairs, and kicked off my sandals. The room was frigidly cold, much colder than the setting on the AC.

After turning the dial up, I opened the balcony door and stepped out into moist heat, heavy with floral scent and the odor of mildew. The backs of three houses were enclosed with high stone walls, the interior gardens crowded with magnolia trees in blossom. One had a cement pool, too tiny to swim in.

Across the street to the left, was the Beauregard-Keyes House, surrounded by cypress trees trimmed into ornate shapes and beyond that the Ursuline Convent, clearly visible from my vantage point.

It was possible to set a chair out on this balcony but in the back of my mind I recalled the master bedroom's balcony being much more spacious. Closing the door behind me I was prepared for the middle door to bang shut, but it didn't.

All was quiet in the master bedroom. The bed was made, the heavy brocade curtains drawn and my suitcase placed next to the dresser. I hid Marie Laveau's gris-gris bag under the pillow. From my suitcase I pulled out a case with cosmetics and toiletries, left my luggage open for unpacking later, and entered the bathroom.

The lion-clawed marble tub in the center of the square room beckoned, but instead, I drew aside the plastic shower curtain and found solace in a warm shower, peeking out every few seconds to make sure no one was there—no psycho with a huge butcher knife ready to make this my final shower. With the tiny jets shooting a steady stream, hitting my head and shoulders like a massage, I began to relax.

My fingers worked the shampoo into my scalp and while the conditioner did its job, I spread chocolate body wash over my skin. The chocolate aroma released pheromones in the air and suddenly I felt great, almost euphoric. Languidly, I rinsed, ready to take it easy before I took a walk to locate Renard's. Wrapped in a fluffy white bath towel I considered the king-sized bed but opted instead to sit on the balcony.

Furnished with a built-in floral cushioned lounge, I climbed up, and piling pillows behind my back, I stretched out taking in the magnificent view of the Quarter. It was like being on top of the world. With the sun settling lower in a clear, cerulean blue sky, I nodded off.

A noise woke me. I didn't know how long I had slept but the sun was now an orange stripe low in a dark blue sky. It was dusk, the moon a sliver directly above. The traffic was practically nonexistent on the street. When I heard a rustling, I sat up. A black bird perched on the far end of the railing.

A rumble of thunder was quickly followed by lightning. The flash silhouetted a round beakless head, tiny teeth and wide spread wings, the bottom edge jagged. In other words, it was a bat.

"Ee-ww!" I leaped off the lounge and scooted to the door. About to slam it shut behind me, a hand grabbed my arm and spun me about. The stranger had a long aristocratic nose and button lips in a narrow face, framed by auburn hair.

"Let go!"

"Belle, don't be afraid. It's me, Raven."

A strange skinny youth was standing in my hotel room, but even worse, there was a bat somewhere. I pushed him aside and checked the ceiling. Everything was normal except for this stranger.

Weighing no more than about one-forty, the young man was dressed in black jeans and a T-shirt, the dark clothing bleaching his already pale skin to a snowy white.

I looked at him curiously. He had the lean aesthetic look of an artist. I could imagine him as the Lord Byron of New Orleans, writing romantic sonnets on a balcony overlooking the Mississippi or a classical violinist, playing his heart out, his large heavy-lidded eyes pensive.

"Who are you?" I demanded, doing my best to appear confident. I was only a little afraid. I could take him out, if I had to.

"Lookin' good, Belle. I'm Raven, remember?"

"No, I don't! Why are you calling me Belle?"

"You were Belle the last time I saw you." Raven chuckled. "Mind you, it's been a century or two."

"I'm assuming you're a ghost?"

He took my elbow and led me into the bedroom. "Why don't we sit?"

"No, not now. I have to get dressed and you should leave." I dragged him to the door and pushed him into the outer room. I figured ghosts needed a firm controlling hand or they'd take over and start throwing things.

Raven shook his head. "No can do."

"Well then, you must wait." I shut the door before putting on a dress and zipping it up. After I stepped into sandals, I slapped on a coat of mascara before calling out, "You still there?"

Raven came into the master bedroom. "Where are we going?"

"I think you will be going back to wherever you came from and I am going to find a restaurant called Renard's."

I didn't think his skin could turn any paler but it did. Somehow all the blood in his body went to his lips, infusing them with a deep merlot red hue.

"Not a good idea?"

Raven's jaw clenched. "Let's walk and I'll talk."

How he figured he could do this was beyond me. Ghosts don't walk the streets with regular people unless they're haunting an area, or do they? "You're not a ghost then?"

"No." Raven took my hand. "But before we go, I must show you something from the balcony." Seeing my expression, he added, "Don't worry, there're no bats out there now."

Once outside, he pointed to the roof of the Ursuline Convent. "That attic was our home. Every one of you girls had a wooden chest to store clothes. They called you casquette girls because those cases looked like coffins. The other girls came from orphanages or convents in France. New Orleans, aptly named after the pervert, the Duc D'Orleans, was a den of thieves and prostitutes. The idea was that all of you virtuous girls would marry into the gentry."

"So, I was from which, an orphanage or a convent?"

"Your mama died in childbirth. You were raised by your father, the best chef in Paris. On your eighteenth year he fought a duel and died. The soldiers took you along with the other homeless girls. All of you were deported to New Orleans but only some came to live in the convent."

"And you? How did you come to know me?"

"You brought me to New Orleans."

"Huh?"

"In the casquette. I'm a vampire."

I backed away to the door.

Raven made a stop motion with his hand. "Belle, be calm. I am no danger to you. I am *your* vampire." He motioned to the convent. "See the upper windows? The shutters are nailed down but every evening some of us break out and fly into the night. Around dawn I have breakfast and retreat to the attic."

His story was ludicrous but I wasn't hallucinating. Raven stood before me a sparkle in his eyes—a Parisian vampire, not Hungarian nor Romanian, and as real as any mythical vampire could be. "But if you're a vampire what's stopping you from sucking my blood?"

Raven snickered. "I would love to suck your neck, darling, but we have a bond. Why don't we go for a walk and I shall explain?"

"To Renard's?"

Raven sighed. "If you must," he said, leading the way to the door.

On the way out, I grabbed my purse and followed him to the elevator. As Raven pressed the "down" button, I said, "Aren't you afraid someone might suspect something?"

"Like what—a clandestine affair?"

The elevator shuddered in its descent.

Raven smirked. "Delicious. I love to be the center of gossip," he said, pausing for a moment before continuing, "There hasn't been a casquette girl with a more interesting life than you."

With a groan the elevator doors opened and I entered the lobby with Raven on my heels. Looking both ways I saw no one either in the hall or at the front desk. I practically flew out the front door into Ursulines. My eyes flicked at Raven. He was huffing to keep up with me. Obviously flying was easier for him.

"Please, Belle, slow down. Oh, I know—" He peered up at white walls of the convent, targeting the attic windows. "You are anxious to see the place where we lived." He stopped beside me and followed my gaze. "It was a nightmare, wasn't it? Twenty girls and their vampires. Oven hot in the summer and chilling in the winter, not to mention liberal doses of religion from early morning until dusk."

From my balcony I couldn't make out whether the windows on the attic level were closed but now I could see they were wide open. "I thought you said they were nailed shut?"

Raven sighed. "The nuns tried, but even the Pope's blessing didn't change anything. It's like wasps. Vampires live where they feel better," he grinned, revealing sharp fang-like eye teeth, "and New Orleans is that place and has been for centuries." He offered his elbow and I locked my arm in. "Why don't we walk on Decatur to the square."

I nodded. "Jackson Square? I'd love to see it."

As we came to the corner I was a little put off by the graffiti on a building, "cat piss" scrawled in sloppy red paint on the side wall of what I supposed to be a gift store. Not something I expected from the Quarter.

Raven frowned. "There's always good with the bad in the Vieux Carré. Look! See the market?" He pointed to the left at an area of stands covered by a wooden roof. "Pralines, clothes, art and jewelry and much, much more. In fact, whatever your little heart desires." Raven pulled me close and whispered in my ear. "Perhaps you'd like gris-gris for your lover?"

"Lover?"

Raven's eyes widened. "Or is it lovers?"

Heat rose to my cheeks.

My Hormone voice chattered excitedly, "And what hotties they are. Philippe's so interesting with all that psychic energy going on. He'd know exactly what you'd want in bed and when and where, eh?"

My Logical Voice interrupted. "Anabelle should choose Markus. He can't read her mind. Philippe's too weird."

"Hey, don't forget the sexy pirate." Hormone giggled. "He's every girl's fantasy. No worries about getting knocked up either."

"Don't blush, Anabelle. You are sexual. If only all women were so inclined." Raven patted my hand. "That's why I stayed in your casquette. As Belle you were famous for more than your beauty, you know."

"Oh? Don't tell me Belle was a skank?"

"No, not exactly."

"A sex worker?"

"You will know soon enough." He pointed across the street. "Cafe du Monde. Remember the coffee we had? They still have it. All the people come for the coffee and beignets."

"I hardly drink coffee and beignets have gluten."

Raven nodded his head. "Beignets affect your digestion. No wonder!"

"What?"

"Anabelle, it's to do with how you died in your last life. I don't want to upset you now with that incident. I see I need to fill you in on some things, but too much too fast might overwhelm you."

Raven knew a lot about me. He was right about the horrible cramping. Gluten was rough on my system or was it lactose in the milk? Either way, my insides were a mess.

I grabbed his chin and turned his head towards me. "What happened?"

Raven pulled away unfazed. He patted my arm. "Be patient." His pace slowed as he surveyed the ink drawings taped to a wrought iron fence along the square. "Nice, eh?" The Creole artist had a dozen or so plastic coated renderings of the cathedral, the market and the Mississippi. "I'm here to guide you," he added. "Hopefully, this time I can do it better."

"How about telling me how I died?"

Raven grinned. "You will find that out yourself."

Irritated as I was with him, I forgot about my gut as we came to a magnificent square. Off to the right an immense white cathedral with sharp black turrets dominated the lush green square. Another building in brown brick was at right angles to the Cathedral and in the center stood a statue of Andrew Jackson.

"The Vieux Carré is about three hundred years old. They named the streets coming from the river after the Saints and the cross streets after the French royals. You've heard of the Bourbon kings?"

"So Bourbon Street was not named after the liquor?"

"No, but to see it after midnight you wouldn't think so." Raven led me to the street corner. The sign read St. Ann. "Why do you want to go to Renard's?"

"I have scary dreams. My past life has to be connected to Renard's."

Raven placed a pale hand on my arm. His fingers were long, almost spindly. "Your life was not exactly pleasant back then."

"I gathered that much. Now, tell me what plans the nuns had for me. Surely, they didn't want me to become a nun?"

Raven smiled. "No, they weren't stupid. You were contracted to marry for a lot of money."

A tall man in a black cape, wearing a top hat was followed by tourists. They stopped in front of the entrance to a red-brick building. The sign above the door read "Renard's.

In a hushed tone the tour guide started a spooky story about the resident ghost. I stopped to listen but Raven grabbed my arm and dragged me inside. "That fool doesn't know the half of it."

From behind a wooden stand a lithe young woman with frizzy black hair popped out to greet us. "Good evenin'. Would you like a table?"

"We're here for a drink," I said.

"May I suggest the bar? Go right on through," she said, indicating an oak bar at the far end of the room.

We walked through a corridor with pillars—a dining room with chandeliers, candlelight and crisp white table cloths to the left. Just ahead was a small bar with dim lighting from the enclosed lamps above the large display of bottles and glasses. A young couple sat at the bar but the other four stools were unoccupied.

I shot Raven a look. "I guess I should have asked. Do people see you?"

The vampire grinned, the tips of his fangs displayed. "Yup, I'm not a ghost, remember?" He pushed a bar stool out for me and took the next seat.

"Two Sazeracs, please," I said, to the redhead behind the bar before placing a few bills on the counter.

"Thanks, Belle."

"I figured a vampire two hundred years old wouldn't have any money."

"Not my usual drink either." This time the tips of his fangs displayed as his lips turned up at the corners.

The brunette barkeep was fast. She set the sparkling bronze cocktails on paper coasters in front of us. "Enjoy," she drawled, before heading over to a couple seated at the other end near the cash.

I watched her momentarily as she spoke to a hawk-nosed lady, glittering like a chandelier with long dangly diamond earrings, a triple gold strand necklace and matching diamond bracelets. A substantial woman like her could pull off the jewelry. I swung around to Raven and said significantly, "Okay, spill."

The vampire raised an eyebrow.

"How you came to be in my suitcase."

"Casquette, Belle." Raven sipped on his cocktail reflectively. "We were targets for all the unscrupulous people out to make a bundle. I was a sous chef. You were trained to be chef by your father before he died. We'd go out for breaks together. When I caught the vampire virus you took care of me and I became yours. Soon I found I had the ability to shapeshift into bat form. It was easy for me to hide in your casquette."

"But why me, Raven?"

"Simple. It's vampire law. You risked your life for me."

I glanced at the bronze hue of the Sazerac. When my attention veered to the kitchen which was separated from the bar by a white wall, the room hazed over with white mist and Raven's voice faded. I was leaving the present and traveling through a portal into my past life.

A force drove me into a large old-fashioned kitchen. Amidst steaming pots on huge ovens I stood in an area noticeably lacking electric or gas appliances.

A heavy-jowled gray-haired man was busy chopping vegetables beside a rotund black woman scooping boiled clams into a bowl.

"Jambalaya. Yum," I whispered at the pot, tying on an apron. The aroma was so rich, my mouth started to salivate.

"Watch that rice, Pierre," I cautioned the teenager at the stove. "It's about to boil over."

"Yes, Chef." A gawky white boy, arms spindly long, his face bristling with what I supposed was his first beard, grabbed a towel and took hold of the lid.

A dusky-skinned man, eyes coal black surrounded by long black lashes shouted out over the voices. "Chef, we have andouille simmerin' with the celery, peppers and onions." He jerked his chin in the direction of several large cast iron pots on the six wood burning stoves attended by a hefty black woman, breasts as large as cantaloupes, hanging low under the white apron.

When the woman swung around to the next pan, her round hips chugged in rhythm as if she was dancing. With her thick body and wide dress she resembled a dark moth, wings spread wide in rest before flight.

I strode over to the pans, reached over and jiggled the contents. "Garlic and tomatoes, Lulu."

"Yes, Chef!" She shouted over her shoulder, "Lattrice, you ready with the garlic and tomatoes?"

A slender girl, curly black hair pinned in a bun raced up with a bowl. "All done."

When a pale lean man, dark curls to his shoulders, his lips wine red, almost as if they were brushed with paint, looked up with soulful eyes, I knew instinctively he was the sous chef and that I knew him well. "I am decorating the gateau with chocolate flowers," he said, in a heavy French accent, setting down a bowl of shrimp on the main counter. "Shirlene said the stock is done."

"Good. And the rice?"

The teenager, Pierre, turned on his heel and scooted over to the burner, lifting the lid, his hands like crab claws in the tan oven mitts.

From over my shoulder a man's deep voice said excitedly, "We're puttin' in the shrimp, Chef."

I craned my neck to see his face, he was so tall—a foot higher than the top of my head. A giant ebony-skinned man, a broad nose in a square face, shiny with sweat, said, "Chef, they say the mayor is here."

"We'll give them a dinner they won't soon forget." I tapped his arm. "Remember the bay leaves need to go in too, Andre." Looking around the kitchen, I was pleased. The staff was scurrying right and left, busy making all the extras, and as for the main course tonight, there would be enough jambalaya to feed thirteen.

It's what they all wanted—to savor the flavors of a Creole dish.

The dinner was a private function hosted by my fiancé. I was excited about being a bride. Someone actually wanted to marry me, a destitute French girl. But was he the "one"?

It was unusual for a woman to have a position of authority, to be the chef in a restaurant, but then again this city appreciated food and I had the good fortune to come from a long line of chefs. My papa had owned the most famous restaurant in Paris. A place the Duc d'Orleans himself frequented. In my mind I pictured the small chateau overlooking the Seine, the riverbank green with foliage.

Apparently, Monsieur Renard, the owner of this establishment had petitioned the nuns to grant his request. I inherited the talent of my famous father and Renard needed his restaurant to succeed. He had paid the nuns a considerable amount to acquire me.

My thoughts were whirling about like a gerbil spinning on a wheel. Who was I really? I rubbed my eyes trying to bring back all the memories. When I lowered my hands I was shocked. My skin was golden. A lady wore gloves to keep her skin white in this century. Surely, I wasn't a free black? If only I could see myself in the mirror.

"Be patient, Chef. It will come back to you."

I turned to my thin sous chef. "I think I know you."

"You do. My name is Raven. I came with you to New Orleans from France." His eyes studied my face. "You inherited the chef gene, Belle. Your ancestors made that wild man, the Duc D'Orleans, delectable dinners."

"And he introduced us to chocolate. Nothing is better than chocolate."

"Oh?" he said, with a wink. "You have something just as tasty."

"What do you mean?"

Before he could answer, Andre approached followed by Shirlene and the other cooks. "We are ready to serve, Chef."

The dishwashers swung the doors open and we entered a cathedral-height dining area, brass chandeliers suspended from the white ceiling and wine-red walls trimmed with ivory wooden panels. Linen table clothes were set with pewter dishes, silver cutlery and heavy crystal glasses for the large party sitting at the round table. Cocktails, wine and beer were the drinks of the hour.

The dusky-skinned lady at the center was elegant, her wavy black hair arranged in a coil above her crown. Arched brows emphasized her startling black eyes. Pouting red lips parted to sip the champagne she tipped back. The low-cut rose silk gown was fit for royalty and she looked the part of a queen.

The woman's long elegant fingers rested on a fair-complexioned man's shoulder—slim in a black velvet jacket over an ivory shirt, equally haughty in demeanor; he demanded the deference of a king.

His dark eyes lit up when he saw the procession of cooks carrying trays. Sporting a pencil moustache and goatee which emphasized his rather pronounced lips, he was attractive but not nearly as much as the devastatingly attractive man beside him.

This man was clothed in a burgundy velvet jacket over a crisp white shirt. His brilliant emerald eyes met mine and a smile played on his lips. There was an undeniable spark between us. He was sinfully delicious like chocolate. My mouth watered for a taste.

The table politely applauded the entrance of the dishes arriving on silver platters carried in by the cooks. But when I brought the jambalaya and set it down, the moustached man with the goatee flew to his feet and pronounced, "We are honored, Mademoiselle Belle. Indeed your fiancé, Monsieur Renard is blessed to have you in his kitchen."

Under his breath a black man built like a barn, laughed showing off a protruding gold incisor. "And in his bed, Jean."

"No need to state the obvious, Paul. Forgive his crude humor, Monsieur Mayor and fellow guests. Our lucky host has the loveliest girl to not only cook but to teach the art of love. Who can be more blessed than Renard should he manage to marry the beautiful Belle?" The man grinned. "But perhaps some smart lad will snatch her away, eh, Alain?" He patted the shoulder of the man of the handsome man beside him.

"Enough!" The tall, dark man growled, "You insult me Lafitte."

A slender blonde seated next to him tugged on his arm in warning. "It's all right, Rene. Jean is joking."

Rene Renard took a deep breath, and announced, "Raise your glass to my fiancée. To Belle."

Glassed clinked and a few men hooted. I took in the group as they stared in my direction.

Although attractive, Rene was vanilla compared to Jean or his friend, Alain. I was smitten with the slightly crooked smile. This man was about as dangerously charismatic as any woman could tolerate. It took all of my will power to resist throwing myself on the floor and pulling him on top.

"No, Belle! Stop flirting before Renard catches on," my sous chef whispered in my ear.

My cell vibrated in my purse and as suddenly as the vision began, it faded. Once again I was seated at the bar beside Raven.

He glanced at my bag. "Answer that. It's important."

"What is exactly going on, Raven? Why were you in my vision anyway?"

"Protection, remember?"

"Hm-mm," I said absentmindedly. I dug into the black slouch purse slung over my stool, and took out my cell. A text appeared.

Dinner? M

"Ah-ha! Told you," Raven said. "Tell him to meet you here. If you tour the upstairs you'll see more of your past life." He winked.

***

Auntie Ruthie was not happy with what she saw. Coffee grinds coated the interior of the coffee cup in an irregular pattern. Hunched over the table she lifted the cup and studied the shapes symbolizing the events around Chuckie Shucker's life.

"You sure it's ready? Maybe I didn't swish it enough?"

"Silence, boy." On one side she saw the spindly image of death extending his long skeletal fingers out.

Auntie Ruthie gasped.

"What is it? You is lookin' scared. Nothings goin' to happen to me, is there?"

The old lady pointed to the figure in the cup.

Chuckie Shucker's eyes grew round. "Someone's goin' to kill me?"

Auntie Ruthie shook her head. "Danger ahead."

"What's about the blonde witch and Doctor Philippe? Do they have somethin' to do with it?"

59

"Dey's in dat cup with you."

"What?"

"In your other life. Right now, you safe. She's not lookin' to find you."

"What's this about another life, Auntie Ruthie? Who was I then?"

"You was octoroon, son of a pirate and a casquette girl. Near white." She looked him in the eyes. "Halfway handsome even. You could play music like an angel. And the gals liked you."

"So that was good, right?"

Auntie Ruthie shook her head.

"Sheet! Is you funnin' wit' me?"

"You had trouble."

Chuckie Shucker leaned back in the rattan chair. "And what about now? Do I get that oyster boat? Them Asians said I can invest with dem if I comes up with the capital."

"Then you needs to follow the witch." She pointed to something that looked like a birthday present. "See here? She has something valuable."

Chuckie Shucker grabbed her wrist and squeezed. "What?"

Auntie Ruthie growled, "Let go, fool. You is foolin' wit' the wrong woman."

Chapter 7: THE SUN

Drink in hand I strolled back to the entrance of Renard's. A tall muscular man was reading the menu in the light of the lantern outside the door. When he glanced up, my heart jumped a beat. I was pleasantly surprised at how much I wanted to see him.

Black waves brushed the collar of a silky shirt he had rolled up to the elbows. The green fabric of his shirt enhanced the sparkle of his enigmatic eyes when he caught sight of me. He was a tall drink of water. Muscular without being one of those neckless weightlifters squeezed like a sausage into his clothes. I would be lying if I said I didn't notice how the black jeans enticingly hugged the curve of his tush.

Only a few hours ago we'd had Bloody Marys in an Irish bar with the rain pouring down outside. He was virtually a stranger but this instant reconnect was uncanny.

Markus drew me into his arms. "You look beautiful."

"Thank you. You look—good," I said, grasping for an acceptable word to describe his sinfully delicious appearance.

"A Sazerac?" Markus glanced at the old-fashioned glass filled with a bronze liquid. "You like it?"

"I'm not drinking for the taste."

Markus grinned. "You had a bad day?"

"This particular drink stimulates my psychic senses." I sipped the cocktail slowly, channeling the energy.

His eyes crinkled at the corners in amusement until he saw my expression. "You're not kidding, are you?"

I nodded. "I had a vision back at the bar and I know it has to do with this drink."

"Happened in Arizona for me, peyote inspired. I decided to return to Louisiana and change my life."

I studied his strong profile. "What kind of changes?"

"I like to write, but a strong feeling made me buy the Nikon."

Just past his shoulder I caught sight of a sign. "Visit our resident ghost upstairs". I waved at the sign. "Do you mind if we go up before we leave?"

"Okay by me." He glanced down at the Nikon. "Not sure if my

camera can capture spirits but let's give it a go." With his hand at my elbow we took the stairs. At the landing he paused and motioned to the oil painting in the guilt frame. "She's so familiar. I'd swear I know her."

The blonde fit into the dress in a way that beguiled any living breathing male but the flimsy chiffon peach gown was one step above a cheesy prom dress. "A pretty face."

"I would have hit on her if I lived back then." Markus stepped closer, his eyes animated. "Captivating the way she stares, yet with a hint of devilish humor that makes me think she was trouble." His eyes swept the painting once more.

For a second I felt a tinge of envy and then rolled my eyes at how insane this feeling was—to be jealous of a dead woman. "Do you ever think of time travel?"

He grinned widely, displaying a dimple. "Rescuing fair damsels and fighting off barbarians? Sure, but knowing my talents I would likely be the court portrait painter. What about you?"

"Wearing a chastity belt, waiting for the knight to return every five years? Not my kind of long-distance relationship. Shooting a long-bow to protect the castle—cool."

Markus' lips curled into a smile. "Warrior princess. Suits you."

When he took my hand electricity sparked. I had a crazy urge to kiss those shapely lips. But at the top of the stairs I put that thought aside as I stopped in my tracks in front of the larger than life Egyptian statue of a Pharaoh. The energy inside the room was eerie. I could feel my hair stand on end.

Markus glanced around. "You okay?"

It was hard to explain. I nodded.

"You know you'd look like a Victoria's Secret model lounging on that settee," he said, his eyes flicking to the leopard print couch.

I glanced at him. He was a bad boy all right.

"Watch out, Anabelle," whispered Logical.

A chill blasted the room like the air from an open freezer door. I couldn't shake the feeling that someone was watching.

In front of a wall-length wine rack filled with red vintages, a square table was set with china, silver utensils and wine glasses for a formal dinner as if the guests would arrive momentarily.

"In photos the spirits present as orbs," I said, as Markus aimed the camera.

Markus smirked. "Dust balls do that too."

"Maybe, but there are ghosts here."

Markus leaned in to hear me. 'So what did they die of?" His fresh scent of soap and lime was like an aphrodisiac, so enticing.

"Suicide for sure, maybe murder," I murmured.

"Morbid girl." Markus took a few shots of the table set for six before we returned to the Egyptian room and made himself comfortable on the red loveseat as I took the leopard settee.

Right above his head there was a painting of a strawberry blonde wearing a blue silk gown cinched at the waist.

"Show me a sign you hear me," I said to the room.

I did a double take when the woman in the painting winked one slanty brown eye. "It's me, Janelle," she whispered.

The room tingled with electricity.

Janelle tilted her head. "Why are you with that bastard?" Her eyes shot daggers at me. "Why is it they all preferred you? Fools!"

"Who?" I waited. "Janelle?"

She pursed her lips into a thin line for a moment. "They died— painfully. All of them."

"And you?"

"My life was horrid." Janelle's forehead furrowed and a tear welled in her eye.

"Anabelle?" Markus touched my arm. "The painting?"

I nodded. "Yes, she spoke. Her name is Janelle."

He glanced over at the painting.

Some noise behind me put me on alert. I lifted a hand in warning. "Is there a man here?"

A tasseled gold lamp shade next to the settee started to sway. The yellowish light flickered, turning a dark cobalt blue. I listened for any activity from downstairs which could have caused the movement but it was deathly silent.

"Show yourself," I said, as Markus took a photo of the area around the lamp.

The lampshade trembled once more.

The woman in the painting puckered her lips in a kiss. The wall vibrated and the painting swayed violently. I shouted, "Watch out!"

The heavy gilded oak framed painting dropped off the wall and clipped Markus on the head, hard enough to knock him to the floor, camera in hand.

A deep voice behind me said, "That shyster deserves that and worse." I glanced at the wall. For a second I saw a man's face and then it went hazy. He was someone from the dinner party vision. I was sure it was Rene Renard.

"Hey, are you okay?" I knelt down beside a motionless Markus. Under a lock of hair, an inflamed area marred his temple. When I shook his shoulders there was no response. I panicked. "Omigod, I'll call an ambulance."

Markus stirred and opened his eyes. "No need for that, Anabelle." An even row of Hollywood whites flashed. "I'll live."

"You scared the hell out of me. Why didn't you answer me?"

"Dizzy, I guess." Markus sat up and felt the bruise with his fingertips. "Deranged creature," he muttered, before meticulously examining his camera lens.

"Should we go to the hospital?"

"I'll heal. More importantly the Nikon is good as gold." He pulled me up with him. "Got a great place for us to eat."

"Wait." Gingerly, I picked up the painting, checking to see if the wire attached to the frame was intact. It was perfect. There was no logical reason for the accident. Carefully, I set it on the floor against the wall. "I'll let them hang it."

"Sensible. Let's go."

I didn't resist, almost too happy to head down the stairs and into the street away from the paranormal room. "Sorry."

"For?"

"The ghosts."

"You've got a regular ghost squad after you." Markus took my elbow and we walked down St. Ann Street.

"Those ghosts want to hurt you, not me."

"Can't figure why."

At the corner of Decatur we stood under a street light. Foot traffic was busy, a line of decorative carriages pulled by mules in fancy harnesses stopped on the side of the road.

"It's not far from here. On the other side of Jackson Square." He took my hand. "Did you get any information from the ghosts?"

I told him what Janelle and the male ghost had said. Markus was quiet but I could tell he was disturbed by this information. As we came upon street artists, prints and paintings of the local sights arranged along the wrought iron rails for a quick sale, we stopped to look. Some artists were exceptionally talented while others floated along content with cookie cutter prints.

Just ahead a small group was blocking the sidewalk. I caught a glimpse of a woman on the pavement, her black skirt jacked up to her waist. I peered over a boy's shoulder. The woman's dusky face was bruised and starting to swell. A police officer was on his knees questioning her. A word came slowly out of her swollen lips. "Juju."

The group around her took a collective intake of breath.

"Who did this?" the black police officer probed, his lips curled downwards.

Her eyes fluttered and rolled back. The tag on her grimy white blouse said "Dee".

I froze.

"What is it, Anabelle?"

"I know her," I volunteered to the officer, pointing at her name tag. "She bartends at the Belfoire Hotel. "Will she be all right?"

The police officer shrugged. Before he could say more, an ambulance zoomed in, siren screeching and lights flashing. When it came to a stop, the crew got out.

"Anabelle, remember what I said about how intuitive I am?" Markus said. "She'll make it. Believe me."

"I hope you're right."

"New O'leans is a big wicked city." Markus led me along past the ferry boat dock. "Look over there." He jerked his chin towards the ship. "It's leaving for the nineteenth ward, called Algiers, across the river. It's a place to be careful. Luckily, we are eating here at a great restaurant where you can forget everything and relax." He pointed at the red sign with a drawing of a king crab in blue, the words boldly scripted "Jumbo Gumbo".

I couldn't just jump into a jovial mood after what I had seen. How blasé for Markus to think so little of the poor woman. What violence had he witnessed to make him that callous? His attitude put a damper on our date. It might be best if I left early and focused on why I was in New Orleans and forgot about this callous man.

"Good evenin', folks." A good-looking black with a shaved head, wearing charcoal pants and a white shirt waved us into a spacious restaurant. Buddy Guy music, ocean photos high on the white walls and ship paraphernalia on the wood panels gave the room a casual atmosphere. Ivory plates and rolled linen napkins were arranged pleasingly on red tablecloths and had just the right level of intimacy had I been in the mood.

"My name is Devon and I will be your waiter tonight." He led us to a round table by a bay window. "Thought you might like the view."

"Are you okay with this, Anabelle, or would you like to sit further in?" Markus' eyes darted to the crowd passing by outside the window.

"No, it's fine."

Markus glanced at me.

I avoided his eyes.

Devon pulled out my chair. "Say, have I seen you here before?" he asked Markus.

"I filled in behind the bar a while back."

"That must be it, then." The server smiled. "What can I get y'all to drink?"

"A Dixie and a..." Markus paused.

"Cranberry juice, vodka and a slice of lime, please."

The waiter nodded his approval. "Here are the menus. Take your time." He strode over to another table.

"You bartend?" My question came out tinged with hostility, my enthusiasm over the date down to zero.

"I did when I first came to New O'leans." Markus shot me a look. "You're pissed at me about the girl, aren't you?" For a moment he looked past my shoulder, his eyes distant. "Let me explain. I was in the military, deployed to Iraq for two years. It did a number on me. Best friends blown to bits. Sometimes I feel I lost a big part of my soul." Markus' eyes looked sad. "That's one reason I returned to Louisiana." He looked around. "Makes me feel alive again."

I placed my hand over his. "Sorry, didn't mean to judge. It must have been rough there. Forgive me?"

He smiled slowly in a way that made me tingle. "Let's start over."

"So, you bartend. We have that in common."

"You mean besides ghosts who don't seem to like us."

"Wrong. A ghost named Janelle can't stand you but a pirate ghost really likes me." I grinned.

"I'm seriously jealous of that pirate ghost and your psychic vibes." He leaned over and took my hand. "What do you sense now?"

My earlier trepidation forgotten, a flame soared down my body straight to my core. Quickly, I withdrew my hand. There was no way I was letting those sensual lips throw me off balance. "I sense you are as hungry as I am."

"Cagey."

"Hm-mm, what?"

"You." Markus grinned, his eyes dancing. "I'd like to get to know you better."

"Do you think there's any point to it? I'll only be here a while and then it's back to Canada."

Markus lightly stroked my hand. "Let's enjoy the experience then."

His touch had set me on fire. I had to focus to speak. "What's good?"

"If you're game we can share the gumbo."

I nodded.

Devon overheard us as he set the drinks on the table. "The seafood gumbo?"

Markus nodded. "Looking forward to it." He held up his glass, "Salute."

"To new beginnings," I said.

Markus clicked my glass with his bottle. "Next time we'll have a bottle of wine, okay?" He turned to me. "Ever had gumbo?"

For a reason I couldn't pinpoint, I blurted out, "African origin, okra used in the roux. I stopped using it when the socialites started coming and complaining about Negro food." I shook my head. "Seriously, I don't know how that came out of my mouth. I've never made gumbo. And Negro? Who says that? It's so racist."

Markus' eyes met mine. "Yet, you knew about gumbo in a way that a stranger wouldn't."

I rubbed my temple trying to clear the confusion.

Markus nodded. "And spirits speak to you."

"You don't think I'm crazy?"

"Do you get these visions often?"

"Intermittently. That vision at the Hotel Belfoire came on after drinking a Sazerac. I was a chef making jambalaya for a dinner party. Strange?"

"Not for a psychic."

"The visions are back in the 1800's." I frowned. "You don't think I'm losing it, do you?"

"Is it usual?"

"Seeing into another life? Not really."

Devon reappeared with a large bowl of thick gumbo and a ladle. He served a portion on each of our plates. "Enjoy."

"Thanks, bra." When Devon left to serve another table, Markus said, "Why Renard's?"

I tipped back my cocktail. The red of the cranberry sparkled in the candlelight. "For the past year I've dreamed of this man who drank a Sazerac. I think he was the ghost who spoke right after Janelle hit you with the frame. Rene Renard."

"Have you seen other spirits?"

"In the Quarter? Yes. At my hotel I saw a ghost woman called Delphine and at the cemetery Marie Laveau."

Markus frowned. "Two ghosts. Interesting. People around here believe in Laveau's powers. Do you?"

"She gave me gris-gris."

"For?"

"Love, I think, or maybe to help." I met his eyes. "I'm afraid to go to sleep because I know I'll dream about Renard."

Markus leaned forward his eyes intense. "How did he die?"

"Hung himself." I stared at a table busy with a group of people celebrating.

"Nasty, but listen, Anabelle, let it go. You'll solve the mystery of your past life eventually."

I glanced at Markus digging into the gumbo. He was right. I was OCD. I would drive myself insane. "I suppose." I forked up some gumbo and let the flavors bite my tongue. They were just the right mixture of spicy. "Very good."

"Glad you like it. Now tell me about your visit with Philippe."

I frowned.

"From your expression I can see it was a bit of a disappointment."

"Not exactly."

"Philippe's one of the best."

"He has this presence which is totally scary. After my reading he said he could meet me for lunch at the Hotel Belfoire."

"And?"

"I had another vision. It was on a ship this time. I was a pirate, or at least had the right outfit."

Markus grinned widely. "Hm-mm, something sexy about a pirate chick—those tight pants and open shirt. You'd look hot in that."

I laughed. "The vision came with a creep. I call him "one nostril"."

"Let me guess...he had the other one bitten off."

I laughed. "No idea. I managed to fend him off with an oar."

"Impressive."

"I'm a martial artist but I think even back then I knew self-defense. Someone taught me."

"Cool. I did some kick-boxing myself." Markus leaned forward and took my hand. "What happened in your vision?"

My hand trembled as a bloody deck flashed before my eyes.

"Are you okay, Anabelle? You know, we don't need to talk about this. I want you to enjoy tonight."

I shuddered seeing the mess of brains strewn over the deck. I took a deep breath and continued, "I survived a horrible attack. A pirate helped me."

"That same pirate who likes you?"

I nodded. "I've seen him twice."

Markus stopped mid-spoon. "On the boat and..?"

"In my hotel room."

Markus' eyebrows rose in the center.

"He's very—nice." I pushed my plate away.

Hormone tittered. "You mean a smokin' red hot male."

I grinned.

Markus looked at me curiously before signaling for the check. "How'd you meet this guy?"

"It was weird. After Sandie left, this pirate appeared."

"Who's Sandie?"

"She works the front desk at my hotel. When I checked in I told her I saw my room in a vision and when I described it she upgraded me to a suite. Funny thing is—she told me it was haunted."

"And you still wanted to stay there?"

"I hoped it might be connected to the dreams."

"Ghosts are promo for any hotel in New O'leans."

"You mean visitors want ghosts?"

"It is the most haunted city in North America." Markus shrugged. "Some would love to see a ghost as long as it's not dangerous—the type who stains the walls with blood. What did she tell you about the spirits?"

"She stayed there with her daughter. There were doors slamming and her daughter saw ghosts."

"And now you have." He looked pointedly at me. "You hadn't been drinking, had you?"

I grinned.

"You're not tellin' me everything."

"Well, Sandie had a joint with her."

I don't know why I expected anything other than a grin from Markus. I was beginning to think he found me amusing.

"Seriously, it made my senses more aware. First I saw a nasty ghost called Delphine and then when Sandie left, Alain Ducoeur appeared."

"The pirate."

"Jealous?"

From across the table Markus grabbed my hand. "You have killer eyes, Anabelle. Anyone, ghost or human would like to know you better."

"Thank you," I said, heat rising to my cheeks.

"Did anything good come of that meeting with Philippe?"

Reflectively, I ran my fingers through my hair. "He mentioned a book, a journal I wrote back in the nineteenth century when I was a woman called Belle."

"If that was two hundred years ago it would be pretty well impossible to find, wouldn't it?"

"Yes, but," I trailed off having a sudden flash of a notebook and a room that looked like my hotel bedroom.

As I tried to envision the location of the diary, Devon returned with the bill and laid it on the table. Markus tugged out his wallet and I quickly opened my purse.

"No, this is a date, Anabelle. I asked you out."

"Let me chip in." Without waiting for his reply I tossed in a bill.

"I'll let you take me out on the third date," he said, sticking the money back into my bag. He placed his camera on the table as he moved his chair closer to mine. "Would you like to look at the photos?"

"Oh, yes. I'd love to see them."

The first few were of the cemetery—the mausoleums white-walled, each architecturally unique in structure. Marie Laveau's tomb was shot from different angles. On the fourth photo he stopped and stared.

"What is it, Markus?"

He didn't answer instead he clicked the zoom button and slid his finger to the corner. I leaned closer. The fresh smell of lime stoked my juices.

"Very strange," he said slowly.

"Look at him," my Hormone Voice whispered. My eyes flicked over his profile. "You need to make sure you get a second date. Kiss him."

"Seriously?" My Logical Voice argued. "Let Markus make the move or Anabelle will mess this up. Men like the chase."

That was probably true and easier too. Who wants to go out on a limb with a new guy? Love needs to grow. I should have questioned my relationship with Sean but I was led to believe he was into me. Stupid.

"No, you're not," Logical said. "Just make sure you don't fall for another guy's delusional fantasy."

Annoying voices. Silently, I told them to put a lid on it.

"Anabelle? You okay?"

"Just thinking."

"Here's another one." Markus' finger pointed at the digital screen on his camera. "See it? Just like the one at Laveau's tomb." It appeared as a large glass crystal bowl floating around the Egyptian pharaoh.

"Yes."

The next photo was of the leopard settee, including the table lamp, its gold shade edged with tassels. This time I didn't have to search to see the orb above the lamp.

"That's an orb surrounding the same lamp that shook!" I said excitedly. "Proof."

"I suppose—if you believe orbs aren't dust balls."

I gave his arm a nudge. "This is not a time for logic, Markus. Say, what about the oil painting that fell down. Did you get a photo of that?"

"No," he said quietly, watching my face.

"Janelle knows us."

"She's trouble."

I laughed. "Now you're the paranormal expert?"

Markus sat back and steepled his fingers. "That room brings back something indescribable. Even the women in the paintings seem familiar." His eyes took on a faraway appearance like a person awakened from a deep sleep.

"Janelle has a beef with you," I said.

"Why?"

A bell inside me chimed in warning. "Cheating," came out slowly from a voice inside my brain.

Markus looked surprised. "I cheated on her? I can see why."

"Oh?"

"She's not as amazing looking as the babe on the stairway." He ran his finger over his bruised temple. "That crazy chick enjoyed beating her men with a heavy hand."

"I think you jilted her or maybe, she's jealous of your beauty." I laughed when I saw the look on his face. "You could have been a woman."

He laughed. "Me? Never."

"What's wrong with being a woman?"

"Women back then in Louisiana were nuns, prostitutes or wives. Boring."

"Unless of course you happened to be a famous chef in Renard's like I was." I was rather pleased with being a chef—creating succulent New Orleans cuisine and all the staff and patrons showering me with praise.

"A rare thing for a woman back then or even now." He grinned mischievously. "I could have been a rich widow."

"The merry widow?"

"Why not?"

It would be just my luck to attract another player.

"I've been searching into my past too." Markus played with the camera cord.

"Oh?"

"An investigator has found my family home."

"You must be excited."

"I don't know much of what it entails." Thoughtfully, he ran his fingers through his hair pushing it off his forehead. "Do you think the person I was back in a past life could have been a relative?"

"No idea. I know Janelle had a beef with you and Renard thought you were a bastard."

"Can't believe everything you hear. But I bet we knew each other." Markus leaned in, hazel eyes flickering emeralds.

"Maybe or maybe not," I quipped, suddenly afraid to taste those shapely lips.

"Get closer and kiss him!" Hormone screeched excitedly.

"Not so fast, Anabelle," Logical hissed. "There must be a reason Janelle lashed out. Think about it."

"How about dessert? I think you like chocolate." Markus laughed softly. "I see from that lascivious smile you more than like it. I found you out, didn't I? You are a chocoholic."

This man could read my mind. I was sure of it. But if he really could, I was in trouble. He would know I had a yen for more than chocolate." I bit my lip and met his eyes. "You're one hundred per cent correct but unfortunately I have a gluten allergy."

"Flourless cake?" He paused, stroking his chin in consideration. "Not a problem. I know a place—"

"Let's keep that for another night. I'll be here for a while."

"All right. Let me walk you back to your hotel then."

On the way, Markus amused me by pointing out quirky art objects or bizarre paintings in the showcase windows of shops on Royal Street. At a wrought iron fence, I posed like a model displaying a couture gown but in such a way he had to grip the camera tightly or his laughter would jiggle the shot. It was a comfortable first date with no awkwardness and as we came to the door of the hotel I stopped not exactly sure how to end our time together.

"A hug would be nice," Markus said softly.

I sprang into his waiting arms, squeezed him tightly and then just as quickly backed away with a wave and popped inside to the safety of the hallway. It was a little abrupt. I wasn't ready for more but on the way up the elevator I started regretting my too sudden departure.

"You blew it, girl," Hormone said sharply. "Why not kiss him? He's hot and funny. What more do you want? Besides, it's a date not a commitment."

I was so stupid, practically running from a sexy man.

"Rebound," muttered Logical, "never works."

"Oh, shut up," I snapped, entering my room. How did either of them know, anyway?

Outside it was pitch black, perfect cover for a bat but when I glanced at the railings on the balcony, Raven was nowhere to be seen. I was disappointed, not only because he held clues to my past life, but I would bet my bottom dollar Raven had information for me he hadn't as yet revealed.

Across the street the Beauregard Keyes mansion was aglow with light, shadows flickering back and forth, as though there were spirits awakening for a midnight haunting. Too tense to go to bed, I popped a sleeping pill to forget about ghosts but with so much tossing and turning I decided to try out the tub and see if a bath would relax me. With the taps turned on, I made my way back to the bedroom and switched on the TV to an old episode of Seinfeld.

As Elaine and Jerry's dilemma at the Chinese restaurant grew more and more frustrating, I hung my dress in the closet and tucked my bra and panties in the dresser drawer before I pinned my hair up. When a car ad came on I peeked into the bathroom and noticing the water rising close to the top, I ran in and turned off the taps. There was no complimentary bubble bath but making do, I grabbed a bar of soap and stepped into the heavenly warmth of the bath water, sinking down deep as I could, leaning against the porcelain tub.

The steamy water caressed my body better than a massage, until I floated off on a virtual cloud. When the water cooled I forced myself to step out. Wrapping a towel around me, I trudged over to the bed and lay down, my eyes heavy and my brain sluggish.

The air conditioner was oddly silent although I remembered I had left it on low. Possibly the maids had switched it off conscious of hydro costs which was strange as most hotels thought their clientele liked an icy cold room. The open balcony door let in a pleasant moist breeze, comfortable enough to let my brain give in to my body's rhythm, drifting into a drug-induced sleep.

***

An eerie bayou stretched over a wide expanse, the muddy banks edged thickly with cypress trees heavily dressed with Spanish moss. Over the brackish water a long-legged egret, snowy white, stood elegantly perfect on one leg. As I watched I felt the bed quiver with a heavy weight. Too tired to wake up, I returned to my dream. In the distance, through the mist, a rowboat approached. I sensed the man on board was coming to take me away from the misery of my life. My heart beat faster in anticipation.

Another jiggle of the bed and I jolted awake. My eyes cranked open to slits and I slowly turned my head almost afraid of what could be occupying my bed.

Comfortably at ease, lying on his side, his head propped up by his hand, Alain Ducoeur said, "You are lovely sleeping, Belle, but even more so awake." His lips came together in an inscrutable smile as his glance swept up and down my body.

"How long have you been there watching me? Don't answer that." I shook myself awake. How creepy was that having a ghost stalker?

"I had to come back, cher."

"And why is that, Monsieur Ducoeur?"

He reached over and lightly stroked my lower lip. "Alain," he said, in a husky voice.

Pushing his finger away, I demanded, "Why exactly are you here?"

His green eyes flashed. "This is our love nest. How could I stay away?" He smiled slightly. "You're doing that eyebrow thing. I've missed that. Enchanting."

"I only do this eyebrow thing when I don't believe someone."

"You don't believe in my sincerity?" He swept a tendril away from my cheek. "Be honest with yourself, cher. Remember how we were together? You read my mind and I knew your every thought."

Hopefully, he couldn't read what I was thinking right now. When Alain looked away to the glass doors of the balcony I was struck by how remarkably masculine his profile was—the high forehead, lengthy nose and significant chin. Everything about him was extremely seductive, especially his lips.

My hand came up almost as if it had a mind of its own and my fingers trailed down his cheek lingering at the familiar feel of the rough bristles along his jaw line.

"I want to kiss those lips," he whispered, leaning in. His mouth pressed against mine as if he was drawing in my energy. I was captured in his net but my brain kept interfering, questioning the sanity of this situation.

"Stop!" I said. "You want something or you wouldn't be here. You need to tell me who I was and in what we were to each other."

I sat up my back against the headboard and glanced down at

Alain's brilliant green eyes sparkling with life. How could a ghost look that good?

But he ignored my words. Light sensuous kisses tantalized my neck as his strong hands stroked from the curve of my waist to the fullness of my buttocks. Tingles shot to every nerve ending of my body. Reaching over, I undid his shirt and helped him pull it off. His body was hard and muscular and not at all flimsy as I would have expected from a spirit. The breeches were next. It was a struggle but when he raised his hips and tugged them down they quickly joined the shirt on the floor.

Underneath, he was commando and ready for action. At that point I was as much part of this feverish exchange as he was. Juices flowed, tongues danced and hands went wildly exploring— his on my breasts and mine on his firm behind. Our bodies rolled and stopped with Alain on top. I could think of nothing else but my needs.

"Ah, cher, how good you taste," he whispered. While he grasped my hips and held them tightly, his tongue trailed over my belly and found its way down. I gasped at the touch of his tongue. I let myself escape with a wave of exhilarating pleasure and screamed.

Loud banging on the door interrupted my blissful state.

A female voice yelled, "Anabelle! Are you all right?"

"What the heck?" The aftermath was destroyed as rapidly as Hurricane Katrina crushed New Orleans. It was then that I noticed how the immense king size bed was suddenly sadly empty. My ghostly lover had vanished. Not even a hint of vapor left. Had I imagined Ducoeur making love to me? Was I going insane?

Hurriedly, I slipped on a robe before running into the other room and opening the outer door. Sandie was rocking on her heels, eyes nervously flitting about.

"Are you all right?" Her glance whipped to 401. "I was just in there checkin' the room when I heard you yelling." She pulled me into a tight embrace, patting my back and muttering soothingly, "I can't believe these ghosts are getting so vicious. They never harmed anyone before, although one scared the crap out of me, but like I told you before, it hasn't happened since."

"Thanks for your concern, Sandie, but I'm fine. Would you like to come in?" I indicated the chair in the sitting room.

"No, can't." Nervously, she ran her fingers through her disheveled blonde strands as she glanced around. "Hair appointment. Gotta go." She jerked around to the elevator and then looking over her shoulder she said, "You can switch rooms if they get too violent." Then, seeing my expression, she added, "Just sayin'."

After I closed the door I was struck by the coincidence of Sandie's more than speedy arrival. Why was she really there? If I sat her down and focused I might be able to get a read on her. Intentions could be sensed but only if I concentrated long and hard.

Back in the master bedroom I sat on the edge of the bed thinking about Sandie but was distracted by the bright sunlight outside. Where was that vampire, when I needed him? Raven wouldn't return to Renard's with me unless it was dark and I definitely had to go. It seemed I had a connection with the building or else why did I have that vision of the kitchen? Quite by accident I noticed a tiny key on the bedside table. A key too small for a door but just right for a diary.

Closing my eyes I let myself drift into a state of heightened perception and when I opened my eyes I was staring straight at the old dresser with the TV propped up next to the mirror—a French provincial piece, definitely antique from another age. The hunt was on!

From the left top to the bottom third drawer there was nothing but my clothes. On the right I was equally unsuccessful but I pressed on. A thorough search called for drastic measures. The room was not a pretty sight after an array of lingerie, tops and pants was dumped on the bed.

Each drawer was inspected. Worn cracked wood on the sides and bottoms. Possibly termites from the tiny holes I found on the edge but nothing unusual unless it was the size of one of the drawers. It seemed smaller at first. Tapping along the top and sides revealed nothing except a suspicious indentation in the corner. As I pressed tentatively on this groove a panel opened, revealing a false bottom and a leather book inside. Upon closer examination it was a journal which required a key. This discovery brought a big grin to my face.

With the tiny key I unlocked the strip of leather which bound the book and opened the journal to the first page.

The first page was blank except for the name "Belle Devereaux Duville" inscribed in flourishing script on the top right corner. The elation I felt flipping through the journal was mind-blowing. If I was right this diary could tell me why I was here and answer all my questions about the nightmares. Quickly, I leafed through, noting entries from aboard a ship, the convent and Renard's restaurant where I worked as the chef. One third of the way along, the name Alain Ducoeur came up and then again a few pages further, yet at that point he must have been an acquaintance, hardly a lover. Periodically, Raven was mentioned as well as Delphine Perdido. Now I knew the angry ghost's last name. Finally, I had some bedtime reading material that could put me on track.

Reluctantly, I set the journal on the counter in the bathroom and stepped into the shower, letting the warm water massage my head and shoulders until the tension left my body. From the bottle on the shelf a squeeze of chocolate body wash coated my palms and I began the slow process of covering the surface of my skin sliding over every nook and cranny, breathing in the hypnotic scent of cocoa I let myself relax, imagining a dark handsome man. He applied the slippery gel, his fingers warm and gentle.

Seriously, I had to snap out of this. Men were everywhere, some real and some ghost. My hormones must be out of whack. Quickly, I rinsed off and wrapped in the fluffy white towel entered the bedroom.

The king-sized bed was strewn with clothes and rumpled from the passionate interlude with Alain. Had I really made out with a ghost?

From the balcony doors a shapely woman in a flimsy white gown with capped sleeves ruffled at the deep neckline stepped forward. With the sunlight streaming in the open balcony door she had camouflaged well. Had I not heard her speak I might not have noticed her. Delphine hissed, "Are you happy now that you've had him, Belle?"

There was no denying the woman was pretty but no one looks good with an ugly on. Had I not picked up on the hostility in her voice, the full lips tilting down unevenly at the corners were a definite clue. She couldn't have looked meaner than if someone had stamped and ground a three inch stiletto into her foot. Of course she was a ghost not an ordinary lady. Although, I'm not sure she was a lady either. What exactly was her deal with Alain Ducoeur?

"Hello, Delphine. So kind of you to come and visit. And yes, I like being with Alain." Something about the woman irritated me. It wasn't usual for me to be deliberately unkind but I have a devilish side that's hard to restrain. "Too bad we were interrupted. He's very passionate. That man knows his foreplay." I smirked to see what reaction I'd get.

A pillow from the bed flew through the air and had I not gained a speedy reaction time from sparring it would have smacked me in the face. Instead I ducked in the nick of time and it hit the floor with a thump.

"Hey, take it easy!"

Delphine's jet black eyes shot daggers. "You'd like to have Alain, wouldn't you?" she snapped. "That would make you happy, wouldn't it? Every man in this town wrapped around your little finger, Jean included."

"Lafitte?"

"Of course! Don't play stupid with me, Belle."

At last I was getting some answers. "Why would I want to be with Jean Lafitte?"

Delphine rolled her eyes. "All the ladies want him for their lover including our so called society whores and you know it. When you came to New O'leans they were all jealous. It was those harlot eyes. You know what you are, don't you?"

"No," I laughed at her serious tone. "What exactly am I, Delphine?"

This set her off even more. In her rage her cheeks flushed pink. "No different than I am. A Creole, but no one can tell with your light golden skin. My skin has a reddish hue from my Choctaw grandmother and obviously I have some Haitian but mostly I am white, yet here in New O'leans I am known as an octoroon. It does not matter that my features are white and my hair is completely straight like the French girls. They don't care. Skin color limits me. I can be as wealthy as any white man but I can't marry Jean." She pointed her finger at me. "Someone like you should have been at the Quadroon balls as a *plaçage* looking for a contract along with the other women of color, not angling to catch a legal husband."

Now I was curious. "How do you know my heritage, Delphine?"

"People talk when they are rewarded. I have slaves who do my spying."

"Why are you so interested in me?"

"Well, believe it or not, I want to rekindle our friendship. We were the best of friends when you first arrived." Delphine smiled beguilingly and nodded her head. "Yes, we were close. After all, both of us are almost white but not acceptable for marriage. Why is it a white man can marry a white prostitute and that's just fine? The situation is most unfair."

"I thought I was to marry Rene Renard?"

"Yes, Rene chose you from the girls at the convent. But he was hesitant. I'm not sure why unless he suspected you had a black ancestor."

"Cut the crap, Delphine. What do you want? You're not here to be my friend, are you?"

"Oh, but I am. I'm sorry I took out my resentment on you. It's not your fault everyone thinks you are white and that men pant for you."

"You're saying you had a hard time getting a man?"

Delphine scoffed. "Surely you jest. Jean showers me with gifts."

"If that's so, what do you want, Delphine?"

"Nothing, really. Don't be so suspicious I just had some questions—" Her voice faded as she spotted my diary on the dresser. "If that is what I think it is I can get my answers without bothering you any further." She swept across the room and reached for my diary.

But I had her there. Karate training tuned not only my skills but my speed and I wasn't about to let Delphine steal away my link to the past. I leaped high, landing in a front break fall, my body flat on the diary. When I glanced up I was relieved to see Delphine had vanished. I must have knocked her vapor away. She was gone, at least for the moment.

Picking myself up I laid the diary on the table while I dressed and when I was ready dropped it my tote before heading out the door. My stomach screamed for a refill. Across the street in the bakery, breakfast was still being served. I had eggs over hard with sausage and coffee, not trusting them to make tea correctly. Once my hunger was satiated I finally began to relax.

The endorphins released from love-making still lingered in my system like a sensuous dream segment, softly willing me back to its closeness and warmth. The sleeping pill I had taken the night before left me dozy as it often did the following morning, but this was different—more languorous yet happy like sex with a human male. Memories of his strong body warm against mine and his hands stroking me into a fever were not about to dissipate quickly. To be honest I had enjoyed my ghostly sexual encounter. It had been a long time since I'd made love and somehow never quite like that. He had a tongue that knew how to thrill. Somehow, this did not seem like a one night stand. I knew now I had to find out more about our connection.

From my tote, I tugged out the diary and opened it to the first page.

August 20. The rocking scares the girls. The moans and stench are making me ill.

Quickly, I flipped through the next few pages and came to her arrival in New Orleans.

September 5. They remind me of large black birds—likely to peck my eyes out. It's a good thing I like wildlife.

I smiled. Belle was a character. How awful to be locked away in a convent.

Sister Marie is my mentor. She was from Paris too and we speak often of our city. She never grows tired of telling me about New Orleans. It was aptly named, she said, after the notorious Duc d' Orleans.

September 9. Sister Marie was the youngest daughter of a count and as such had to enter a nunnery.

September 10. Rene Renard asked for my hand in marriage. He is a good-looking older man but hardly anyone I would choose.

Sister Marie helped move me to Renard's hotel. I am cooking in the restaurant tomorrow.

September 12. Rene is like the perverted royals Sister Marie told me about. Janelle is his slave. She says she wants to be my friend but I don't trust her.

September 18. Janelle is pregnant.

As I read that passage, I shoved my breakfast plate away and my thoughts returned to the handsome pirate, Alain Ducoeur. The droning vibration of my cell pushed away the memory. A text message.

Drop everything. I want to whisk you away. M

Chapter 8: THE EMPEROR

The leather seats in the Mercedes were white, plush and luxurious as all get-out, and especially comfortable with the cool air fanning my face and arms. "Nice car," I said, admiring the classic interior.

After an SUV passed, Markus pulled out into the road. "Borrowed. To be honest I haven't needed a car since I came to New O'leans. A bike does the job better in the city with these narrow streets."

"A motorcycle?"

"You bet."

"For photography?"

"When I'm wearing that particular hat. I'm a freelance journalist. It pays the bills but lately I've started to follow my dream. New O'leans has great opportunities. With the bike I get shots almost anywhere and no problem finding parking either."

"Do you do work inside as well?"

"I'm set up on Decatur living above an Italian restaurant. So far the work is mostly portraits and ads. I want to do other jobs but it's early days yet. I've been taking photos for a book I plan to do about the Vieux Carré or maybe even Louisiana."

"Sounds exciting. Everything I've seen in the Quarter is beautiful." I couldn't take my eyes away from the activity in the streets, feeling like a dog, head out the window, panting with excitement. When we turned on Esplanade Avenue and drove until we turned left on Claiborne, I finally asked, "Where are we off to?"

Markus patted my hand. "Sorry, I was focusing on the traffic. I didn't mean to ignore you."

"It's okay. I am enjoying the city."

"I think you'll like the change from the city. We're heading into the country."

I stiffened. Really? Was I stupid getting in a virtual stranger's car going who knows where? A tourist is a prime target for serial killers. No one would know they're missing and the police would not care about a woman from Canada turning up dead. Was I crazy trusting Markus?

"Hey, Anabelle. You all right?"

"Yes." I said, hesitantly. Then I thought about how he could have offed me already in the cemetery at closing time if he was a psychopath. I was just being paranoid. Even a psychic without much practice gets danger signals and I had none with Markus.

"I'm glad you wanted to spend the day with me."

I glanced at Markus—tough competition for Alain Ducoeur but there was no comparison between a living, breathing man and an attractive apparition.

The road veered to the left. I checked the sign. "The Metairie is a suburb?"

"People move for the lower house prices. But for me, it's the Vieux Carré. There's nothing like the Quarter and the food."

"Hm-mm. I agree. The food is delicious and if ever a place looked European it's the Quarter. I was seriously considering renting a place."

"Glad you are liking it."

As the road merged into I-10W, he asked, "Top down, okay?"

"Sure." Now that we were on a highway, I was becoming more curious. "What exactly is our destination?"

"Sorry. I should have explained. You know how I was looking into my family origins. Well the detective I hired turned up with the jackpot." He shot me a look. "You didn't have anything else planned this afternoon, did you?"

"No-oo, but I'm getting closer to finding out about why I'm having these nightmares. Something came up with Doctor Philippe. You'd never guess..." I trailed off seeing a sign for Baton Rouge. "Are we going to Baton Rouge for lunch?"

Immediately, Logical piped up. "Piggy! You just ate, silly. Did you forget?"

Hormone drawled, "So what? With all the sex she'll have later, Anabelle will need the extra energy boost. Those calories will be gone with this one. Have a good look at that buff bod. And don't forget Markus is real—no ghost here. His parts will give Anabelle a workout better than karate."

"Hungry?' Markus' shapely lips tilted up at the corners as if he'd heard the voices in my confused brain. "If you can hold off a bit I know of a great place."

Next to the road in the bright blue water amongst the cypress tree roots and tall grasses long-legged egret stood on one leg. It reminded me of my dream with the bayou, waking next to Alain Ducoeur the pirate but here I was with an equally charismatic man, Markus.

"See that?" Markus jerked his chin in the direction of the bayou. While my eyes shot to the log floating near the shore, Markus added, "Looks like a log but it's a gator." Markus switched on the radio to a mixture of fiddle, harmonica and washboard.

"Zydeco?" I asked.

"Ya, cher."

I laughed. "You're a regular Cajun."

He nodded. "My people were Acadians from Canada."

I smiled at him. "So you're Canadian, nice." But I wasn't thinking about our Canuck connection. He was delicious like chocolate—sinfully decadent, loaded with exhilarating cocoa. While the breeze ruffled his thick waves, I pictured him rolling in bed with me, my fingers in the tousled hair pulling his head to my lips. Maybe an affair was just what I needed. A little dalliance might make me sleep better at night. Rest was good for the complexion, as was some great sex.

The scenery began to get monotonous with the green fields, trees and patches of bayou. After a while, the warm air lulled me into a drowsy state. I sank back into the comfort of the plush leather and after a bit dozed off.

When I opened my eyes the scenery wasn't green or picturesque. Outside a silver monstrosity towered above an array of buildings, glimmering in the sunlight. "An oil refinery?"

"Provides jobs around here."

"Ugly."

"True, and is hardly environmentally friendly or at all safe."

Markus turned left onto road 22. Through the tall leafy trees alongside the road the fields beyond were lush and green. He kept his eyes on the road. "Out in the Gulf there's always danger of chemical and asbestos contact."

"Lung cancer?"

"Or birth defects."

"How awful." Judging from his expression the plight of refinery workers affected him personally.

"You seem to know a lot about this. I thought you lived out west."

"I lived here until my late teens. When my father died from asbestos exposure, mom moved us to Colorado."

"Sorry to hear that. Is your mom still living out there?"

"No. Just my brother. Mom died."

"Oh, so sorry. I keep bringing up painful subjects."

"It's all in the past." Suddenly, Markus brightened, his eyes on something ahead. "Hey, we're almost there, Anabelle."

I smiled. "And what is this mysterious place?"

"You'll see. We're in Ascension Parish now." A dirt road veered off to the right and we took it.

"Parish?" I fidgeted, trying to stay focused on the conversation but my stomach was crying out for nourishment.

"Louisiana was settled by the French and the Acadians. They split the area into parishes because of the church. Everyone was Catholic back then." Markus' eyes twinkled mischievously. "Hungry?"

"You are beginning to know me, aren't you? Of course, you have to understand, a chef is always interested in food."

"So that's your excuse for your food obsession, piggy."

When I poked him, he flinched. "Hey!"

"You deserved it."

"No need to be violent, cher. I have your needs covered."

"Do you regularly call your dates names or am I especially privileged, big guy?"

Markus' lips curled up at the corners. His eyes still on the road, he picked up my hand and gently gave my fingers a quick kiss. "I respect and appreciate the lovely, Anabelle. Now take it easy, woman."

I sighed. Markus was hotter than Bourbon Street in midsummer. Not a patient woman, I was eager to experience a real kiss. In fact, my mind raced imagining more—his lips pressed hotly on my mouth and neck, and our bodies locked in a killer embrace, nothing stopping us—clothes falling to the floor in a frenzy of passionate exploration. I drifted off with the sounds of Zydeco, opening my eyes a while later.

"Tired?"

"A little."

Markus grinned. "I noticed you keep nappin'. I must be boring you."

I yawned. "It's not you. My room is spooky. Can't seem to sleep at night. I'm awake now."

"Attagirl. We're almost there, Anabelle."

From gigantic trunked leafy trees white lace draped the dark branches, in intricate patterns like spider webs, brushing the brilliant green grass below.

"What are those?" I asked, taken aback by the beauty of the shrouded branches on the dark green foliage.

"Live oaks. You haven't ever seen them?"

"They look so mysterious."

"It's the Spanish moss hanging down from the boughs. Gives them that ghostly appearance."

"You know Markus it's odd but seeing the trees feels like déjà vu." I stared at the towering oaks. "Strange, but it's like I belong here."

Markus glanced at the green fields splashed with blue where a narrow bayou met up with the Mississippi river. "I know. Been feeling the same thing ever since I drove out here the first time."

A bar called "Big Papa's", part of an attached wood frame general store appeared ahead. On the narrow porch, a couple of grizzled old men, wearing straw hats, checked shirts and overalls sat smoking pipes, swaying rhythmically in wooden rocking chairs. A group of young boys in T-shirts and jeans playing marbles looked up as we drove past, their dirty faces shiny with sweat.

About a mile down the road split and we took the dirt road.

"It's not far now. Thanks for being so patient," Markus said, his expression serious.

Huge live oaks with immense trunks, lined the road equally

spaced, almost as if someone had measured the precise distance from one tree to the next. Up about five hundred meters ahead a large house with ivory Greek columns came into sight. Six columns were spaced evenly on either side of the front steps. Large rectangular windows lined the veranda which stretched the width of the mansion. Doors opened up on the second floor to a balcony edging the front of the house. The stately mansion was impressive but the white paint, peeled and rippled, belied its stately presence.

"Indigo Oaks Plantation House," Markus said quietly, shifting into first gear. He brought the car to a stop.

With the manners of a southern gentleman, he came around to my side of the car and opened the door to help me out. In the dirt parking lot in front of the building, the Mercedes looked wrong, somehow misplaced like a time traveler lost in a past century.

I closed my eyes. Four sleek thoroughbreds appeared in my vision. Harnessed to a two passenger carriage they stood in wait for the master and mistress of the plantation. I shook my head to push the vision away and listen to Markus.

"It's old. Built in the late 1700's and changed to Greek revival in the 1800's." Markus jerked his chin. "Andre Cadeaux, my great, great-grandfather lived here. The investigator discovered it almost by accident. By the way, it's about twenty miles from the oil refinery where my father worked."

"Odd to think your father owned a plantation and didn't know about it."

"He had a falling out with his family. When I was young, alcohol was his only friend. Want to see inside?"

"They gave you a key?"

Markus smirked. "No, but it's simple enough to open."

There was a touch of larceny in this man. It was kind of appealing. Bad boys usually are. Unless they cheat and lie, of course, using and abusing a woman before they're off in search of greener pastures. Men could be pleasant and romantic at the beginning, leading a girl on, but eventually they revert back to the primitive mould they came from.

Markus took out his keys. On the chain there was something pronged and metal which he inserted into the key hole. Amazingly, it worked. Markus held the door for me to enter and a spider web tore open leaving part of it in my eye and mouth. When I brushed it away it stuck to my fingertips.

"No one has been inside to clean since I last saw it, I'd bet."

My nose twitched and I sneezed to confirm his conclusion. From my pocket I dug out a tissue and put it to use.

"Bless you, cher. Sorry about this." He waved his hand around at the draped furniture. "I had no idea they'd neglected it with a realtor showing the house to clients. Wait," Markus said, picking out fragments of spider web from my hair.

"Thanks, not quite prepared for that. I hope the spider's not still in there?"

"No, it's on your back."

"Ew-ww!" I reached behind to brush it away, not knowing exactly where my target was.

"Relax, just joking."

When my finger poked into his chest Markus stopped smiling.

"Still think it's funny?"

"Violent woman."

"You deserved that and you know it, so don't tell me your other girlfriends loved spiders."

"One had a pet tarantula, but I had to stop her from letting it sleep with us."

"Yuk. Was that the fat girlfriend?"

"No, the anorexic one. She was into the Goth thing. Black eye shadow and lipstick." Markus glanced around. "What do you think?"

The immense wide hallway, the aquamarine vaulted ceiling, the marble flooring, a row of twelve foot long windows in forest-green walls were an impressive abandoned luxury from another century. A gap in the heavy drapes shut out the light from outside leaving only a thin veil of sunlight to illuminate the floating dust particles. On the floor, dust bunnies gathered around the base of the dining room hutch.

"Can't get good help nowadays, eh, Markus?"

I walked over to the French colonial hutch and ran my fingers over the smooth oak. The portion of the cabinet under glass stood dusty and empty but when I opened an empty drawer, I saw a thick paper wedged inside the crack. Curious, I picked it up and straightened the heavy paper. Cupids were etched in purple and gold on the upper left hand corner. A flowering script was penned in black ink. It appeared to be an invitation.

I read aloud. "His Majesty Proteus, God of the Sea, King of all Creatures Therin, reigns with his Krewe in Vieux Carré." As my eyes shot ahead to the next line, my jaw dropped. "Omigod," I gasped. "This is unbelievable."

"What is, Anabelle?" Markus turned away from the window and came over.

I shook my head in wonder, still in shock.

From my hand Markus snatched the invitation and in a voice barely above a whisper, he read, "On Monday before Shrove Tuesday in the year eighteen hundred and thirteen, Proteus extends greetings to Belle Devereaux Duville and requests her to grace His Majesty's Court on this occasion as Queen. A carriage will arrive at eight if consent is given to this invitation." It was sealed and signed Hippocampus, scribe.

Markus shot me a look.

"It's my link to the past," I said softly. "Belle was my name in my past life. Her last name very similar to my surname now, which is, in case you don't remember, is Sommerville."

"How could I ever forget?" Markus grinned. "This invite is definitely for you and it's here in the Cadeaux home."

"Makes me wonder why it was stuffed in the drawer and why I happened to open the drawer."

Markus grinned. "Because you are curious?"

"Get serious. Do you think this card was a Mardi Gras invitation?"

Markus shook his head. "It's before Mardi Gras. The parades with floats came later. Probably a party, I'd think."

"How'd you know that?"

Markus shrugged his shoulders.

I recalled the opulence of the wine red walls and sparkling chandeliers in the formal dining room where I served Alain Ducoeur and Jean Lafitte their dinner. Were either of them

Proteus? "Doctor Philippe said my saint was Yemaya, Goddess of the Sea. And Proteus..."

"Is a Sea God. The Krewes have names from Greek mythology."

"Belle and the man who called himself Proteus went on a date. I'm sure of it!"

"If there is more to it, we will find it." Markus indicated the staircase with a sweep of his hand. "You game for a little exploration?"

"Why not? Maybe there'll be something interesting up there. A clue even. You know, this is the second odd thing that happened while we were together."

"You think the ghost throwing the painting is someone Belle knew?" Markus said, starting up to the next floor.

"Her name was Janelle." Following behind Markus on the winding staircase, I held my breath, hard-pressed not to sneeze. "She knew us. I'm getting the feeling you had a past life with me."

Markus thrust his hand to the arch of the hallway to clear the spider web away. "That's cool, isn't it?"

"Maybe," I said. Pushing past him, I entered a small room. The floors were planked with oak and even though dusty, the beauty of the room shone through. There was nothing else to see. Further down the hall was another room. "Should we continue?"

"Be prepared for rats." Markus said with a straight face.

"I'm safe with you, Superman. You've fought off worse. Open it."

From behind him, peering over his arm, I waited as the door swung ajar. I don't know what I thought I might see, but I was glad it was only an empty room.

"Come on, let's look down there," Markus said, taking my hand to lead me further along the hall. The spacious bedroom was furnished with a large chest of drawers and a four poster bed draped with a sheer flimsy material. Light streamed through from the ceiling-high glass doors leading to the exterior balcony. It was amazingly clean compared to the rest of the house.

"Wow! This is so 'Gone with the Wind'."

Markus glanced at the bed. "Want to try it out?"

I didn't have a chance to reply. Suddenly, Markus swooped me up in his arms and carried me to the bed, my stomach fluttering nervously. When he held my face, stroking my cheeks gently with his fingertips, a liquid heat awakened my core. His lips pressed down on mine eliminating all thoughts of anything except him.

"I wanted to do this ever since I met you," Markus said, his voice husky.

Lost in the fascinating depths of green in his hazel eyes, I forgot the pirate who had left me wanting more. No matter how much I delighted in his ghostly lovemaking, he wasn't a warm breathing man.

A trail of caresses down my neck trailing to my shoulder sent tingles down my spine. When Markus brought his hand to my neckline and slipped it into my bra, I felt my body respond, shutting off my mind, the energy rushing through my body as powerful as a drug. His lips and tongue feathered to the valley exposed by my dress, and gently cupping my breast, he said, "You are so lovely, Anabelle. I want you."

Nothing in me was saying no. This was meant to be. Hadn't fate intervened in the form of Sue and brought this handsome man to me? Just as my breathing became heavier, footsteps sounded on the main floor. On the stairs, male and female voices carried up.

Chapter 9: THE HIGH PRIESTESS

"Sounds like Gen." He jumped off the bed, giving me a hand. "She's the realtor."

"Markus, is that you, sugar?" A high-pitched female voice trilled from the hallway.

I straightened my dress in the nick of time. A voluptuous woman, her wide mouth coated with glossy scarlet lipstick and matching bottle-red hair rushed in wearing a snug tan dress accessorized by chunky jewelry, followed by an ugly bald man, his face flushed from the stair workout. His flat face, short wide nose, small eyes and drooping skin reminded me of an old warthog.

The red square handkerchief he used to wipe his face was stained wet with sweat. Weighed down by a few extra pounds, a roll over his belt, and a holster, the attached keys jingling as he pushed by the redhead. He wore an issue dark gray shirt and pants, and a pair of heavy-duty boots coated with mud. In his hand he held a motorcycle helmet. From the star on his chest, I gathered he was the law.

"How delightful to see you again, darlin'," the redhead said.

"Hey, Gen," Markus said, with a smile.

Gen's eyes swept down from Markus' T-shirt to his jeans and then focused on me, "I'm Genevieve Severe," the woman said, a trifle stiffly. Her eyes took in the ruffled state of my hair. "I'm afraid I didn't receive your text, Markus. If you wanted another viewin', you needed to contact me first. You had me quite alarmed. I called Deputy Malone."

The big man spoke up. "Miss Severe reported a break-in."

"As it happened I was drivin' by and noticed a car parked out front," the redhead said steadily. "I should have known a burglar wouldn't drive a Mercedes. How silly of me."

"Miss Gen said no one was given a key to Indigo Oaks." He stared at Markus pointedly. "Comin' in like that is breakin' and enterin', boy."

"The door was unlocked, Deputy," Markus squeezed my hand reassuringly, "and as I wanted to show my friend, Miss Sommerville, the view of the property, we went on in. By the way,

Gen, my lawyer has forwarded the information to the bank. I am the owner."

"Yes, I understand, darlin'," Genevieve said, her forehead furrowed in twin vertical lines, "but I am showin' the house until I'm informed otherwise. If you want to view it again," she arched a finely penciled brow, "you have my card."

"No need. It should be legally mine today. My apologies about this, Deputy, but I'm sure you can understand how Miss Sommerville is intrigued by my house."

"I am a student of Greek Revival," I improvised. "I was interested to see how the columns extended to the upper level."

"Entering a house without the owner's permission is illegal in the state of Louisiana."

"I gave myself permission, Deputy," Markus said. "And, I have a good reason to be here."

The Sheriff grimaced, glancing at the rumpled bed. "Enjoyin' yerself showing an attractive woman a view is not any good kind of reason. Hardly within the boundaries of the law. Since you don't have title, as yet, it's trespassin' as far as I am concerned."

I blushed, feeling like a teenager caught making out.

The fat man puffed out his chest, wedging his thumbs into his belt, rocking on his heels. "You aren't from here, are you, boy?"

"I was born in Ascension Parish."

"Don't sound it." He tugged out a half smoked cigar from his shirt pocket and lit it. He paid no attention to the rest of us as he inhaled and then puffed in a fiendish frenzy to keep the flame going.

"I've been away. Lost the accent," Markus said slowly. "Have you heard of the Cadeaux family?"

"There was Cajuns livin' in a cabin up the river. Worked at Tyron." Malone blew out an acrid cloud of smoke in our direction, his mouth twisted. "You one of those gator hunters?"

Digging out a pair of dark glasses from his shirt pocket, Markus slipped them on and stepped in front of the deputy. "My great, great-grandfather owned this house. My lawyer has verified the deed as mine." He glanced at the realtor. "It's a waste of your time and energy, Gen, to show this property."

The deputy squinted his eyes through the smoke, listening to the exchange.

"Until I'm notified officially it will be business as usual, Markus." Genevieve Severe nodded, as if to reaffirm her statement. "We should all leave now. I have other clients to see. Ever so nice to meet you, Miss."

"Sommerville," I said.

The redhead nodded succinctly, ignoring my partially extended hand. I let my hand drop. We weren't about to become besties anytime soon.

Genevieve Severe turned her attention to the deputy, pursing blood red lips, she glared at Malone. "Deputy, I'm afraid we don't have an ashtray available." She jerked her chin at the deputy's cigar, the ash at the tip growing longer by the second. "These floors are very old and fragile, easily damaged so I suggest," Genevieve made a motion at the cigar, "you put that thang out."

The big man waved her away with the glowing butt of the cigar. His eyes flicked towards the ceiling high doors to the balcony and with two quick strides, he swept by us, undid the latch, and swung open the doors. "No problem, darlin'," he said, flicking the ash over the railing. Speaking over his shoulder, he growled, "I am tryin' to be reasonable here, Cadeaux. You need that deed in your hands to enter the premises." He swung about, his stance menacing like a bull straining to charge. "There's a cell with your name on it if you come here again without it. Understan'?"

The burly deputy was trying his best to goad Markus into doing something he might regret. But my photographer friend took off his sunglasses and stared, his gaze cool as ice, a slight smile on his lips.

As for the Southern Belle, batting long lash extensions at Markus whenever he glanced in her direction, she was getting excited, her face flushed to a pleasing magnolia-pink. It was my guess Gen was hoping one more flip of her locks might land him in her net.

Smiling beguilingly, the redhead's blood-red fingernails smoothed her cinched floral skirt over her thighs. "I'll always take time to let you tour this ol' house, Markus. Just text me."

"There you go, boy. Make an appointment with Gen here and

you can come back." The sheriff waved his cigar indicating the door. "Why don't you and the lady head out? There's nothing left to see here."

"Sure thing. Have a good day, y'all," Markus said evenly.

***

Two men watched the tall dark-haired man and the blonde come out of the house and stand by the Mercedes parked in front. Right after them a voluptuous redhead, followed by a bulky man in an Ascension parish uniform appeared at the door. They spoke briefly before the redhead teetered over to the Lexus and drove off in cloud of dust leaving the deputy behind.

The deputy slipped on his sunglasses and helmet, before he mounted his motorcycle. In no hurry to leave, he withdrew a cigar and lit it.

"That's the po-lice," the thin man called Doobs mumbled. He swatted at a mosquito on his arm but it eluded him buzzing around his head.

Beside him, the heavy-set dark-skinned man grunted, "That dude is a deputy, Doobs. What if Cadeaux told him about us?"

"We good, Shuckster," Doobs said. He was as dark as coffee and blended right into the shadows of the early evening. "Nobody knows we here. Besides, looks like they in trouble not us." He tugged out a joint from his shirt pocket and flicked a lighter, flaming the tip. Quickly, he took a couple of drags to keep it burning, letting the thick, sweet smoke fill the air.

Sometimes, Chuckie wanted to smash Doobs in the face. He was so tired of hearing himself being referred to as Shuckster or just plain Shucker. The put-downs made his blood boil but when Doobs passed on the reefer, Chuckie welcomed it. He sucked in deeply waiting for that mellow feeling to hit.

Auntie Ruthie said he would get rich if he found the blonde's diary. The oyster ship could be his. He inhaled deeply and held the harsh smoke, and then exhaled as if regretting to let it go. The marijuana was rough on his sore throat. A cough exploded, rumbling choking noises that didn't stop until he spit out a glob of phlegm into the river bank. Beady eyes narrowed, Chuckie said,

"Ya think he caught sight of your pickup, Doobs?"

"Quiet. They hear us." The scrawny black man bopped on his heels. "This ain't the city. Sound carries."

"Yer paranoid." Chuckie passed the joint back. "Look, bra, the deputy must have another call. Looks like he's goin'."

The two men watched as the deputy drove off down the dirt road disappearing around the bend.

"That good, Shuckster."

Chuckie curled his hand into a tight fist and punched him square in his back. He snorted a laugh as the thin man doubled over, dropping the joint into the long grass. It flickered for a second before going out.

Doobs gave him a bewildered look. "What the fuck did ya do that for?"

"Don't call me Shuckster."

Doobs massaged his lower back with one hand, trying to ease the sharp pain in his kidneys. "Didn't mean anything by it." His eyes returned to the Mercedes parked in front of the house. "Police didn't take them in. Must be something else going on in the parish. Could be trouble at the refinery."

"Only trouble is if they let yer baby mama out," Chuckie sneered. "The ho's certifiable."

"Leave Yolissa out of this. You don't know fuck."

Chuckie turned away to the river. He unzipped his pants. "Hey, Doobs. Bet I can hit the water." A stream of urine shot out in a high yellow arch to the sandy bank. "Shit!"

A bark of laughter escaped Doobs' lips. "More like piss, Shu...Chuckie."

Chuckie sighed and zipped up. "Damn used to do better than that. Gotta start drinkin' water."

Doobs poked Chuckie in the ribs to get his attention. "They gone."

"Huh? Where they go?"

Doob's eyes darted to the trees. "Over yonder. By the river." Fingers in a "v", he pointed to the two figures disappearing behind a live oak shrouded with Spanish moss. "The dude's hot for the blonde. Ya think they doing it?"

Chuckie felt a stirring in his pants. It had been a while since he'd had a woman and the blonde was doable.

"We need to find out what she knows about my money," Doob said, his jaw tight.

"Your money? Doobs, let me explain it to ya. Auntie Ruthie say I get da money. Nobody say anything about you."

"If I help ya, the money be half mine, ain't it?"

Chuckie Bateau glared. "I said you git twenty per cent."

"Twenty-five, Chuckie. Besides, how do I know Auntie Ruthie wasn't funnin' ya and I be wasting my time?"

"She was serious, all right. That dude there is a Cadeaux and they's the same as a Ducoeur. They shared treasure with my folks. All of it was in my tea cup reading. I know one thing for sure—" Chuckie stared into space lost in thought.

"What dat?" Doobs glanced up at Chuckie.

"The Quarter be small. I got eyes and ears watchin' their every move."

Chapter 10: THE DEVIL

Raven was sitting on the stoop of the Hotel Memoire when I returned. He was wearing a black T-shirt and jeans. He wasn't alone. A pale thin carrot-topped teen was perched on the stoop beside him swigging a bottle of red wine.

It was dusk, the sky a dark blue streaked with crimson from the departing sun. The lamp light above them illuminated their faces, cheeks blotched pink.

The boy beside Raven was a sloppy drinker. Red wine trickled from the corner of his mouth and spotted his white T-shirt. He paused to look up as he passed the bottle to Raven. Wiping his mouth with his hand he said, "Where y'at?"

I took the New Orleans' greeting in stride but couldn't remember the customary reply. "Good, thanks," I said, and turned to wave goodbye to Markus sitting in the Mercedes parked at the curb, already regretting my decision to take it slow. His car pulled out. I followed the headlights until they faded into the darkness.

"Gabe, this is my lady, Anabelle," Raven said, in a hushed tone. "He came over from France around the same time as we did."

Raven's friend grabbed the bottle and raised it. *"Laissez les bon temps roulez."*

I caught some it, but if I don't hear the language often enough I forget words. Besides, New Orleans has a way of changing any French word into a hybrid of American English. At the puzzled expression on my face, Gabe added, "Let the good times roll. Want some?"

I am a big fan of shiraz, especially the Australian kind, but when it comes to sharing wine with strangers, I'm a bit of a germaphobe. Still, I had to be careful not to get on the bad side of a vampire.

"Sure, thanks."

"Come join us." Gabe made a space on the stoop. Luckily I was skinny enough to fit between the two of them, squeezing in on the stoop with an inch to spare on either side. "You look so young," I said to Gabe.

"It's my narrow frame." He glanced at my biceps which were more muscular than his. "You probably workout." He dug a wrapped candy out of his pocket and offered it to me. "Praline?"

I shook my head. "No thank you. They're sweet like fudge, aren't they? I'd love to try one but I've been eating too much lately. Don't want to gain weight." On the way back from the plantation Markus had stopped at a restaurant. I'd gorged myself, burning my tongue on cajun fish in my enthusiasm.

Raven offered me a tiny box closed with a shiny round sticker. "This would be more to your taste. A chocolate praline. And believe me you will need this when your visions are too powerful. Keep it handy. Belle had visions too. For her only chocolate could bring her back to reality. This place," he said, flinging his arms out wide, "is full of paranormal activity. You can't even imagine how controlling it is. You don't want to be lost in the spirit world forever." He shook his head, black curls tossing about with the gesture. "I want you to have a better outcome than Belle."

"You know, Anabelle," Gabe said, interrupting sharply. "I'm not *that* young. I'm fine-boned, and the same age as Raven."

I grinned. "So barely two hundred years old?"

Gabe rolled his eyes like every teenager I'd ever met. "Funny," he said, his voice dripping with sarcasm. "You're lucky, Raven. You might have had to wait another hundred years before meeting another version of Belle."

"I am, lucky, Gabe. Anabelle is a jewel in the rough." Raven ignored my offended pout and grabbed the bottle. "Gabe's story is a bit like mine. Came from France with a lady—a real wildcat. When you started cooking at Renard's and became betrothed to Rene, Gabe's lady, Janelle, was also given a position at the restaurant."

"Wait a minute! This woman, Janelle, worked at Renard's?"

Gabe grinned. "She was the best."

"In the kitchen?"

This cracked the guys up. They laughed, faces infused with color. It was strange considering the pallor of their vampire complexions. The only red otherwise was their red rimmed eyes and blood-red lips.

My eyes flicked from one to the other. "What is it you're both hiding from me?" When they stared into space ignoring my question, I grabbed their T-shirts and pulled. "Tell me!"

"Let me go," Gabe whimpered. "Raven!"

"Okay, you win," Raven said. "I'll explain."

He took the bottle from Gabe and slurped before he said, "Janelle was Rene Renard's mistress until Belle came along and then he decided he was 'in love'. After that Janelle was demoted to entertainment director."

"She was a dancer?"

Gabe snickered.

"Oh, a prostitute."

"No, a touch better than that. I'd call her a skilled courtesan," Gabe explained haughtily. "And she was good! For a while she took up with a wealthy pirate, exclusively." He shrugged. "Pirates had money, more than most. But Belle, she lured the men in with those witchy eyes and eventually my poor Janelle lost her man. Other men treated her badly too, but relentless in ambition, she became a powerful woman." He hung his head. "I miss her."

Raven took a swig of wine. "It's not easy for us vampires, you know. We have a duty to find our ladies. In fact, news has it Gabe's girl is here in the city. Of course, she's no longer a courtesan and her name is not Janelle either. It won't be easy to find her."

"Last I saw her she had a brothel on Rampart Street. It wasn't easy for her to start over." Gabe brightened. "The new Janelle will be drawn to return to the Vieux Carré. It's not easy to forget this place—the music, the dancing and the romance. I will sense her approach."

Raven nodded at that and took a swig. He was much neater than Gabe, not spilling a drop. Tonight, he was especially crisp in a white button down shirt and ironed jeans. His hair was gelled back revealing a small widow's peak.

"What have you been up to?" Raven eyes flicked to my messed up hair.

I grinned.

Raven's eyes widened. "You didn't?"

"I took a trip into plantation country with Markus and we explored his house until the deputy and the realtor arrived."

Raven's eyes widened. "You have been busy, chérie. I'm definitely seeing a sparkle in those big blues of yours. Good things happen to those who wait. You'll see."

"There's more." I hesitated. I was worried about Doctor Philippe, Alain, and the visions.

Raven patted my hand. "You've got it under control. Say, did you find the key?"

"You left that?"

"I'm helping you solve the mystery."

I raised an eyebrow. "Oh, which one?"

Gabe giggled. "She's got you there, Rave. I was thinking you've been shirking your duties lately. What's with all that dancing in Congo Square?"

"That was two centuries ago, Gabe. Not doing that any more. Say, Anabelle, let's walk over to Frenchmen."

"Where?"

"The music street. Clubs, bars, restaurants, all the rage. It will be fun." Raven grabbed my elbow and pulled me up. He fist bumped with Gabe and we headed down Ursulines.

He whispered, as we headed towards the river, "Some things need to stay strictly between us."

"I thought you were friends."

"Friends, loosely. Keep your friends close and your enemies closer. That way you can discover the past."

I shot him a look. "You, seriously don't know what happened to Belle?"

Raven shook his head. "She disappeared at times."

"Where did she go?"

"She knew some sketchy individuals. Went into pirate training, along with Delphine and Janelle. They had this Asian martial arts expert teach them take-downs for protection when they were involved in dicey activities."

"Why do you say that, Raven? You mean Belle was part of Renard's business?"

"She probably assisted from time to time. Renard had a thing for her." Raven nodded as if considering what he'd just said. "She had reservations about him. Renard was an addict."

"Belle accepted the marriage proposal knowing he was an addict?"

"She had to. There were only three choices—marriage, prostitution or the church."

"And she was involved in criminal activities?"

"I don't know for sure." Raven pouted. "Belle didn't let me live with her."

"And the police? They allowed this?"

"Corruption was rampant. Not much different than today, chérie," he said, his eyes on the drug dealer standing against the wall on Ursulines.

Raven made sure I was close as the crowd thickened like roux in a gumbo—quasi street people mingling with the crowd hoping to lighten tourist wallets in a quick brush-by swoop.

Further on up Decatur, lights beamed bright. I had the feeling petty crime would be low on the police priority list so with my purse between us we trekked east a few blocks, crossing Esplanade over to Frenchman's.

On the street corner a band of teenagers in sweats and jeans gathered together, saxophones and guitars in their hands. There was a box for contributions. Already a crowd gathered on the sidewalks and the street.

"You missed this party for years. Too bad you had to be reincarnated a Canuckster. Recognize it?"

I listened, taking in the words sung in a deep gravelly voice by the big black teen in the center. "When you walk through the garden..." I repeated. "Is it Tom Waits?"

Raven squeezed my hand. "Uh-huh. Keep the devil down in the hole. It's a good lesson. Don't trust anyone." He jerked his chin to the club ahead. "We can talk there."

A sign flashed "Blue Bayou" above the door. We walked into a dark dingy room, wood tables and stools, a stage area where the band was setting up at the far end. It was already filling up with a mishmash of people, old white gray-haired hippies with ravaged faces in ripped jeans and pony tails, bald blacks, tattooed arms exposed in muscle shirts, and women of all sizes and color in sundresses.

We took a table at the window. The boy band's sax rifts drifted in through the open door, the rhythms smooth and sultry. "Beer for us, please," I said to the server.

"Blackened Voodoo," Raven added.

***

Sandie steadily contemplated her thumbs. To her they seemed larger than yesterday. Maybe she was having an ego boost since visiting Anabelle. It was an insightful session with a psychic and even better, Sandie thought, she gets me, which made her wonder if she was flipping into dykehood. She shrugged. Nothing unusual about that in this part of the Quarter. It would be stranger to believe aliens were abducting her and bringing her to a land of sexy male strippers. Yes, that would be unbelievable.

Sandie took another hit of her doobie and settled back against the wicker swing, periodically kicking her feet out to propel the mechanism to oscillate in a steady back and forth rhythm. It was quiet in the perfectly manicured garden, the shrubs sculpted by a professional gardener and maintained weekly, the full moon behind backlighting the treetops into silhouettes.

It wasn't like her, a Louisiana girl from the Quarter, thinking sensuous thoughts about a woman even though this was the "gayborhood". Sandie always had her eye on tall dudes—black, white, didn't matter. If they had the height they had a good-sized package and might have the know-how to please a lady.

In the case of her ex, Carlisle Brighton DeLouisa, the new state's attorney and the next governor of the state of Louisiana, he had a large man's package. Unfortunately, that thang had shriveled from frequent coke usage, along with his brain. But that wasn't her problem any longer. Louella Babboon Waters was his new sweetheart and her daddy's oil money made Carlisle's black heart pitter-patter extra hard. Carlisle was like a pig rolling in mud, his political aspirations going strong as long as he followed their directions.

The evening was warm and breezy at the back of the Beauregard-Keyes mansion with a full blown harvest moon beaming down, like a great big orange globe suspended in the sky by a fishing line wire. As for bugs, there was not one mosquito buzzing tonight. It felt like she owned the place. Especially since the guide was off on vacation and the owners were relaxing in Italy.

Heck, she lived here more than the owners did. Sandie closed her eyes a moment and imagined herself in a long white dress, a fan in hand like the southern belles of another century. Sandie's people came from the Quarter, well to-do shopkeepers back in the day.

When she was offered the part time security guard job for the house, she accepted. She had taken the security guard course after all, what more was there to think about? It paid the rent. If worse came to worse and someone took it upon themselves to investigate the Confederate ghosts marching on the main floor, she was prepared to defend the property. On her lap she made sure the Winchester was loaded and ready to fire. She also had a backup. The Remington 1100, a semi-automatic twelve-gauge, an excellent bird gun that held up to five shells but she would use the Winchester and place the Remington on the lounger beside her, just in case.

It wasn't what everyone thought a woman should have. Some of those little gun shops on Bourbon Street thought a tiny nine millimeter Glock was right for a petite woman like her. After all, it fit into a purse.

Had her plan been to conceal the gun, the Glock would have worked, but for the security guard of the Beauregard-Keyes estate it was way too lame. The Model 70 Winchester packed a punch that would drop even the meanest psycho in his tracks. A few pellets from the Glock would only penetrate his junk and make him angrier than a hornet. Not a good idea.

The guide didn't know she carried serious heat. He was only here during the day when he walked the tourists through. The French Quarter was chock-a-block full of pathetic drug addicts and thieves, not to mention the rapists lurking in the shadows looking for a powerless woman to violate. That dude had no idea what she had to contend with.

Did she have the guts for it? Oh, yeah! Last spring she proved it to the low-life peeking in the window.

When the druggie broke in through the back, she was ready.

106

Sandie fired straight to the chest, the way her daddy had taught her back in the day. The loser hightailed it out through the bushes leaving a trail of blood. Sandie didn't bother to call the police. Things happen in New Orleans.

When she thought about it, this type of life was not what she had imagined for herself—alone, living in someone else's mansion. Her sweet baby was now permanently residing with crater-faced Carlisle and snotty Louella Babboon Waters. Sandie's ex had hired a stripper to babysit Dana while his precious Louella flirted with society and he romanced politics. The stripper's part time job was to get Carlisle's mojo back and ready him for action.

Earlier today, Sandie lit a candle. Papa LaBas would help find her money to pay a top notch lawyer to represent her in the custody case.

A rustling in the bushes interrupted her thoughts. A branch cracked and broke. It could be an animal but then she heard what was in all certainty muffled men's voices. Confidently, she raised her Winchester, and aimed at the garden.

Two figures popped out from the bushes—a husky no-neck and a string-bean, less than a hundred and forty pounds if she wasn't mistaken. They were waving guns around, and stomping on the plants like a herd of Texas longhorns. Sandie couldn't make out what they were saying but she was sure those mofos were up to no good and it was no use taking chances.

Sandie yelled out at the top of her lungs. "Stop right there or I'll cancel yar birth certificates." Her voice was strong like a lion's roar in the stillness of the jungle, fiercely penetrating the darkness shrouding the porch where she stood. She shot a round into the grass to emphasize her point.

The no-neck screeched, "Hey!"

"Drop yar weapons," Sandie said steadily. "Kick 'em out here, close to the veranda."

For a moment the two men argued and no-neck started back to the bush. Sandie shot a round between the man and the bush. "Now!"

"Stop that! You crazy, lady?" yelled the weightlifter. "I paid good money for my gun. It's staying with me. Besides we mean no harm."

Sandie glared at the men. "Ya came here to rob the place."

"Bullshit," Chuckie said.

"Drop them weapons on the lawn, maggots."

"No need to be rude, girlie," the big man resembling a giant potato head said, "We're leaving, okay? Forgit we was here and we'll go."

"Stop and drop yer weapons," Sandie said, and blasted another round. "Kick them over."

There was a glint of silver as the guns skimmed the surface of the grass. "Step forward, and explain yerselves." She kept her eyes on the men and gingerly picked up the weapons dropping them one by one into her tote. "I'm waitin'."

Holding up his hands in surrender, the skinny black scratched his scalp in between the corn rows. "We wanted to get to the top floor of this building to see across the street. Didn't think anyone would be here. We weren't plannin' on taking anythin'."

"Don't pee on my back and tell me it's rainin'." She pointed at the deck chairs on the lawn, "Sit down, y'all."

The men sat on the loungers and looked at Sandie expectantly.

"Talk. I don't have a month of Sundays." Sandie looked at Potato Head. "Well?"

"M'am," Chuckie said, "it weren't like that. We were plannin' on doin' a little detecting work."

When Sandie said nothing, Potato Head's skinny companion added, "There's a witch staying in the Hotel Memoire across the street and we thought we'd—" Doobs' reply was muffled as Chuckie firmly placed his big paw over the little guy's mouth.

"He don't know sheet from shinola," Chuckie Bateau explained. "We're detectives—private. Just watching the building."

Sandie clued in. They were talking about Anabelle. It was also clear they were lying. "What for?"

"Just observin'," Chuckie said smoothly, trying to keep his voice steady with confidence.

"Why?" Sandie asked.

"Well, it's like this." Doobs took a step towards Sandie.

"Stay where you are, cotton picker," Sandie said, waving the barrel of her rifle. "Now talk."

"Don't tell that cracka-ass-cracka anything," Charlie growled, getting out of his chair.

Sandie shot a round, hitting the ground a few inches from Doobs' foot." Doobs yelped and jumped back.

Not knowing exactly how many rounds she had left, Sandie took up the Remington 1100 and said, "That's for not talkin' fast enough."

Doobs crouched down to finger his toe. "I felt that. That bullet took the leather clean off," he said to Chuckie. He sniffled loudly.

"Keep yar hands out where I can see them." Sandie felt like a Confederate captain capturing a Yankee interloper. The ghost inside would be proud as punch.

Chuckie glanced at his partner's face, gleaming with tears. "Grow a pair."

Sandie barked, "Y'all are perverts—watching a lady in her room."

Chuckie pulled himself up taller his bald head gleaming as it caught a ray of moonlight. He knew he'd better work this. Maybe he could sweet-talk the racist ho. "We'd be willin' to pay ya for yer trouble."

"How much?"

"Well, we don't have nothin' yet, but it's comin'. My Aunt Ruthie told me to watch the witch. Ya know Auntie Ruthie on Rampart Street? She's gifted. Says I was entitled to treasure."

"Treasure?" This was interesting to Sandie. She needed money to get her baby back. "How ya getting it?"

Chuckie frowned. "Just thought if we watch," he said, jiggling the binoculars around his neck, "we'd get a clue. The witch has a treasure map."

"Huh?"

"That witch knew pirates. They gave her—" His voice trailed off.

"What?"

"Not sure, but couldn't we go up there a while and watch?"

"And why would I jeopardize my job for a couple of loony tunes like y'all?"

Chuckie smirked. "Bet you'd like some of the money."

Sandie rolled her eyes. "Like I could count on you to pay." She pointed at the binoculars. "Give me those."

Chuckie hesitated. "Why?"

"You would if you trusted me."

Chuckie squirmed uncomfortably.

With a grimace, Doobs reached over and pulled the binoculars off Chuckie's neck.

"Hey, watcha doing?" Chuckie protested.

He tried to stop Doobs but the skinny guy was strong, cranked up with meth. It was easy for him to pull them off. Tightly holding the binoculars he crept closer to Sandie, one step at a time.

A bullet tore into the ground in front of him, spraying tiny stones and fragments of grass in the air.

"Stop there, mister. Set them on the porch step." Sandie pointed the rifle. "Now back up and go out the way you came in. Come back, and I'll call the police on speed dial."

"But!" Doobs protested.

Chuckie spit on the ground.

"Go, I said." Sandie shot a round and watched the men run. "The next one will hit yer asses."

She kept an eye as they ran to the back gate, disappearing behind the hedges. A good hour passed before Sandie picked up the binoculars and made her way inside to the top floor where she settled on a couch, aiming the night vision binoculars at the top floor balcony window. Sandie could see perfectly fine but the room was dark and empty. She would wait.

***

"I'm not sure if I'm ready for another vision, Raven," I said, studying the bronze hue of the Sazerac. "Maybe, I should read Belle's diary first."

Raven grinned, flashing his pearly whites. "That's why I left the key."

"Smart. I had planned to, but this morning Markus took me out of the city."

"Ah-huh."

I blushed thinking of that aborted moment of passion in the

master bedroom of the Indigo Oaks Plantation. A tingle of arousal remained, reminding me of what I had missed. "After what you said I get the feeling Belle's life was a lot more adventurous than mine, at least her last few years."

The club had filled up with a mixed crowd of whites and blacks, partying to the upbeat rhythm of the band. I glanced at the dancers shaking to the blues, wishing I had someone to love. Raven was not Markus. And goodness knows if he became excited he'd give me a love bite.

Raven slouched in the wooden stool. "Don't forget, everything back then ties into your present."

"What did she die of?"

"All I know is Belle lived at Renard's upstairs, worked as the chef and got involved with men." Raven's face darkened. "One day she left and never came back."

"How did she feel about Rene Renard?"

Raven shifted uncomfortably in his chair. "I bumped into Belle at the market. She had bruises on her arms."

"You think—"

"He could have. Rumor had it, Renard was into kinky sex, you know with multiple partners. Janelle made Renard's a place where all sorts of desires could be satisfied. She was the hit of the town back then."

"Lucky Janelle," I said dryly. Eying the bronze glow of the Sazerac, and with the band playing loudly, I spoke into Raven's ear. "You know, sweetie, I'm not anxious to go back to Belle's life but if I drink this I will."

"You'll have to go back eventually and find out what happened to Belle, won't you? And the Sazerac seems to do the trick." Raven squeezed my hand. "Come now, chérie, be brave. You know there is no other way."

I let out a sigh. "I suppose, but not here, okay?'

Raven nodded. "I understand," he said glanced at the dancers having fun. He waved over a waiter and asked for "go cups".

"I'm afraid of what I'll find." With my fingertips I pressed and rubbed on the knots at the back of my neck. "You have no idea how these nightmares frighten me. I wake up my body coated with sweat."

The waiter brought us the cups and we poured our drinks in.

Raven patted my shoulder. "You have to solve the mystery of her death, Anabelle, or you will suffer even more."

"I know," I said unhappily, "but the vision I had when I was with Doctor Philippe was terrifying."

"What happened?"

"I was on a pirate ship. There was so much blood and death. Alain Ducoeur was there to save me." I shook my head. "I get the feeling Belle's life is linked to Alain Ducoeur."

"Gossip had it, Belle had lovers. We were close but she was secretive about the men in her life. I know from the tidbits she told me she had something special going on."

Burning warmth flowed to my core thinking of Ducoeur's tongue caressing my skin.

"You're smiling," Raven said slyly. "I'd bet Belle had an extremely hot session with Lafitte."

I pursed my lips. "I don't know about him but Alain visited me. On a scale of one to ten it was an extremely delicious encounter of ten."

Raven threw his head back and laughed.

The crowd was beginning to feel claustrophobic. I tossed a twenty on the table and stood. "Let's go."

Cups in hand, we pushed our way outside into the warm evening breeze. Frenchmen Street was swarming with tourists and locals.

"I want to go back to the hotel," I said to Raven.

"And try for another vision?"

I grinned. "If not, at least I'll enjoy my drink."

"I advise you to read the diary and then drink the magic potion."

Where I come from the sidewalks are rolled up at ten but here in the Quarter it was as if the night had just begun. Music charged the air with energy. From every bar—reggae, blues and jazz mingled like a potent Hurricane cocktail. Through the throng like salmon swimming upstream against a strong current we made our way, stopping once in a while to window shop at the art, novelty and crafts stores. Street people with stringy hair and dirty clothes sat on stoops. One of them played a bluesy rhythm on the harmonica. I maneuvered a bill out of my purse and dropped it in the open guitar case.

Raven glanced down at my plastic cup, upright and full of a Sazerac's potent juices. "Good for you, Anabelle. No spillage."

"Too important to lose one drop."

I recognized the Italian bar at the corner of Ursulines and Decatur and we turned to go north. It was a short walk to the hotel from there.

Raven sighed. "Drink the Sazerac, Anabelle, but be careful. Have a chocolate handy to return if things go sideways." He flashed his fangs. "Not to be selfish here, but I must fly."

In the lamplight on Ursulines Avenue, Raven's face held a sickly pallor. I was worried. "Are you sure you're all right?" I said, brushing the vampire's curls back with my hand.

The vampire glanced into the night sky. "I will be once I get a bite to eat. The selection increases later, after they leave the clubs." He handed me his cup. "Take mine. You might need another hit."

***

The door opened no problem. Call it instinct, something was making the hairs on the back of my neck stand up. My eyes searched the room trying to pinpoint what was off. What I saw was not exactly ghostly in nature but I knew spirits made their presence known. The water-stained black and white family photo hanging above the day bed in the outer room was slanting precariously to the right. I wasn't convinced it was the doing of a spirit, but the drawer in the cupboard below the mirror was a fraction ajar. Spirits do that sort of thing but when I saw the middle door connecting the two rooms shut, I was suspicious of the human kind of intruder.

The heavy oak door would block any noise from this side but my dilemma was opening it without putting the thief on the alert. This was a city of violence and just because the hotel was old and quaint didn't mean that I couldn't be a victim of a crime.

That ridiculous row of nails sticking out from the upper portion of the frame, ready to dig into the upper part of the wooden door, would crush any chance of a silent Ninja entrance. This suite was not a Howard Johnson. An old building like this could be the target of a criminal or an axe-wielding psycho ghost.

I had a big swig from the go-cup for courage and picked up a heavy golden lion bookend from the table before pushing the door open.

The master bedroom was tidy and seemingly undisturbed. There was no place to hide with the box spring low to the carpet and the closet too small.

I breathed a sigh of relief and sat on one of the chairs. Setting Raven's Sazerac on the table, I sipped my drink. Courage in a cocktail. It was justifiable considering the situation. Thoughts raced through my head like a bag full of M&M's—different colors on the outside but each interior held the same tasty, crushed chocolate. Alain Ducoeur and Markus Cadeaux were my candies, although Philippe had a certain allure as well. My personality is addictive whether chocolate or sinfully sweet men. Leaning my head back I drank from the "go cup". From where I was the fabulous bathtub on clawed feet beckoned as forcefully as a siren lured sailors to their death.

Sauntering over, I ran steamy warm water into the tub and then returned to the master bedroom to strip off my clothes, laying them on the chair. I was tempted to grab the diary from the drawer to read but I have this unfortunate habit of spilling water or wine on my paperbacks and this was not the time to ruin the diary.

When the tub was filled, I took the Sazerac and perched it the ledge in easy reach. I allowed myself to sink deeper into the soothing welcoming water. The golden liquor glittered in the dim light of the lamp as if urging me to drink. Drifting into a comfortable state of relaxation I took the cup and tilted it back letting the liquor trickle down. When I set the drink back on the ledge I closed my eyes and became part of the water, a tiny molecule spinning over the supercharged surface to connect in a moist droplet. And if that wasn't strange enough, I was like a bead of water vapor rising above and dropping down on something solid yet slippery and wet.

Jolted awake, I stared into Alain Ducoeur's magnetic green eyes. My hands rested on his strong well-developed shoulders, my legs pressed around his while I sat firmly on top of him.

"Wow!" I said. Energy had thrown me in cowgirl position on a drop-dead sexy male and yet I was determined not be side-tracked.

"We need to talk," I whispered. "I have to find out how Belle died."

He looked up at me his eyes shadowed. "There were too many of them against us. They blamed me for ruining their lives."

"How?" I murmured, aware of his hands stroking my back. Responding would have sent me into a tailspin so I focused on the bump on his nose, avoiding those compelling green eyes.

"It's been broken," Alain said with a frown. "Lafitte attacked a ship and someone hit me with a plank. This was before we parted ways."

"Why?'

Alain laughed. "Why did we part or why did a plank strike my nose?"

"Both."

The pirate stroked my cheek. "Lafitte took possession of Spanish galleons no matter what the cargo, including the human kind. When I had my own vessel we parted company. After a while I wanted to leave the life behind. I set up a shop and helped those with medical needs using herbals. Of course, I could sew up any blade wound and knew enough to cleanse it. Workers and pirates gave me plenty of business."

"And Lafitte was okay with you leaving?"

"I was paid. He wanted to leave for South America. Lafitte wasn't any worse than people buying from slavers up north. Other states were breeding slaves to be sold in Louisiana. Believe it or not, here in New O'leans, people of color were often freed and had their own businesses, some of them very successful."

"And the plank?"

Alain kissed me softly on the mouth before he said, "I didn't move fast enough." Suddenly, his eyes widened. "Anabelle, duck!" he yelled.

I felt a sharp pain, followed by dots—red, blue and yellow, and then everything went black.

Chapter 11: THE WHEEL OF FORTUNE

In the darkness, a faint fragment of light filtered through a narrow crack running from floor to ceiling. Stiff and numb from being cramped up, knees close to my chest, I was naked—a faint residue of soap and bath water coating my skin. The question was, where was I and why was I here? All right, that's two questions, but equally important in the weigh-in. So here I was in gloomy darkness. Any visual clues were eliminated yet lingering in the air I was aware of the familiar musky scent of the Hotel Memoire.

When I tried to stand, clothing and wire brushed against me and I was suddenly aware of constricting duct tape wrapped around both my wrists and ankles. Sometimes as a psychic I have trouble dealing with reality as opposed to my perceived reality. My sixth sense is a rogue player surfacing when least expected, often throwing me a curveball but this time it helped.

Cleverly deducing I had been stored in a bedroom closet, I groped the wooden surface for a door handle and found one. When it turned, I gathered I was lucky enough not to be locked in. Could it be my attacker was demented but not violent otherwise I'd be minced meat. On the other hand, I'd seen enough movies of serial killers to know they store their victims alive, and come back later to torture and kill. That last thought was enough to propel me out of the closet and hop out like a steroid-injected kangaroo into an empty master bedroom which luckily happened to be mine.

It was a chaotic mess. Whoever ransacked the place had pulled out every drawer in every cupboard and dresser. Contents were heaped on the rug and the bed. Costume jewelry consisting of necklaces, bracelets and earrings were scattered in every direction on the floor. Luckily, my wallet was safely stored in the front desk safe. He or she had nothing to steal, yet, I couldn't get rid of the feeling that there was something amiss.

It wasn't as if I was a wealthy woman but he might have thought anyone staying in the hotel's suite might have a hefty load of cash. I had to wonder what I was waiting for? The intruder was either a robber or worse.

Furthermore, the fact that a perv saw me naked made me as

angry as a hornet. With every bone in my body I wouldn't let the creep get away with this.

A light clicked on in my brain. There is a way of getting out of duct tape which works eighty per cent of the time even without being Houdini. Straightening my spine and pushing my chest out, I raised my hands above my head, and took a deep breath before I swung my hands violently down and out. It was a Wonder Woman move.

The duct tape broke and my hands were free, the gray sticky stuff hanging from one wrist. Hair removal, as in eyebrow shaping or a bikini waxing has to be done with a quick snapping action. Same here. With a quick jerk I tore off the remainder of the tape along with the tiny hairs on my wrist and let out a groan. My hands free at last, I hopped my way back to my makeup bag in the bathroom, grabbed the scissors and sat on the floor to work my way through the stubborn tape restrictions around my ankles, my mood more hostile by the second. Whoever had done this was sadistic and I wouldn't let them get away with it.

Finally done, I stood, aware of the ache at the back of my head. Gingerly I touched my scalp. It felt sticky. In the bathroom mirror, a pale woman with smeared mascara stared back.

From my makeup bag I dug out a cotton pad and blotted the back of my head where I figured I'd been hit. It soaked up the blood. A few tries later, the pad came up clean. After tossing out the pads I wiped away the smudges under my eyes. There was a tinge of red in the bath water. The realization of what had happened was so overwhelming I plopped myself down on top of toilet seat, my elbows perched on my knees, and tried to pull myself together.

Finally, I go up. Figuring there was nothing worth stealing, I assumed the intruders were after information. That meant it was the diary.

First things first. I dressed simply in jeans and a T-shirt and leaving my feet bare, I cleaned up, filling the drawers up with my things before pushing them back in the dresser slots. As I slid in the bottom drawer it suddenly occurred to me that I hadn't checked to see if the diary was still there. My fingers found the small groove and pressed. The secret bottom creaked open. The brown book was inside where I had left it after breakfast. I sighed with relief.

Just as I was about to take it out a movement caught my eye. On the floor under the edge of the duvet a patterned cream and brown snake appeared. When it fully emerged it was close to four feet long. Poisonous or not, I am not a snake person. I screeched and then getting control of myself I backed up. From the closet I located a coat hanger, and in the bathroom I found a woven laundry basket with a hinged lid.

On the plus side the snake was a python. These snakes eat rodents by squeezing them and then swallowing them whole. This thing was big but harmless unless it hadn't eaten for awhile.

A tapping on the outside door broke my concentration. "Anabelle?"

Carefully, keeping an eye on the python I stepped backwards still holding the basket and the coat hanger and swung the outer door open.

"Anabelle? You all right? You look strange."

"I will be just fine when we take out the snake."

"Snake?" Sandie peered over my shoulder.

"In there," I said, pointing to the floor of the master bedroom. "Help me get it out. We can put it in the basket."

"You're kiddin' me." Sandie pushed past. She stopped dead in her tracks. "It's a python." She stared at me suspiciously.

"It's not mine."

"You said you're a witch."

"I'm not a Voodoo Queen." I grabbed her arm. "Come on. It will be fine. The python is someone's pet. Hold the basket open on the floor and I'll herd the snake in."

"Okay." Sandy spoke so slowly, her head tilting in a peculiar angle, I figured she was high. When I looked into her hazel eyes, the red rims confirmed it.

One of us had to do this and from the looks of Sandie's quivering chin I figured it had to be me. Surprisingly, it wasn't as hard as I thought. The python was a curious snake or maybe a tired one. The patterned reptile saw the basket with the cloth lining and crawled in, curling up into a coil without me having to nudge it with a coat hanger.

As I stood back to admire the python's patterning the room phone rang. I closed the lid and traipsed over to the night table. "Hello?" Out of the corner of my eye I saw Sandie leaving, holding the basket gingerly in her hands.

"Miss Sommerville, this is Warren from front desk. A man called for you."

"Oh?" I said into the mouthpiece.

"A tall, good-lookin' gentleman I was told. Don't have his name."

So Markus couldn't stay away. I felt all aglow thinking of his kiss. This time I wouldn't let him leave. "He's not there now?"

There was a pause before Warren replied, "Wait, there's a message."

"Could you read it, please?"

"It says: *I need to see you. It's important. I'll drop by.* It's signed 'P'."

Philippe? My stomach somersaulted. The Voodoo priest frightened me. That vision had been ghastly—brains splattered on the deck of the pirate ship. And who's to say it was my vision at all? Doctor Philippe could have reached into his box of tricks and cycled in some Voodoo magic.

I took a deep breath before I said, "Thanks, Warren. When did you get this?"

There was a pause on the other end. "A few minutes ago. I'm guessin' you don't want to see him?"

Fingering the cut on my scalp, I said slowly, "Maybe not."

"Well, have a pleasant evening, Miss Sommerville."

I heard the receiver click as it was laid down. I glanced at the bedside clock: 9:55. The outer door was locked to non-residents at ten. Doctor Philippe wouldn't get in tonight.

Grabbing a protein bar from the dresser top I took the diary with me to the balcony and sitting on the built-in lounge, I glanced up. In an otherwise navy blue sky, heavy black clouds hung low, the pale full moon revealed as they shifted away. For a moment my eyes lit on the attic of the Ursuline Convent. From where I sat, it looked as if one of the shutters was open. Vampires flying out to feast on tourists. Raven had been happy enough to hand over the Sazerac and rendezvous the streets for a suck of bloody nectar— finding just the right throat to dig his pointy fangs into.

The protein bar was packed with vitamins but hardly a meal like Oysters Bienville. As I swallowed a bite of nuts and chocolate granola I heard a knock on my door. Wary of my attacker returning, I hid the diary in the drawer and picked up a red high-heeled stiletto from my closet on the way to the door. Holding it behind my back I opened it a crack. When I saw who it was, I tried slamming it shut, but he was too fast, jamming the tip of his leather shoe in the opening.

Chapter 12: THE HANGED MAN

"We need to talk," Doctor Philippe said, his steely gray eyes intense. "Really, darlin'." He leaned on the door, wedging it open further. "It's important!"

"About what?" I asked, my curiosity getting the better of me.

"Let me in, Anabelle."

"No."

"Please. This concerns you just as much as it does me."

Against my better judgment I opened the door wider. Handsome in a denim shirt and jeans, Philippe brushed past. If I liked men with shaved heads, I would have thought he was extremely sexy.

To me, hair is a turn on. All that aside, I was seeing his purple aura spread, the inner color too murky to perceive. The Voodoo doctor was deviously blocking my intuition. I felt like Little Red Riding Hood with the Wolf character. Getting close to this man was like playing with fire.

Doctor Philippe made his way into the master bedroom. "May I sit?" He motioned to the wing chair.

"You will anyway," I said, sitting across from him. "Why are you here?"

He twitched his nose. "Something happened in here, didn't it?"

"Unfortunately, yes. Someone hit me on the head." I said, touching the back of my head, "and shoved me into the closet."

"Do you need a doctor?"

I shook my head. "No."

"You should call the police."

"Nothing was taken. I have the feeling it wasn't about my ten carat diamond earrings."

"Were you hurt?"

"No."

He stood, leaned over, and ran his fingers through my hair. "A bump."

Flinching, I said, "It's okay."

"You could have a concussion, Anabelle."

"I'm okay, really. Tell me why you're here."

Doctor Philippe rubbed his chin reflectively. "Dreams, darlin'. His expression clouded. "Disturbing dreams." Doctor Philippe got up and wandered outside onto the balcony. Prompted by his sudden exit, I followed and standing by him, watched the sky. In the distance blackbirds circled. But no, they couldn't be birds. They had to be bats.

"The convent," he said, his eyes focused on the attic windows of the Ursuline Convent. "Do you know its history?"

"The vampires you mean?"

His eyes flickered like silver moonlight. "And?"

"They search for human prey." I wasn't sure if he knew about Raven but I wasn't about to discuss my vampire. Besides, I've always held my cards close to my chest. My attention strayed back to Doctor Philippe's lips. If I kissed him perhaps he would reveal all his secrets. Or not. Either way, I might enjoy it.

I don't know if it was the blow to my head or this hotel but my Voices started a discussion. Hormone spoke first. "Markus and now the mysterious Voodoo guy." Hormone was having a field day. "You can make up for all the pleasure you missed when you were in that farce of a relationship. You go girl!"

Logical whispered, "The Voodoo man is not interested in you. He wants something. Be careful."

Doctor Philippe's voice was hushed, barely audible. "The vampires appeared with the arrival of the casquette girls in the early 1800's. Story has it they guarded the young ladies but pedestrians need to be careful walking around after dark. They found people dead near the convent, fang indentations in their necks." He took my face in his hands. "You don't walk out there alone at night, do you?"

"No, not usually."

The energy from his hands flowed through my body. It was almost as if the blood coursing through my veins had turned to liquid Jello and my will was now his. He was certainly a powerful Voodoo priest and that in itself was reason enough to be wary. Yet, when I searched his face I read nothing but honesty. Still, I was suspicious. "But that's not why you are here, is it, Doctor Philippe?"

"You think I have an ulterior motive?'

Hormone spoke up. "This guy is super sexy, Anabelle. Flames are flicking out of his body. Give him a test drive."

I nodded, not sure if I was answering Hormone or the Voodoo priest's question.

"You're right," he said slowly. "I didn't think I could pull one over on you, pretty lady. It is very obvious you have some amazing psychic ability. I was hopin' you could siphon into that and come to my assistance."

That was a shocker. The Voodoo priest needed help?

"Yes, I do," he said, as if he heard the words inside my head.

"Come," I said, taking his arm and leading him back inside. "Sit." I indicated the wing chair. "Tell me what is bothering you."

"I've been havin' dreams. A coincidence that you are also havin' them? Or have you stopped havin' nightmares?"

"My sleep seems more tranquil with sleeping pills. Unfortunately, New Orleans is not giving me the answers I need."

Doctor Philippe's jaw clenched. "Are you seeing spirits?"

"And visions."

"I recall the ship we both saw. It got me thinkin', wasn't sure at first, but now I believe I'm pickin' up your past life," he said, his lips turning down at the corners.

"How do you know?"

"Tell me somethin'. What do you know of Belle?"

My jaw dropped. "You saw her?"

"We both have. She's a gorgeous blonde with luminescent golden skin and mesmerizing eyes. Sound familiar?"

My mind drifted back to the portrait of the blonde on the stairs of Renard's. Could that be Belle? "What do you propose?"

"We need to time travel." He met my eyes. "It's the only way."

I took the plastic cup filled with Raven's Sazerac and filled the two small glasses provided by the hotel with the golden liquid. "All right," I said. "Drink up. The Sazerac has given me visions ever since I arrived in New Orleans."

"Curious, wouldn't you say?"

"It was invented in the early 1800's. But don't ask me why this cocktail spins me into a state of altered consciousness."

Doctor Philippe clicked my glass. "May this Sazerac bring us there."

Cautiously, I took a sip.

"Let me tell you how this started." His gaze was thoughtful. "I was strollin' in the cemetery trying to get a moment alone when a gauzy figure in a white dress and red turban approached."

"Marie Laveau."

Doctor Philippe shot me a look. "You've seen her?"

"Yes, in the cemetery. She gave me something to place under my pillow."

"Gris-gris."

"I assume so, although I didn't open it." I grinned. "She thought I needed a man." Marie Laveau was right, but I regretted saying what popped out of my mouth the way Doctor Philippe's gaze swept down my body. Voodoo priests were men after all. Now what had I done?

"Love is necessary for everyone." Doctor Philippe tossed back the rest of his Sazerac and glanced at me expectantly. "Drink up." He tugged out a purple candle from the satchel he had brought with him and after placing it on the table, lit it. "The light will help us find the past. Focus on the flame and wish for clarification. We have to get to the bottom of this. It's not just your past I'm worried about. This is much bigger."

"How?"

"I think you know and if you don't, you should shortly," Doctor Philippe said softly. "I will try to tell you what I am seeing as it occurs. Will you do the same?"

I nodded, eyes on the lit candle.

"Say these words after me." Doctor Philippe chanted, *"Redde preterito, redde preterito, redde preterito."*

"There's nothing to confirm we will have a connected vision." But as I spoke the flame grew stronger and the peculiar bronze shimmer of the Sazerac came out of the glass, swirling of its own volition around the candle flame like a whirlpool.

When I looked up the room was a haze. "I'm seeing something."

"A muscular form coming out of a cloud. By his appearance I'd say he is something other than a man."

As I drifted into Doctor Philippe's vision I saw this god-like being. He had an athletic body, his face lean with strong features and far-seeing strange pale green eyes like a cat's.

"Who are you?" I whispered.

"Morpheus, the God of Dreams," he said softly. "I am taking you to Renard's."

Doctor Philippe spoke up. "And will you take me?"

"You must come," Morpheus said, his face suddenly stern. "Your past life is connected."

As if by magic we were swept through a cloud and dropped into an opulent Egyptian room flooded with gold and reds hues, velvet settees accented with tasseled pillows. There was the painting of Janelle, the tart with makeup to the heehaw who had dropped a killer blow to Markus' temple like some avenging angel.

From where I stood I could see the dining room was busy—men and women dressed in evening wear, the ladies in low cut satin dresses and the men in fancy suits and cravats drinking wine and eating seafood dishes. Somehow I knew the oysters, shrimp and fish were Creole dishes I had prepared. For once I was interested in the people at the table rather than the food.

A man with shoulder length dark hair called out, "I'm enjoying the shrimp, Belle. You've outdone yourself. You are a lucky man, Rene." His voice was sexy and very familiar.

"I am." An older man with a thick head of gray hair smiled in a superior fashion. "Belle's skills in the kitchen have made us the most talked about eatery in the city, Ducoeur."

"Or was that her bedroom skills, Papa?" a man chortled.

"Belle is a fabulous woman, son. Unfortunately, she will have the arduous task of being your stepmother, Robert."

At the table I caught a glimpse of Alain Ducoeur. My pulse raced. How ridiculous to be aroused by a spirit man. Hormones again. It was better to ignore them.

"Concentrate on your vision and forget him, Anabelle. You need to discover the major players from Belle's life," my Logical Voice hissed in my ear.

"You can have fun for a change. You're the siren Belle now. Sample the sexy men she has lined up!" Hormone said, with a giggle.

Beside me, Doctor Philippe took my hand. "This is strange." He pulled me close. "A kiss for luck."

His lips smoldered on mine. Whoever he was, Doctor Philippe had a ton of magnetism. "If you need to return, use the antidote."

"Which is?"

"Chocolate." His icy eyes met mine. "Careful. Remember you are Belle and it could be dangerous." He handed me a bonbon wrapped in gold paper which I dropped into the tiny purse at my waist. " Ready?"

I nodded. His hand gripping mine was dangerously hot almost lethal in its intensity, so much so I wanted to leave Renard's and go back to the safety of my present life. But that was wrong. My stay in New O'leans had become all too dangerous and I had a head wound to prove it.

Following the Voodoo priest I was dumbfounded. The vision had not only changed me into Belle but it had altered Doctor Philippe. He was older and thinner. Long curly dark hair brushed his shoulders. He sported a pencil thin moustache and pointy beard. Though he wore a suit and cravat as did the rest of the men in the room, it was clear Doctor Philippe was the famous Louisiana pirate, Jean Lafitte.

When I glanced in the mirror in the hall I was clothed in an elaborate pink dress, my skin was tawny and I had a longer nose. I was Belle now, not Anabelle.

The dining room was lit by candles from the table casting shadows on the faces of the diners surrounded by a heavy, black vapor—negative energy reaching to the corners of the room. I had that same feeling when I first viewed the painting of Jesus and his disciples at the Louvre, the famous "Last Supper". One person seated here had betrayed me just as Judas had betrayed Jesus. One of these people murdered Belle. I was sure of it.

My eyes wandered past Alain Ducoeur to the woman who sat beside him. She was the ghost spirit from the hotel. Tonight, Delphine was sensational in white, her ebony hair and dusky skin contrasting with the gown. The other woman was Janelle, the strawberry blonde floozy who flew off the wall and struck Markus.

When we entered the chatter ended abruptly. As we trod over to the empty seats the men at the table rose to their feet. It was something I didn't see too often—gentlemen standing for a lady. It was a shame women lost the pedestal after entering the man's work world. Wouldn't it be wonderful to be treated like a princess for a change with flowers and chocolates?

"Here she is. Thanks for bringing her back from the kitchen,

Lafitte. Rest yourself, my dear. The food is exceptional, by the way. Wouldn't you agree?" the gray-haired man at the head of the table said, raising an eyebrow to which the other guests responded with applause. "Renard's is the best restaurant in New O'leans, thanks to you."

"Thank you."

"You outdid yourself, cher," Alain said, his green eyes filled with warmth. "You were gone for quite a while. No matter how delicious the oysters, I'd rather have the pleasure of your company." He held out my chair and I took the seat in between him and Rene.

"You've kept my betrothed much too long," Rene Renard declared, an edge in his tone, staring narrowly at Lafitte, formerly Doctor Philippe. "If I didn't know the lovely Delphine was your lady I would be jealous," Rene said, his glance settling on the dusky-skinned beauty on his right. "Or perhaps I should be anyway." Rene Renard lifted the decanter and refilled Delphine's glass. "Drink up, my dear."

"It tears me in two when you betray my trust," Delphine took up a table knife to emphasis her point and waved it at Lafitte, her eyes blazing coal embers.

Alain Ducoeur grabbed her wrist. "Easy now, Delphine. No one is taking him from you." The squeeze and downward push to her hand must have dialed up her pain. She gasped loudly.

I knew from my defence training if he pushed any harder he would break her wrist. When the knife clattered on the table, Ducoeur added, "Well, Lafitte? Your heart is with this lady, is it not?"

Doctor Philippe, aka Jean Lafitte, laughed. "Of course. The proof of my love is that sparkly necklace I appropriated from a wealthy Spanish countess. You have nothing to fear, Delphine. I admired you long before I became a devotee of your favors." His bright smile sparkled in the candlelight his gold front tooth reflecting the flames. Perhaps, I shall take you with me when I leave New O'leans."

The news surprised everyone. Rene Renard was the first to speak up. "But why?"

"Why Delphine, or why leave?"

"Get serious, man." Rene glared. "Something happen?"

"There are some that want to hang this particular pirate, so," Jean Lafitte sucked up an oyster, "before things get out of hand I made plans with the Colombian government to fly their flag. The men will be happy about that."

"And you, Ducoeur?" a younger swarthier version of Rene at the other end of the table cut in. "Are you going with him? Father would like that but maybe not so much the lusty Janelle."

"I am sick of your attitude, son." Rene Renard's eyes were like black holes in a frozen pond. "Janelle is my assistant and as such receives a hearty chunk of the profits. She doesn't need any man."

Janelle, from the painting was seated next to Alain Ducoeur. She was attractive in a slutty way. Her dress was so low cut she was in danger of wardrobe malfunction. If one of her milky-white breasts fell into her dinner plate I was not exactly sure what the conscientious hostess should do.

Her plump generous lips suddenly curled back from sharp fang-like teeth and along with the thick liner around her coffee-brown eyes, she resembled a hungry raccoon on the prowl. She was the kind of woman who talked too much and laughed too loud with every man in the room.

"I like to make us both happy, Rene. It's a profitable business with me running it." Janelle squeezed Alain Ducoeur's arm in an intimate fashion. "You're a wild mustang. Quite the challenge for any ordinary woman but I'm up for it."

"You would be."

"Not like the sweet Dina. Charming little thing, isn't she?" Jean Lafitte chimed in. "I'd like to spend some time with her when you're done, Ducoeur."

"Who?" Rene Renard asked.

"Janelle's virginal sister." Jean Lafitte grinned.

"None of you will be seeing her," Janelle hissed. "My sister is innocent and I intend for her to stay that way."

"What's this about a sister? You are a little minx for not telling me," Rene Renard slurred, his eyes half-mast. "Bring her here tomorrow night, Janelle."

Janelle poured wine into Renard's glass. "You have Belle now. Be happy with her." Tipping back her wine she glanced at

Delphine. "Breakups are difficult. Lafitte is an amazing man. I sympathize."

Delphine stared at the pirate who avoided her gaze and scooped up a shrimp.

Rene's laughed so hard he choked on his cough. After a sip of wine he managed, "Delphine, you are any man's dream girl. Don't worry. You will find another pirate. Now, in warning I believe Lafitte needs to look elsewhere. He can't have Belle. And Robert, if you learn what stirs New O'leans desires you can take over my restaurant someday. As for Janelle, she takes whatever she wants, when she wants." He raised his glass. "To success."

"And Alain?" Janelle purred. "What about you?"

"You are leaving New O'leans, Ducoeur?" Delphine asked.

"I am staying right here in the Quarter," Alain said, with a big grin. "Jean has settled his accounts with me and I shall start my medical practice in the Quarter."

"While still keeping the store loaded with pilfered items I'd bet. You have made a pretty penny from piracy. Pays well, why ditch it now?" Robert asked, picking up his wine glass.

"A difference of opinion."

"Slaves." Jean Lafitte shrugged his shoulders. "We captured that ship not knowing what was on board but if I hadn't supplied the Negroes from the Spanish galleon for auction, the Virginia plantation owners would have brought in their own slaves to auction anyway."

"They breed negroes," Delphine said, disgust in her voice.

"So you hate the concept of slavery, Delphine?" Robert said.

"Of course. I have African blood, back several generations."

"And yet you have house slaves whom you beat regularly."

Rene poured himself another glass of wine. "Everyone with slaves abuses them on principal."

"That's not true, Rene! I am kind to my house servants whom I have freed." Delphine dug an oyster and tossed it in her mouth. She smiled with content. "These are so delicious, Belle. I should have you working in my kitchen. There are many fine gentlemen who would love to sample these goodies."

Robert snickered. "Belle's goodies in your brothel?"

"Belle has a job waiting for her if her betrothal goes sour which it well might, knowing Rene's mood swings. I think you overindulge, Rene," Delphine flicked a dark curl away from her forehead with a long pointy fingernail. "Do I detect some envy, Robert? You and Belle are about the same age. She would be your new stepmother. Very cozy."

"Like Oedipus, he beds his mother and kills his father? Delphine might have something there," mused Lafitte.

It was hard for me to remember that this man was Doctor Philippe. He was much more flippant and carefree. Only when I looked into those icy gray eyes did I see the Voodoo priest surfacing.

"You have a thing for Belle, don't you Robert?" Lafitte said.

"Like you do? Oh, wait, you already have a woman." Robert chortled. "How stupid of me—you have a stable full of women, all of them insane. And as for my papa, he sealed the deal with the nun himself. Paid her off plenty. He's the only one entitled to Belle now. No use discussing it further. Besides, I'm not a boy. I have two years on Belle." Robert glared at everyone seated. "Let's not upset my illustrious father. He is not a well man."

"Nonsense," Rene spat. "Nothing wrong with me. I have speared a hundred women."

Robert twirled his fork, muttering under his breath, "More like a thousand."

"Tell us, Lafitte, did no one complain about the slaves?" I felt a hand on my leg. It wasn't Rene's. With the smirk on Alain Ducoeur's lips I knew it belonged to him. I tried to ignore it but the man was so magnetic, a flush fired my cheeks and lit my core like a blast of dynamite. When his hand crept up to my thigh I brought my hand down on top of his. I hardly knew what women behaved like in the nineteenth century in New Orleans but a girl living in a convent had to be a virgin. Ducoeur was way out of line!

Lafitte shrugged. "They like whatever goods we capture. New O'leans is not Paris, Belle."

"Delphine, you hardly uttered a word when Lafitte sold the cargo. The profits must have been more than enough to keep your lips sealed," I said pointedly, staring at the diamond-sapphire encrusted necklace adorning Delphine's neck. I wasn't too keen on the dusky beauty. As a ghost with a gripe she could have knocked me out and stuck me in the closet so that she could search for Belle's diary.

Janelle smirked. "Rene bought me a fabulous necklace from the very same collection, Belle. So we all have one. Oh, wait a minute, darlin'. You haven't been so fortunate, have you? Perhaps if you play nice Rene will get you one too."

"No need. I like simple jewelry." I fingered the single strand of gold around my neck.

"A pretty wench like you would look enchanting with a ruby pendant. Red for love. Who would like to buy one for the temptress Belle?" Jean Lafitte grinned like the Cheshire Cat.

"Shut up, Lafitte. You forget she is mine now," Rene slurred, his fingertips on my cheek.

Casually, I pushed his hand away. "Tell us about your adventure, Lafitte."

"I would love to but isn't it time to sample the house drink? You promised us Sazeracs, Rene."

"All right. I will make some for everyone. Belle, come help me."

"I prefer her company," Jean Lafitte said, a twinkle in his eye. "She should stay here and entertain us whilst you prepare our drinks."

Rene's eyelids, half-mast like a lizard's in the tropical sun glared at the pirate. "You owe me a game of bourré, my friend."

Alain Ducoeur pulled a small box wrapped with a gold ribbon from his pocket and set it on the table in front of me. "Go make the drinks, Rene, but leave the charming Belle here. You can handle the job alone, can't you?"

Rene shot him a look but ambled over to the door next to the bar on the other side of the room and entered.

"Where's he going?" I asked puzzled.

"Rene has a weakness for the hookah, remember?" Janelle peered at me from half mast eyes. He goes to his opium den. I will be surprised if he brings back any drinks or if he returns at all."

From the other door a group of young men entered holding instruments. They set themselves on the chairs and tuned up before playing a lilting tune that reminded me of wind and waves.

"They are a fine band," Delphine said.

Lafitte glanced casually at the boys. "Aren't you the proud

mama."

"And you are the daddy. That boy in the middle is yours, isn't he?" Janelle said.

Lafitte laughed. "Delphine has numerous lovers and accordin' to the women of O'leans I have at least a dozen scattered about. Which one is yours, Ducoeur?"

Alain Ducoeur grinned. "None that I know of. Of course ..." He trailed off as if contemplating the possibility, glancing at me.

I was appalled. These men were incorrigible. "Don't any of you use birth control?" I blurted out. Omigod, did they even have such a thing in the early part of the nineteenth century?

"*Coitus interruptus* or does she mean a glove?" Robert winked at Alain Ducoeur.

"There isn't a man alive who likes the feel of the animal skin of the *baudruche,* Belle," Alain said seriously.

"Papa doesn't use them, does he, Belle?" Robert said, a smile playing on his lips.

Alain Ducoeur's glance swept to me. "Treat her with respect, boy."

"Soon there will be a baby, I'm sure," Jean Lafitte said, with a chuckle.

Stupid men. They thought Belle was a virgin raised by nuns, secluded from men but if I was truly Belle right now, I didn't get the feeling she was so innocent. "I'm not a cow Rene just purchased for breeding. Tell us about the jewels," I reminded Lafitte, glancing at the box in front of me, wondering if it came from a Spanish galleon and if it might be a necklace.

"Diamonds and rubies. Unfortunately, the Virginians didn't like me bringing in the slave cargo. They had their own to sell."

Robert snickered. "So the governor wants you gone?"

"The governor appreciates how my men fought to defeat the British. He's hardly in a hurry to exile the pirates when everyone in New O'leans likes the fancy goods from Spain." Jean Lafitte glanced at Ducoeur. "I feel very lucky tonight. Shall we play a game of cards?"

"Why not," Alain Ducoeur agreed. "I'm on a winning streak."

"Which should end tonight." Robert laughed, his dark eyes glittering.

Ducoeur met my eyes. "As there is music, I would like to dance with the ladies first."

"Belle, this wine is so good." Robert drank deeply. "What is it?"

"It's a very old cabernet from the cellar," I said crisply, wondering about Robert. His aura was an olive green. Too dark and gloomy for a boy of twenty.

My eyes lit on the package next to my plate. "What's in the box, Alain?"

"Something for you."

"I shouldn't accept." The way Rene had given me the evil eye before made my skin crawl. One minute happy, the next depressed. It was playing with fire to accept anything from another man. His mood swings made him a loose cannon. It was so much simpler to be Anabelle. I wished I could leave the nineteenth century behind and have dinner with Markus—a man who was hot and alive.

Alain Ducoeur's eyes shimmered brightly green like the hues of an exquisite emerald. "A gift for the hostess. Surely that's acceptable?"

"Open it." Janelle smirked. "Alain has certainly brought you some fine lacy underthings from Paris. Of course Rene will get to see them on you first."

That woman was trouble on red stilettos. I glanced over at the musicians playing a lively tune. "The music is excellent. Where ever did you find these boys, Janelle?"

"You can thank Delphine. Her son is the tall one with the guitar. The others are his band. He has a fine singing voice."

"He is talented."

"Barely thirteen."

"Wait, your glass is empty, cher." Alain stood. "I will be right back."

Janelle's eyes flicked to the others at the table. When she was sure they couldn't overhear us, she leaned in closer, whispering, "They will want to kill you when they know you are carrying his child, just like they took my baby and killed him."

"What are you saying?" I grabbed her wrist. "Are you drunk?"

Janelle tugged her hand away. "No, it's true."

"Here we go." Alain thrust the box in my hands. "And before you open it, some wine to make the taste perfect," he said, refilling my glass.

"Who killed your child?" I whispered, when Alain leaned over to top Delphine's glass.

Janelle shook her head.

"Are you filling Belle's head with nonsense, Janelle?" Alain frowned.

As I lifted the lid, my thoughts raced. Who was she afraid of? The tissue parted to reveal six decorative chocolate truffles. "Oh, how sweet of you."

Alain Ducoeur swooped one out of the box. In a husky voice he whispered, "Addictively delicious as are your lips."

I hesitated, remembering chocolate had the power to bring me back to the twenty-first century. I decided to have a taste but not swallow. The chocolate melted slowly on the warmth of my tongue. Holding it in as long as I could, I closed my eyes a moment to savor the creamy rich, delicious tones of cocoa. Lifting the linen napkin to my lips as if to wipe away the chocolate, I deposited the velvety morsel.

"Are you seducing my betrothed with chocolate, Ducoeur?" Rene Renard set a pitcher of Sazerac down on the table with a thud. "Can you not find your own woman? Perhaps you need to consume oysters." Rene Renard chortled. "Or try some of my very fine cocaine. Gives my mojo a perk."

With the glazed look in Rene Renard's eyes I could sense a fight brewing. Quickly, I passed the chocolates over to Janelle. "Thank you, Alain. The ladies will love them as much as I do, I'm sure."

"They are for you, but share if you wish." Alain Ducoeur sent Rene a disdainful glance. "You need to ease up on the drug cocktail. Opiates make for a pitiful bedroom romp. Remember, it takes a thoughtful lover to make a woman happy, Renard."

"She will be happy in the kitchen, Ducoeur, and the rest is not your concern." Slopping the liquor mixture into glasses, he passed them to the guests.

"It's hardly necessary to squabble over a woman, Papa. If Belle displeases you can send her back to the convent," Robert said with a superior air. "You are getting on in years. Why not wait for grandchildren?"

"Belle is carrying my child," Rene slurred. "And Robert, this woman is special. Her gourmet cookin' has done wonders for the restaurant." Rene stood unsteadily and trudged out into the hall muttering under his breath about writing a poem.

Janelle rolled her eyes. "Long, boring poems about genies in pink clouds."

"His inspiration is Morpheus and the hookah," Robert added. "Is he serious about the baby, Belle?"

I shook my head in confusion.

"Excuse us. I need to speak with Janelle." I took her hand and stood, pulling Janelle up. "Come with me."

"No, I've said all I have to say."

Lafitte appeared behind me and handed me a Sazerac. "Drink up, darlin'." He whispered, "It not only opens the portal but it will keep us here longer."

As I speculated how to corner Janelle, a very handsome trim young man, auburn curls and coal black eyes with a pale complexion came to the table. He was followed by a slim transgender type with limp orange hair and narrow shoulders. My jaw dropped.

"Miss Belle, may I have this dance?" Raven said politely. He motioned for Gabe to go rejoin the musicians.

People did not dance as couples I soon found out. We did some sort of square dance, hips swinging and arms bouncing. Belle knew the steps even if I hadn't a clue. But all this changed with the next piece, a waltz which was definitely a risqué dance back then—not like grind in the clubs now but with Raven's hand firmly around my waist we twirled around the floor careful not to collide into Delphine and Jean Lafitte. Raven swept me into the room behind the bar and I confronted him.

"Why are you here and why are you looking so goo-goo eyed at me?"

Raven's full lips curled up at the corners. "I'm your biggest fan and you look lovely in that gown. But I'm not here just to dance, chérie. I want a kiss." With that he leaned forward.

I was shocked but flustered even more so. It was something I hadn't even considered—Belle romantically involved with Raven.

"Hey, I have feelings, Belle. It's not like it's the first time, is it? You always liked a kiss." He leaned over and planted a kiss on my neck. Um-mm," he moaned. "Such skin."

"Forget it, Raven. I'm not your next meal." Listen," I said, placing a finger on his lips, "What's up with Janelle?"

"Hm-mm?"

"Janelle said someone killed her baby."

"Never mind her." Raven peeked into the main room. "I have to show you something." He took my hand and led me to the top of the stairs which opened to a luxurious bedroom—a massive draped bed, mirrors on the ceiling and champagne on ice.

"Where are we?"

"Rene Renard's bedroom."

I drew the curtains around the bed aside. Handcuffs were attached to each bed post.

"What's going on?"

"For you, dear Belle," a woman husky voice said behind me.

I swung around to face Janelle holding a six shooter, the pupils of her eyes tiny pinpoints in muddy brown water.

She waved the gun. "Get on that bed, Belle."

I looked around. Raven had disappeared behind the velvet curtain. I could see the tips of his shoes peeking out.

"What's wrong, Janelle? You look awful."

"Shut up! Do as I say or you will regret it."

I wasn't close enough to disarm her so I slipped off my shoes.

"Quit stalling, Belle." She pointed the gun to the headboard. "Up you go."

She needed taking out but I wasn't sure how to do this as Janelle was standing out of reach and trigger happy, judging from her agitated facial tick. If I could get a hold of something heavy I could throw it and disarm her but Janelle was smart, staying a safe distance away.

"Handcuff your wrist."

Not having a better plan I edged up to the pillows and locked my right hand into the cuff. If she came close I'd kick her in the face.

"Now, bring your other hand up to the handcuff."

When I hesitated, she screamed, "Do it or you'll be gettin' a third eye." She kept her distance and waited. Having no choice, I clicked the cuff shut.

Janelle leaned over tugged the neckline of my dress down,

pronouncing, "He will like this."

"Who?"

"The master, of course. He will be here momentarily. Oh yes." She picked up a glass flask and dabbed the liquid onto her palm and commenced spreading the scented oil on my neck and cleavage. Then, picking up the pistol from the night table, she strut out the door, swinging it shut as she left.

"Raven," I yelled. "Where are you?"

The vampire stepped out from behind the drapes. His eyes widened. "What a waste to give those to Renard."

"Boobs are not things. They are parts of me. Get your head out of your butt and help."

Raven waved his hand in a stop gesture. "Okay, I'm on it. Where is the key?" Raven's eyes shot to the bedside table to a metal object. With a quick motion he clicked open the lock.

Pulling my hand out from the cuff I shook it to regain circulation. "Quick. The other one."

When Raven released the mechanism, I said, "Perfect. Do you have an escape plan?"

Footsteps in the hallway put an end to our conversation. I pulled my dress higher and sat up.

Raven shot behind the curtains once again as Rene Renard entered, a small whip in his hand. His pupils were dilated like a cess pool in Mississippi mud.

"You're loose? Oh, well, no problem. Handcuffs or not, there is no stopping me tonight, Belle." Renard leered at me. "It's time for some fun, eh?" He laughed raucously. "Janelle knows exactly what arouses me." Snapping the whip in the air, he chortled. "Sweet flesh aching for the pain of the lash." He stared at the whip. "Lovely, isn't it? I had a mare I whipped regularly with this and now you, my filly, will receive the sting. Prepare yourself for exquisite delight."

Renard belonged in an S&M porn flick, not my bed. He made me so angry I was ready to grab that whip and wrap it around his scrawny throat. First chance I had I would make sure I would or go out fighting. Where was Raven when I needed him, anyway? I formulated an attack plan for the druggie. If he came closer I would give him a kick to the groin he wouldn't forget but though I was ready, the slimy freak was keeping his distance prancing around the room like a circus pony.

As I braced myself, a heavy thud followed by a loud moan, and yet another, brought Rene lurching forward, his eyes rolling back in his head. A sound, a lot like a man's orgasmic groan spilled noisily from Rene Renard's lips but I had an inkling he was not getting his jollies. When he dropped like dead weight, face down on the bed, I retreated to the headboard.

Alain Ducoeur rubbed his fist with his other hand. "That lunatic needs a lethal injection but having none to give him I thought a punch to the kidneys would cause him some well-deserved agony." He glanced at the unconscious form of Rene Renard. "I was careful not to injure him permanently. Now come here, Belle. You don't have much time."

I remembered I had hidden a truffle in my dress but my clothes were strewn on the floor.

"Don't worry. I have what you need." With that he tugged out a chocolate truffle from his pocket and thrust it to my lips. "Swallow the chocolate and wish yourself back. I would take you away from all this but for now, Renard has claimed you and I can do nothing." Alain Ducoeur stroked my lips with a finger. "You make such a delightful feast. I wish I could taste every bit of you." He leaned in and kissed me gently. Then he murmured softly, "*Redde praesenti, redde praesenti, redde praesenti.*"

Chapter 13: THE EMPRESS

"Wake up, chérie! Are you all right?"

A stinging slap brought me into a state of painful consciousness. The bedroom was shrouded by night. Through the open balcony doors, red beams streaked the inky horizon. I was sitting on the wing chair with Raven hovering over me. He was about to slap me again but I blocked him with my forearm.

"Enough, already. What do you think you're doing?"

Raven pursed his lips. "I thought you were lost in the past. You had me worried."

Perusing the room I spotted Doctor Philippe's candle on the table but there was no sign of the Voodoo priest. The purple candle had burned down to a tiny pool of wax.

"So he was here. I didn't dream that. And you were too?"

Raven nodded.

"How did I get back?"

"Remember the chocolate Ducoeur gave you? For you, it works."

"Not for everyone?"

"No, Anabelle." He grinned mischievously. "It only works for chocoholics."

The taste had been rich and sinfully delicious just like the man that gave it to me. Ducoeur was drop dead sexy but definitely unavailable in this century, yet he had information that might solve the mystery of Belle's death. She must have been murdered or I wouldn't be getting nightmares. "Is Doctor Philippe still back in the nineteenth century? I feel bad leaving him behind."

"A man like him has time traveled before. He'll know how to return." Raven stared solemnly at the sky, fragments of color rendering it indigo. "Shape-shifting is a Voodoo priest's strength. Surely you've heard stories of Madame Laveau and her powers? Although he might not be on par with the Voodoo Queen, I'd think he's probably right now sleeping happily in his bed on Governor Nicolls. I heard he has an apartment there."

"With the rich and famous. He can afford that?"

"Made a mint from his psychic HBO series."

"He came prepared, bringing a purple candle. I wonder why Doctor Philippe needed me to come along?"

Raven clicked his long fingernails on the railing impatiently. "I'd bet you anything the Voodoo priest has tried unsuccessfully to return. It must be harder going back that far in time. Meeting you, however, was his ticket for a safe return."

"What do you think he wants to know?"

"You're kidding me, right?" Raven laughed. "Lafitte was a big player back then. Richer than the governor. He had it all— adventure, women and money."

I raised an eyebrow skeptically. "You think Doctor Philippe wants to experience the pirate life?"

Raven shook his head. "Rumor has it Lafitte hid treasure all over Louisiana."

"And he thinks I know the whereabouts of this treasure?"

"Belle does. She slept with him."

"I thought he and Delphine were in a relationship."

"Lafitte was never exclusive."

As we spoke the city was coming alive with brilliant rays of pink, spilling on the roof tops, yet the buildings themselves were still dark with night.

"Lafitte seemed to like me when I was Belle."

"Not any different than Doctor Philippe liking you now. You were especially ravishing lying in Renard's bed." He coughed. "Not that I have designs on you. Just saying."

"I'm Anabelle, remember?"

"You look so amazingly alike, sometimes I forget. You see, I felt especially bad I couldn't prevent Belle's death. She was a free spirit like a butterfly. Every man could see how she was. I think in a way she loved us all."

"What? Even Rene Renard?"

"Poor man was bi-polar, a child of abuse. With his addiction to morphine and cocaine, he seldom saw anything clearly, but he knew Belle was the best woman in New Orleans. She made him see he could change."

"But he didn't, did he?"

"You think Renard killed her?" Raven shook his head. "I don't know." He took my hand and looked tenderly into my eyes. "Would you like to make love, Anabelle?"

I rolled my eyes. "Seriously? Obviously, we need to talk." I placed a hand on his arm. "No offence but we have no chemistry." Then seeing his frown I added, "Not that you aren't attractive or anything but—"

"You like Markus or is it Doctor Philippe?" He scratched his chin. "They are fine healthy specimens."

I shot him a sidelong glance.

"It's because I'm a vampire. That's the problem, isn't it?"

I stared at him suspiciously. He was up to something. "You aren't thinking sex with me will make you a human?"

"It's possible." Raven grinned widely. "We'd have to do it a few times to test it out." He eyed his pants. "I have everything you need."

Grabbing Raven by the shoulders, I shook him. "You're losing it, Raven. Now get real, I have a situation here and you are supposed to be my vampire, right?"

"True, but I can't help thing thinking..."

"Well stop thinking." I stared at him. "It's human life you want, not me. You realize humans die, don't you?"

"Of course." A shadow crossed his face. "But I think it's you I need, Belle."

"See? You're mixing me up with her. I'm not Belle. She's dead." "Sorry."

"Do you honestly think sex would help you transform?"

"Maybe, who knows? It might be fun." Raven stroked my cheek. "You don't think we could be happy together?"

"No! I came here to solve a murder and this crap doesn't help."

His coal black eyes sparked and he stamped his feet petulantly. "Which one of those men has ruined my chances?"

"It isn't them," I said, but I got a little hot thinking about Markus on the bed in the old Indigo Oaks mansion. "I have to discover the cause of Belle's death." I pushed aside a strand of hair from my forehead. "Don't you need blood to survive?"

"I do. But maybe, if I have a normal sex life, and get away from the blood-sucking, I'd become human."

I gave him another eye roll. "Vampires need blood to live. If you don't want to feed on humans, try the blood bank. It should be easy since any blood type would do."

"You don't have to be so sarcastic. I have feelings, Anabelle."

"Are you sure you want to be a man?"

Raven frowned. "You think I'm fem? Gabe thinks we're both gay. I am attracted to women but in a way he's on to something."

"How?"

"I feel I have the soul of a woman. If I can transform into a human perhaps I'd like to be a woman."

My eyes were getting tired from the rolls. "I know we're in New Orleans, and it's trendy here to be transgender, but really?"

Raven shrugged his shoulders. "Okay, maybe not trans. I've only had it bad for Belle, but when you showed up, I started to think about you."

A yellow streak appeared on the horizon. "Look, I get you're confused and there's a lot we need to talk about, but your vampire dilemma has to wait. From the look of the sky, I'd say our time is running out. Who do you think murdered Belle?"

Raven's brow furrowed. "You saw the usual suspects. Belle's life was complicated."

"Don't I know it! Thanks for helping me out of the cuffs. I will think about your blood situation, besides raiding a hospital, that is, but first something has been really bothering me."

"What?"

"Did you see who knocked me out and stuck me in the closet?"

"Huh? Who would do such a thing?"

"The question is why. I'm almost certain it's because of the diary."

"Ah-ha! That's it. Belle had secrets." Raven took me by the shoulders. "You need to read that journal, chérie."

"True. I should have done that before tonight's adventure." The tips of the buildings were alive with dancing gold beams. I had to hurry before the sun rose. "Something else. There was a snake in the room when I got out. Any ideas?"

Raven scratched his head. "Voodoo stuff. Lots of that in New O'leans. Root workers and Priestesses carry them around to use in ceremonies, fertility rites mostly, but all of them have snakes for pets."

Madame Laveau came to mind. She was in the cemetery. The gris-gris she had given me was tucked under a pillow, but why would she visit? I should be thinking of my time travel and connections there.

"Ask Gabe if he knows who killed Janelle's baby. It might be important."

"Sure." Raven peered up at the sky. "I must fly, Anabelle. Luckily, it's a short flight."

"And if you fly in daylight?"

Raven shook his head. "Vampires die with light, chérie." He pecked me on the cheek. "Adieu." With that he leaped onto the railing, he transformed into a black bat in the blink of an eye, and flew off before I could reply. Raven was on his way to the Ursuline Convent where the attic shutters were conveniently open.

When I saw a speck of black disappear into the convent window, I turned back into the bedroom and from the bottom drawer released the latch to open the secret drawer. The diary was inside. I breathed a sigh of relief that it was still there and lifted it out.

After I set it down on the duvet, I traipsed to the outer room and flipped the sign from "Clean my room" to "Do not disturb" on the outside of the door before locking it. Throwing off my clothes on the chair next to my bed, I climbed in and pulled up the covers. Pure luxury. Soft yet firm. Can't beat that for a bed.

Although my eyes were heavy, I forced myself to read as much as I could. The diary was loaded with information—French recipes, Cajun recipes and the restaurant organization. It didn't get detailed until Belle started taking on lovers. She didn't seem to be too concerned about getting knocked up either. This woman had an insatiable sex drive.

November 12: Jean is interested but I prefer his friend.
December 4: Alain Ducoeur is the lover I've been waiting for.
December 17: I had too much wine. Jean seduced me. Rene will kill us both but I have no regrets.
December 18. A nurse took the baby away. Janelle is weeping like a crazed woman.
December 30: Rene is insane. He had Janelle cuff me to the bed and forced himself on me but the drugs left him impotent and angry. Could Janelle have told him about Jean?
January 5: Jean Lafitte has passion but Alain has tenderness.
February 13: I was tied to the bed once more and drugged this

time. I hate Rene.
February 14: Alain brought me flowers. How romantic. I melt
inside. I want him all the time.
February 16: Getting sick every day.
March 15: Robert keeps leering at me.
April 16: Rene is gambling excessively. I think he is greatly in
debt. Alain wants me to leave Rene. He has given me directions to
his treasure.

Belle was a busy girl, all right. Lafitte and Ducoeur were her
lovers while Rene and Robert were left chafing at the bit. Even
though she seemed to have conquered the art of bed hopping, that
didn't make her a slut. In fact, I felt bad for her. Here she was
stuck with old Rene Renard, an addict whose idea of making love
was handcuffs and rape.

When I flipped to the midpoint of the journal I came upon
several pages filled with incantations for love, money and revenge.
Belle had learned to make her own gris-gris. Finally, I came to the
page I wanted.

Time travel: Going back to another life requires caution. Light a
purple candle and focus on the flame. Drink a potion which has the
power to transport. Mix lime, bourbon, and absinthe to make a
Sazerac. Chant the spell three times: Redde preterito. Let yourself
travel through time to the place where you loved the most. To
return eat chocolate and chant three times: Redde praesenti.

A beep alerted me of a text. When I picked up my cell I saw it
was from Sandie. *Want to come over for coffee and beignets with*
friends?

I texted back: *Sure, thx.*

It was impossible for me to sleep now anyway. I'd take a nap
later.

I hid the diary, and took a shower. After a touch of mascara and
lip gloss, I donned a short white skirt, lacy black top and a
turquoise bracelet to complete my ensemble. I was ready to rock it!
The woman in the mirror looked awesome if I said so myself. Who
would have thought I had been partying all night, dancing, and
tossing back wine, not to mention doing a Houdini act with
handcuffs. All of which made me think a psychic trip into the past
must be similar to REM sleep—like a long chaotic dream where

much time is spent tossing, turning and unpleasantly sweating. And what was up with Janelle, the happy hooker? The way she was tugging on my dress, made me wonder if men were her thing but the bigger question was, who killed her baby and why?

***

I was sipping a cup of Joe heavily laced with Jim Beam trying not to knock them back like Sandie. The hostess, with the mostest, had invited Shotgun Sue and Jacqueline from the Voodoo Emporium to her garden party. We were seated in comfortable wicker chairs around a glass table on the back deck facing the elaborately sculpted gardens of the Beauregard-Keyes house. Sandie was busy stuffing Cheetos out of a large bowl in her face in an unrestrained eating frenzy. The rest of them were gorging on chocolate beignets still warm from the bakery on Ursulines. I restrained myself, knowing indigestion would be my reward with my gluten allergy.

"The fatter I am, the more I need these," Sandie said, gleefully popping a Cheeto into her mouth. Some crumbs had dropped off her daffodil trapeze blouse to her jeans. She flecked off the orange specks with a fingernail. "Eat and be happy is my motto."

Sue's wide-brimmed garden hat flopped over one eye. Her round freckled face was moist with perspiration. She glanced at her pale arms exposed by the floral green cotton dress she was wearing. "Holy shit, it's hot today. This sun is killin' me. You sure about coffee cooling us off, Sandie?"

"If the coffee don't, Jimmy Beam will." Sandie chuckled. "You won't notice after a couple anyway."

"These shots sure are eye-poppin' strong," Jacqueline said. This might be Sandie's place but Jacqueline was the most important person there. The Voodoo lessons had paid off and she was the center of attention. There was nothing like a tarot card reading, everyone nervous with anticipation, hanging on her words. In a purple midi-dress splattered with fuchsia sequins, Jacqueline looked the part of a sorceress. "Bet you were surprised to see me here, Anabelle. Do you remember when we met?"

"Doctor Philippe's Voodoo Emporium."

"Right on. Say, I heard you two had a date—you and Philippe." Her blue eyes widened just like a kid's in a candy store stocked with brightly colored lollipops.

The other two perked up and leaned in closer, all eyes on me.

I was beginning to feel uncomfortable. "Why do you say that?" Now I knew why I didn't like lingerie and sex toy parties. The mean girls would guilt trip me into buying something and dish dirt about me for months afterwards speculating about who I was using it on or wearing it for.

"Tell!" Sandie squealed loud enough to be heard by two old ladies tottering past the convent across the street. They stared at her, frowns on their shriveled faces.

"From the look on Philippe's face when he came back to the shop, I'd say he was smitten as a kitten." Jacqueline nodded confidently. "Yup."

"Really? When, yesterday?"

"So you've seen him more than once?" Jacqueline grinned knowingly.

I watched her take a bite of the beignet.

"But what about Markus, Anabelle? You dumped him?" Sue asked. "He's so hot! That man is smokin'. Why would you do that?" Her eyes narrowed.

Jacqueline nodded. "Markus is one hot tomale but you have to admit Sue, Philippe gives you the chills."

"In a creepy way," Sue said. "Like in those horror movies when you are strangely attracted to the stalker killer. Count me out. I like the way Markus rolls."

Sandie giggled. "So, what's the scoop, darlin'?"

"You mean, which one do I like?"

Sandie poked my arm. "Don't play dumb, girlfriend."

"I haven't got a clue. They're both nice."

"Nice? A Voodoo priest?" Sandie curled her lip. "You've got to be kiddin'."

"Markus is hot, Sandie." Sue fanned her face. "He sizzles more than eggs frying on Bourbon Street in the August sun. Have you seen him, girlie?"

"I sure would like to," Sandie murmured. "Hm-mm, Anabelle, what do you say to me checking him out? You need a stamp of approval from your bestie."

"Mm-mm," I muttered. Sandie had given me a fine suite with a view, and a calming whiff of Blueberry weed but in all honesty her concept of reality was foggy at best. And she was not my bestie. "So, tell me, how do you all know each other?" I asked quickly. Three women I'd met in the last two days all knew each other coincidently?

"It might seem weird but stay here longer and you'll know everyone in the Quarter," Sandie said, fluffing up her blonde hair distractedly. "I thought you might be interested in a tarot card reading, being you're a witch and all, so I asked Jacqueline to do one for me." Sandie smiled. "If you like how she reads, Jackie will read for you after I get my answers."

Jacqueline nodded. "I am good. You'll see." She reached in and took out a pack of super-sized cards and gave them to Sandie. "These are the Swiss tarot," she told us. "A pack has seventy-eight cards but I'm only using the Major Arcana for your reading." Jacqueline jerked her chin at Sandie. "Shuffle."

The interpreter of the tarot had to be psychic. It wasn't simply an interpretation out of a book to memorize and repeat if it was to be successful. Jacqueline was after all, just a young girl, maybe twenty at most, a Voodoo Priestess in training. It didn't mean she had the sight. What the third eye sees beyond the real world isn't an open door for everyone, no matter how cool she might think it was to tell fortunes.

"Cut them." Jacqueline had the pained look of someone chopping onions, feeling the sting of harsh vapors. It was not easy to read the tarot and I couldn't believe she could do anything in the condition she was in. Wasted for sure. One too many Jim Beams. With my height and a slender build, Jacqueline couldn't down much liquor before it would hit her hard.

"Are you sure you want to do a reading?" I asked.

"Because I've been drinkin' you mean? I live on Bourbon Street, remember Anabelle?" Jacqueline lit a purple candle and placed it on the table top.

"It's hard to forget, considering Doctor Philippe has been helping me with my visions."

"You had lunch with him. I saw the strange look on his face that men get when they like a woman." Jacqueline took the cards from Sandie and placed them on the table in a spread, face down.

"Okay, so we connected." I'd had two journeys to the 1800's, neither of them pleasant. I didn't know what I thought of either the Voodoo doctor or Jean Lafitte.

"That's all?" A dreamy look came to Sue's eyes. "That Voodoo man has a hard, sexy bod." She glanced at her own sturdy arms. "That's the kind of man I need. Strong and powerful so I feel like a real woman."

"Don't we all," Sandie said, licking her lips. "You okay to read, Jackie?"

"Sure, no problem. You three join hands." In a stream she sang, *"Pape LaBas, viennent à nou. Come to us. Help us find Sandie's journey.* Say it with me two more times. *Pape LaBas, viennent à nous. Aidez-nous à trouver le voyage de Sandie. . Pape LaBas, viennent à nous. Aidez-nous à trouver le voyage de Sandie."*

We chanted the French words in unison.

With a steady hand, Jacqueline turned the cards face up. "I'll start with the present." A gaily attired young man in a Jester's hat with bells smiled back at us. Jacqueline pursed her lips. "The Fool."

"What does that mean?" Nervously, Sandie tapped a rhythm on the glass table top.

"It's been happening for a while now. You, acting irresponsibly—partying." She glanced at the card with a sun and two lovers. "Once you were in a loving partnership. You had a child."

"My little Dana," Sandie murmured.

"And you had a marriage. I don't think he was all that, but you could have made it work had you tried harder." She pointed to a red devil card. "I don't like that one. Black magic is working its force on your life. It could go down badly." Jacqueline glanced up. "Watch out. Negative energy is coming closer."

"What should I do?"

"See this card?" A man played a guitar for a girl on a balcony while below a giant crab crept up the wall. Overhead a moon shone yellow. "Deception. It could be friends or a situation. Be sensible. Think before you act. Wear a protective amulet. You can't trust anyone."

Sandie sighed. "I was afraid it was like that."

From where I sat I could see changes in Sandie's aura—black rivulets creeping into the yellow and green. It was almost as if I could see the danger attacking her.

Jacqueline pointed to the last card with a crumbling wall, bricks flying off. "I don't know how to say this any other way but you have false friends. On the good side the Tower card means change but not always how you want it. That's all I'm getting today."

We released hands and looked at the cards grimly. There was a decided pallor to Sandie's skin. When sweat appeared on her upper lip and forehead, I was worried.

The others were taking this reading seriously, but I had to wonder if Jacqueline knew her stuff well enough to predict such a doomy outcome.

With one large jeweled hand Shotgun Sue patted Sandie's tiny one. "Have a chocolate beignet. Things always look better with chocolate. Right, Anabelle?"

Chocolate did alter moods, releasing pleasure and feel-good chemicals in the brain. Cocoa beans could only help. "Sue's right. Remember you are in charge of your destiny. Find out who your false friends are and beware of what they ask of you."

It didn't take Sandie long to scoop up a beignet and gobble it down. With a swipe of her napkin she knocked the crumbs from her lips.

"I am curious. Why did you invite the three of us?" I asked.

"My suggestion," said the Voodoo apprentice, "the power of three. You should know that as a witch. The triangle and the reader."

Of all the women I couldn't believe Shotgun Sue with her freckles and red hair was the mystical type waiting for word from the psychic world, yet that room in her house cried out occult. "I didn't know you were interested in readings, Sue."

"Call me Shotgun." She perked up. "Makes me feel strong."

"Do you believe in visions?"

"The longer I lived here in the Quarter the more I believe. Things happen here."

"Shotgun makes beads for the shop." Jacqueline pulled out a string of white and blue beads. "Some are Voodoo and some are Santeria, like this one. Here," she said placing the necklace over my head. "Yemaya is your saint. Goddess of the sea and all gods."

"When Sandie told me you were coming today, I had to see how it's going with Markus." Sue turned to the others. "That man is a rocket charging up the financial ladder at breakneck speed. The photography book he put together is on point!"

"Pardon?"

"He's perfect," she said, "and that isn't just his body. Markus' fame as a photographer has spread, besides the fact that he's rich. You saw his Mercedes didn't you?"

"We drove out in the countryside to see his property." The memory of us making out on the bed made me feel all warm and tingly. "When I asked about the car he told me it was a friend's. He said motorcycles were more his thing."

Sue smiled knowingly. "Markus is testing you to see if you are a gold-digger. You like him?"

I nodded. Markus was that unusual combination of heat and creativity that made my juices flow.

"That much?" Shotgun Sue chuckled. "But you're leaving soon, aren't you, girl?" Sue's glance swept the table. "I've always been in tune with Markus. Now that I've lost weight I've got the energy for a man."

Shotgun Sue had the satisfied grin of a gator gulping down an unsuspecting duck happily perched on Mississippi riverbank.

Lips pursed, Jacqueline stared. "You look like you are coming in for the kill."

"Might be." Sue giggled. "Anabelle will be leaving New Orleans and then, well, I'm ready. I've been told men like the voluptuous type." She glanced down at her 38 triple D's and smiled. I have a figure eight body. Classically beautiful like Venus de Milo. Um-hm."

"Sure, honey," Jacqui said soothingly.

Sandie studied my face. "You okay with that? Sue taking Markus when you leave?"

I shrugged. "Markus has a brain. He can decide what to do."

A ding sounded.

"Your cell?" Jacqueline glanced at my purse.

"It's a text," I said, reaching into my tote, tugging out my cell.
U at the hotel? M

Yes. I texted. I was close enough.
Can you meet me at Lafitte's Blacksmith Shop? M
Now?
Right away. M
Ok. I'll be there in 5. A

"I have to go. Sorry, girls. Markus wants to meet with me."

"Sounds like trouble—a good kind." Sandie smirked. "The kind that calls for lube."

"Cut it out, Sandie. He wants to talk about something important. Did you hear me? I said, *talk.*"

Jacqueline pretended to light a match on her butt and said, "Sizzling! I want that."

"Is he psychic, Anabelle?" Sue said, her eyes narrowed.

"He is what I'd call a 'sensitive'. Has he spoken much about his family's plantation house?"

"A little," Sue said. "Do you know his plans for it? Will he sell?" I shook my head.

"Jacqueline sighed. "My lady parts get a boner thinking of that hottie." From her pink cloth bag she pulled out a massive cigar, and with a small device clipped and lit it, a bemused expression on her face. Clouds of smoke filled the air, sweetly aromatic and not at all unpleasant. "Wanna hit?" she asked, looking straight at me?

"Thanks." This was kind of like high school. If you didn't do things with the group, they could turn on you. At the same time they might share secrets. I had a feeling Jacqueline might tell me something. "Say Jacqueline, do you have a python?" I drew in the smoke and watched her expression.

She glanced down at the cards. "No, but I am lookin' to acquire one."

"What did you do with that snake, Sandie?"

Sandie frowned. "I took it to the front desk. I have no idea what happened to that thang."

Voodoo priests slung pythons around their necks to summon up fertility spirits all of which reminded me of Janelle and her baby story. It was like a puzzle with the pieces not quite fitting.

"Look at Anabelle suck that cigar," Sandie said, her eyes popping. "She is good!"

Chapter 14: THE TOWER

On the uneven sidewalk, the hot September sun beat so intensely tiny beads of perspiration coated my skin within minutes. The conversation had gone south rapidly after the Bourbon shots. Markus texting was my opening to escape.

The girls were just kidding around yet I sensed an undercurrent. My guess was it came from Sandie, psyched out by the reading, her thoughts dark about the husband who had taken her daughter. A quirky sense of humor concealed her angst which showed in her aura. Slivers of green bordered by black. The others weren't as easy to read. Possibly, reading a witch's aura is more difficult and from what I gathered, Shotgun Sue and Jacqueline were occult practitioners.

I wasn't far from my destination. Once I hit Bourbon Street, I made a left. The building had seen better days. Predominately wood, black doors and a gray roof, a sign "Lafitte's Blacksmith Shop", hung from a chain.

Out front, a man as tall as he was broad sat smoking a cigarette on a bench. A red T-shirt emblazed with the Lafitte logo was stretched tight over his gargantuan chest and shoulders. A thick neck held up a square head shaved into a buzz-cut resembling a landing strip. Squinty eyes gazed at the building across the street, but flicked to me as I approached the door.

"Where y'at?"

"Good, thanks."

He looked me up and down appreciatively. "Y'all enjoy yourself, gal. Call me if one of those boys gets crazy on you. I'm Cal. Gets wild in there after a few of our house drinks. Hurricanes are powerful. Watch yerself."

"Thanks, Cal." I gathered he was the bouncer. It was good to have a big man on my team.

Inside the bar it was crowded, gloomy, and candlelit as it had been centuries ago. After taking a walk about I saw Markus sitting at a round table in the corner. "Hey!" I yelled out, but he didn't hear me.

He seemed to be talking to the empty chair across from him. I heard him muttering something in Latin as I approached. I could hardly believe it. Markus was totally smashed. This was something

I wouldn't have expected, especially from a man I was attracted to. A few hours ago I had been contemplating bringing this relationship to the next level. Now I had my doubts.

Hormone giggled. "Haven't you done that already?"

She was right. The Indigo Oaks Plantation house had a rumpled bed to prove it. Of course the test drive had been rudely interrupted by the flashy realtor with a yen for Markus.

Logical growled. "Look at him. A secret drunk. After dealing with her ex, Anabelle hardly needs a follow-up with an alkie. Dump him."

Hormone laughed. "Get over yourself, Logical. So the guy was celebrating."

"It's better to put a nail in this coffin before she's in too deep, Hormone. Stop seeing him, Anabelle. Now. Tonight."

"Shut up! " I muttered to the irritating voices. I wasn't about to ditch this hottie, at least, not until I knew what was going on.

"I'll talk to Belle," Markus said to the chair, oblivious to the fact I was standing behind him. "It couldn't have been her fault. Now please go."

"Hello," I said tentatively, waiting for him to focus on me.

Glassy green eyes glanced up. "Sit with me, cher." He pulled out a chair and pushed his leather case aside. "We need to talk."

"About?"

"Janelle said you were pregnant with Renard's child but I disagree." Markus took my hand. "Tell me the truth. The baby is mine, isn't it?"

"Pregnant?" Logical was right. I had to throw this one back into the muddy Mississippi. One nutcase ex in my lifetime was more than enough.

A waiter suddenly appeared with two plates. "Po Boys, folks, one with no bread and extra shrimp for the lady, and a glass of wine." He set the plates and the wine on the table along with a fork and napkins.

Markus pulled out a chair. "I know you don't like bread, cher."

I plopped down in the chair. We'd had shrimp at that roadside diner in the country in Gonzales with rice. That was a strange thing to say. How did he know about my allergy?

"You must eat, especially in your condition."

Gazing at the sizzling shrimp hot from the frying pan I became aware of how very hungry I was. Too much coffee and booze at Sandie's. I needed to sober up.

Against my better judgment I attacked the shrimp and beans, flushing it down with the wine. I was a firm believer in the wine weight loss program. Antioxidants in the system push out the fats and leave behind proteins to slim down the waist and define the abs. I was in heaven except for the fact that my handsome lover was a raving lunatic.

"You seem very concerned about my heath. What about you? Are you all right?" It was only polite to ask when someone offers good food and a full bodied cabernet. The aroma was intoxicating and the finish lingered of tart berries and chocolate. A pleasant warmth spread through my body like the aftermath of an orgasm.

"I am happy now that you're here." Markus lifted my hand and gently kissed my wrist. "Mm-mm, you smell like the spices of the Orient. "Here," he said handing me a drink, "A friend bought me a drink earlier. Have a sip of this and see what you think."

I downed a bit of the golden liquid and set it down. "A Sazerac made just right."

"Renard stole it from Antoine and you perfected it, right? I don't regret winning at bourré and stealing you from Renard. Now that you are mine I want you to be happy." He frowned. "What do you know about the disappearance of Janelle's baby?"

A smoky haze appeared and I knew I was conjuring up a vision. A pregnant female looked accusingly at me. "The blonde girl."

"Whenever she decides not to be a redhead. Yup, that's her." Markus steepled his fingertips.

"Was it yours?" I asked.

"She told me the baby was Renard's."

In the cloudy mist Janelle was yelling at me, only I wasn't Anabelle. I was Belle.

"Janelle slept around."

"With you?"

Instead of answering Markus picked up his glass and tipped back the golden liquid. "Janelle thinks you should be cautious. I understand that but really, Belle, why didn't you tell me you were with child?"

"I'm not Belle. I'm Anabelle and you are Markus."

"Funny girl." He laughed. "My name is not Markus."

I was worried with this talk about pregnancy and a kidnapped baby, not to mention a woman that cuffed me to the bed for her master, Renard, to violate. I was also concerned about this man sitting beside me. A Sazerac had opened the portal for him just like it had for Doctor Philippe when we ended up at Renard's. This cocktail could transport psychics. This had to mean Markus had the "power".

Then it dawned on me. His reference to Belle and Renard. He wasn't Markus right now. He had time travelled two centuries in his mind yet was still here physically in the present. Something clicked. I had read about the state of limbo. It was the danger of being in one life and going back to a past life yet staying in the body of the present life. An incomplete transition that could cause the soul to stay in the past life.

"Am I the father?"

"We haven't had sex."

Markus patted my hand. "You loved it, cher. As for Renard he has accepted your departure."

"I bet he has, if you think suicide is acceptance."

Markus threw his head back and laughed. "Where do you come up with these things? Renard is alive and well, enjoying himself with women and opium as we speak. You, and the restaurant are mine, so you must live with me."

"You want to marry me?"

"I'm not the marrying kind, cher. "

"Tell me what's happening with Renard."

"Don't worry about that degenerate. He has holdings I didn't win. He can start over."

"And his son, Robert?"

"He will marry a woman with money."

"Listen to me." I squeezed his hand. "You have time travelled. This is the only explanation for your present state. You drank a Sazerac. It opened a portal to another time period where we both lived two centuries back. Right now you think you're there but this is a bad situation. We need to get you back to the present."

From inside my purse I tugged out my cell and clicked Jacqui's name.

Markus believes he is in the 1800s. How do I get him back? I sent the text hoping she'd help me. Markus was being screwed over by someone, but why?

Just then a tall shapely woman, auburn hair straight out of a L'Oreal hair color box of vibrant reds, swooped into the room commanding everyone's attention. Her eyes cased the room slowly but upon seeing Markus charged straight to our table where she pulled out a chair.

Settling in, she said beguilingly, "Darlin'. So glad I caught up with you again. I have news about the property. Tyron wants it and will pay you well. Your lawyer said you had the rights, you lucky darlin'." She tugged out some papers from her briefcase. "Look at this figure! Can you believe it? Sign where I placed the sticky notes and you will be wealthy beyond your dreams. Oh," she said, noticing me, "maybe I should have been more discreet. Hello, there." She smiled thinly. "I think we met at the mansion."

How could I ever forget that gushing voice and those eyelash extensions flipping rapidly like wet butterfly wings?

"Anabelle Sommerville," I said.

"Genevieve Severe. Markus and I have private matters to discuss, so if you will leave us?"

"No, I don't think so," I stared at her defiantly.

Markus' forehead furrowed.

I squeezed Markus' shoulder. "Come with me. I'll explain later." In his state he could give something away to the estate agent.

"Genevieve, we need to go. Markus is not feeling himself. He is too ill to deal with this right now. I'm sure you understand." I captured Markus' elbow and brought him to his feet. "Come on, honey." From out of my purse I tugged out a few bills and tossed them on the table.

My cell vibrated. I glanced at Jacqui's text. *He needs soil.*

***

Through the open balcony doors, mellow blues rhythms floated up to the master bedroom of my hotel suite. For a moment Markus' eyes sparkled brilliantly before his lips pressed to mine. With a push he propelled me to the wall. His hand slid down from my waist to my hips, stroking my legs as he drew me close. "This is quite the risqué dress, cher," he said, leaning down to kiss me, lips molding passionately to mine. Heat rushed down my body, sparking a flame at my core.

I felt his fingers on the zipper of my dress tugging it down.

"You are so beautiful I want to taste every inch of you." Lightly, his hands pushed the fabric off my shoulders and the sundress dropped to the floor. His lips brushed my neck, trailing to my shoulder. A flame lit my core.

The buttons of his shirt snapped open under my eager fingers. As I pushed the fabric, he tore it off, tossing the shirt on the bed, followed by his pants. His body felt firm and muscular, yet lean around the waist and hips, the way I like a man. With one motion his hands caught up my legs and I latched onto him, clinging to his hips with my legs. The wall felt cool on my back but my body burned. Our lips moved softly, an internal fire raging below the surface.

From the wavy dark hair, the strong chin and nose, to the sparkle in his sea green eyes, I was magnetically drawn to him as if a powerful force had entered my body. Everything about him was the masculine to my feminine—the yin-yang balanced. Inhaling his soapy scent touched with lime, my fingers threaded through his thick hair. He was Markus, but different—especially his eyes having lost all hint of hazel.

When his lips brushed my breasts a flame ignited, leaving me breathless. And though I cared to find out about his time travel, a conversation to find out why was put on the backburner. Right now I needed him.

I brought his head down until his shapely mouth met mine in a hard kiss. I had a hunger for more and lost control, nibbling his upper lip aggressively, breaking the skin.

He licked the spot. "Tiger cat."

"Mm-mm."

Skin to skin we explored, our fingers caressing, our mouths spilling a chorus of moans. Markus carried me over to the bed where he eased me down before joining me, arms closing around my hip and shoulder. His lips brushed my neck ever so lightly.

Suddenly, he stopped. Sudden spasms jerked his body with alarming intensity and then he slumped, a dead weight in my arms.

Chapter 15: STRENGTH

My fingers felt for a pulse. The faint beat alarmed me. "Markus!"

I slapped his cheek lightly but there was no response. With all my strength, I turned him on his back. His face was unusually pale. Surely, he was too young for a heart attack? He was virile and fit and no matter how mind-blowing the experience of the two of us together it shouldn't have sucked the life out of him.

Sitting back on my heels I groaned, "What have I done?"

"Looks good to me," a voice said softly behind me.

I whipped my head around to face the lovely brunette standing behind me in a white diaphanous gown. "Delphine!" I grabbed my robe and slipped it on. "What are you doing here?"

"You'd think you had enough of that man. Did you kill him, Belle?"

"I did not!" At least I didn't think so, but it wouldn't be the first time men had heart attacks during foreplay. "Now get this straight, Delphine, I'm Anabelle. What did you mean, back then and now?" Gently, I pulled a sheet over his hips, covering his amazing display.

"You don't know who this is? Get a grip, girl. This is your lover, the infamous Alain Ducoeur, the pirate. Ring a bell, Belle?" She chortled. "Oh, so funny."

"Shut up, Delphine. This is Markus, not Alain."

Delphine peered at the man on my bed. "Take a good look and you will see Alain. This one has been time travelling, hasn't he? That's why he has Alain's soul residue."

"But Alain is a ghost."

"True. You need to find his murderer to set this lovely man free."

On the bed, Markus lay as still as death, paler than a ghost.

I tried to grab her hand but it slipped through the misty air. "What happened to Markus?"

"He's caught between two worlds, I imagine. Someone wanted him to go back to the past but he may have resisted and he stayed here while his mind went to nineteenth century New Orleans."

"Why would anyone do this?"

"Love or money. It all leads back to that."

"Is he going to be okay?"

"Alain might stay like that unless you cast a counterspell, Belle."

"Markus, that's his name, not Alain. What should I do?"

"You're the witch." She grinned maliciously. "Now, give me my necklace."

I lifted an eyebrow.

"Alain may have given it to you but don't forget it's mine. Look in the diary." She pulled out a knife from her waistband and brandished it in a threatening manner. "Find out where it was hidden."

"Go away, Delphine," I said, stepping back.

The spirit woman's eyes narrowed dangerously. But just as I thought I would end up a blood-splattered mess on the carpet, Delphine slowly dissipated into thin air, leaving behind a remnant of her mouth contorted in an ugly grimace. Like the Cheshire cat's grin in "Alice in Wonderland" it faded seconds after her body had vaporized. My eyes flicked about searching for her but she was definitely gone—at least for now.

Tugging on my underwear, jeans and a top, I was ready to get help, if necessary. Trouble was I wasn't sure what to do. Opening the balcony doors I stepped outside.

Dusk had arrived, the dark blue sky streaked with crimson rays. Staring at the Ursuline convent down the street, I telepathically summoned Raven. A dozen black birds shot out of the attic windows, approaching with a flutter of wings. It was evident they were bats. One in particular was quick to land on the wrought iron railing.

"Raven?"

The tiny creature's wings spread and the whiskered mouth opened and closed with a faint squeak. Not overly fond of bats I was about to make a run for it when Raven materialized into the form of a man wearing a long black cape to his knees. "*Bon soir, chérie*. At your service." He clicked his heels together and made a tiny bow with a flourishing hand gesture.

"Am I glad you're here. I am desperate. Come with me," I said, heading into the bedroom.

"*Mon Dieu!*" Raven's eyes widened at the sight of Markus on the bed. "Exhausted the man I see, but what do I have to do with this?"

"Nothing. It's not sexual, well, it was, but what's happened is more like a purgatory trance. Markus was drinking a Sazerac thinking he was back in New Orleans in the nineteenth century. When we made out, he collapsed. I think it has to do with not being fully transported."

Raven's body trembled like a tree in a storm.

"Are you all right?" I said with concern, before I realized he was laughing. "Stop that! This is serious. Markus is in trouble. I think someone is playing us."

Raven tilted his head like a bird and frowned. "Playing?"

"A person with magical powers wants something from Markus."

Raven nodded his head solemnly. "A spell. Markus has an enemy."

"Delphine recommended a counterspell."

"You have twenty-four hours, I believe."

"Who would know what to do?"

"A Voodoo practitioner."

"You think I should ask Doctor Philippe? With any luck he might still be in the shop."

Raven pursed his rosebud lips.

"You don't trust him, do you?'

"He was Lafitte, remember?"

"Yes, okay, I get your point," I said. "Well, if not him, who else?"

"Hm-mm. The Voodoo Queen of New Orleans will be haunting the cemetery," he said, pulling me outside. "We must fly."

"How's that possible?"

"You are a witch, remember? You can shapeshift with an incantation, can't you?"

"Maybe Belle could."

"Think hard and dig deep into your soul."

He was right. The knowledge of Wicca was internal and so was my power. I could make this happen.

I waved my arms, incanting, *"Alis, alis, alis."* My outspread arms transformed into black wings.

We were both bats now, communicating with echolocation. Catching an air current we shot over the buildings into the evening sky. Down below, the Quarter flickered with a rainbow of lights—the narrow streets thick with the evening crowd on Bourbon Street, go-cups in hand, on the way to the next bar. Music blasted up as we soared over the street but once we headed north the city grew darker and quieter, the street lights few and far between. Closing in on Basin Street, we neared the marble mausoleums of St Louis Cemetery No. 1, filmed in a fog.

In midair, hovering like a hummingbird, I allowed a moment to search the area, alert to the presence of the white-robed figure of the Voodoo Queen of New Orleans, but she was not there. When we landed, our bat bodies transformed instantly back, both of us human in appearance.

Slivers of moonlight illuminated the tops of the tombs. Stone angels on a ledge cast black shadows on the grassy path leading to Marie Laveau's monument. It was hard to see anything but the roses scattered at the feet of the tomb. I slipped on the coins left on the dewy grass, grabbing onto Raven's arm in the nick of time.

"Take care, Anabelle. There are broken beer bottles around."

I nodded. "Now what?"

Raven's eyes narrowed. "Go over there."

A person dressed in white moved swiftly through the maze of tombs as if on a mission.

"Hello!" I called out.

The figure stopped dead in his tracks and swiveled around. "Anabelle? What are you doing here?"

"I could ask you the same, Dr. Philippe."

His teeth flashed white in the gray of twilight. "Please, call me Philippe. I think we are past the formalities. You realize it is dangerous to be here."

"I was looking for Marie Laveau."

"She left." He reached over and took my hand. "Why are you here alone?"

"I'm not—" my voice trailed off realizing I was indeed alone. I had no idea where Raven was. In the pale moonlight Philippe's eyes were eerie as if a force occupied his body. "I'm sorry I left you back at Renard's. I hope it wasn't difficult for you to re-enter the portal."

Philippe's expression was bemused. "Did you leave me behind intentionally? Is there something you didn't want me to know?"

"No! Of course not." A memory of Janelle tying me to the bed, followed by the Renard and his whip had me silently thanking Alain for my escape from a kinky bondage experience. "My friend said you knew how to return."

"What friend was that?" he said sharply. "You went back there with me, and ended up with Jean Lafitte. Oh, wait. You had a thing for Alain Ducoeur, didn't you? Here I was so enamored I didn't realize. We have different lives now but did you ever think that we journeyed in time to have another chance at love?"

Philippe was cool, almost an iceman compared to Markus, a man with an incredibly hot undercurrent. Yet, this man was different from Jean Lafitte. And as for Belle, I was afraid she was not at all like me. "I don't think Belle loved Lafitte," I said.

"Maybe not, but there was considerable chemistry. When you disappeared at dinner, I spoke to the ladies. They told me Belle was a woman of mysterious passions."

"And Delphine and Janelle were crazy for you too?"

"I was wealthy. Women love men with money."

"Belle's passion stemmed from your money? And Ducoeur?"

"Ducoeur and Lafitte shared, as friends do."

"Both treasure and women?"

His expression was guarded.

"You don't trust me?" I asked.

"I hardly know which woman you are." He stepped in closer, his lips tempting me. "There's the wild uncontrollable jaguar, kisses burning with desire and then there's the temptress who lures men into a quagmire letting them die a slow and painful death as she kicks them down with one delicate foot. And there's the spirited witch who beguiles me with her intellect. Those are Belle's personalities, but now I know the psychic Anabelle whose power is incredible. I believe we have chemistry, don't you?"

"Tell me, Philippe, what women did you share with Ducoeur when you were Lafitte?"

"Lafitte was a sensual decadent man."

"Not like you."

He ran a finger over my hair. "Sensual, but not as decadent."

"And Alain Ducoeur?"

"You are a better judge of that than I am."

I felt heat rise to my cheeks.

Philippe stared into the night. "Lafitte paid Ducoeur the money to buy the estate in the country. The ladies came in droves to the parties. There would be dancing..." His voice trailed off.

"Booze, sex, and rock 'n roll."

Philippe laughed. "Drugs too. Louisiana was totally uncivilized, remember? Somethin' like the bands today with groupies."

"Well that explains a lot." Was I being paranoid about Philippe? I wished Raven was here to give me his spin on it. Where was that bat when I needed him? "Do you come here often?"

Philippe smirked. "It's one way to meet attractive women."

"Better than Matchwitch.com?"

"I had a dream where Marie Laveau appeared. She wanted me to bring a recovery gris-gris to the cemetery for a lady." He took out a small velvet bag from his jean pocket. "Little did I imagine that it was for you."

I shook my head. "It's not for me. My friend is in a bad way. He opened a portal and went back to nineteenth century New Orleans but somehow he wasn't there physically. He's stuck between two worlds. "

"Sounds like this was no accident. The spell was meant to hurt him. Someone doesn't like your friend." Philippe's clear gray eyes narrowed. "Who is he?"

From his look I wondered if he was jealous. "Markus. You know him, don't you?"

He nodded. "He's a clairvoyant besides being a photographer."

"He's living in a state of limbo."

"In twenty-four hours his breathing will cease and he will die."

"That sounds rather unsympathetic."

"I've seen a lot of suffering in my line of work."

"Is there anything you can do?"

Philippe's eyes narrowed. "You care about Markus."

I nodded.

Philippe handed me the velvet bag. "Prepare the drink that sent him into the portal and sprinkle in a touch of this gris-gris. That should do the trick."

"Easy enough. I'll stop at a bar. Are you sure it will work?"

"No," he said, offering me his elbow, "but it's worth tryin'."

Chapter 16: THE MOON

The walk through the Quarter was not as awkward as anticipated. Philippe was the epitome of old Southern charm. For a while I forgot he was a Voodoo priest and began to see him as a well-aged bourbon—drinks rich and smooth, the finish long and elegant, the aromas as yet unknown. I began to wonder what his kiss would taste of.

"Did I ever tell you how your eyes gleam like the azure waters of Lake Pontchartrain on a sunny summer's day?" he slurred Pontchartrain into a sexy "Poncho train" as New Orleans' natives do.

"No," I said, the accent triggering a tiny buzz of excitement, "but I think you hardly had a moment for thoughts like that. As I recall we were busy putting together the puzzle pieces. My nightmares, remember?"

"And your troubles are important but darlin', there should always be time for complimenting a beautiful lady."

"True," I whispered, curiosity getting the better of me.

Philippe took hold of my shoulders and leaned closer, lips almost touching mine. "Give me some sugar."

Hypnotically drawn to his mouth, my energy flamed like a shot of bourbon tossed down my throat. My lips brushed his. Breathless, I stepped back regretting my loss of control. "Give me a reason to go back in time."

"Seems we need to solve the nightmare problem—yours and mine."

I twisted a lock of my hair. "And once we find out what happened in nineteenth century New Orleans, these dreams should go away and we can be happy in our present lives."

Philippe sighed. "That's what I assume."

"What did you find out about Lafitte?"

His eyes were suddenly sad. "We were good together, Belle and Lafitte, that is. Far better than Delphine and Lafitte. It's possible you were a virgin when we had relations."

"Seriously?" I raised an eyebrow. "Are you sure we even had sex?"

"After we took our trip through the portal to the nineteenth century I started having recollections of my past life. I was the lover you deserved—kind, considerate of your needs, and adventurous. I made a mistake not to pursue you. I should have tried harder to win you." He shrugged his shoulders.

"Everyone has regrets on how they dealt with love one time or another but we need to move forward."

Philippe took me in his arms. "Were you in love with me?" His kiss was soft, yet sensuous. The emotion in his eyes surprised me.

I pulled back. "You mean when I was Belle and you were Lafitte?" I shrugged. "I'd imagine she'd like a dashing pirate."

From the diary I gathered there was a romance going on with both the men, Ducoeur and Lafitte, but I felt cautious about revealing any more. I had a feeling he knew too much about the diary already.

Philippe grinned. "Maybe you're feelin' it now?"

"Not so fast, Voodoo man. I don't fall easily."

"Were you pregnant with my child?"

"Not you too? If I was pregnant I wouldn't know who the father was. I'm Anabelle, remember?"

"In a dream Belle told me she was in love with Ducoeur but only after she was pregnant. I think she wanted Ducoeur to be the father."

"What about Renard?"

"Not likely."

"The drugs."

Philippe nodded imperceptibly. "I, on the other hand, wasn't a good person."

"You mean Jean Lafitte wasn't."

"Exactly. I'm not sure any of us were. Ducoeur fooled everyone. Under a cloak of respectability lent by a doctor's education, he was still a pirate. I always wondered how he could afford an education but I think as a youngster he manipulated women to gain the capital he needed for schoolin'."

"He was a gigolo?"

"Rich older women gave him presents, enough to provide for his food and ale. But he was not a keen student. In those days medical school was mostly theoretical and he was all about experiencing surgery. When he became a pirate, the injured people from captured ships became his patients. Of course, this was all before he captained his own vessel."

"You shared treasures?"

"It was the pirate code."

"Kind of ironic, isn't it? Alain Ducoeur was a doctor back then and now you are a Voodoo priest, bringing healing gris-gris."

"Which reminds me," he said, pointing at the wooden sign "Trois Frere", painted in flourishing gold script. "I'll run in and get a Sazerac."

When I nodded he scooted inside reappearing with a go-cup. "All set."

We continued east on Royal Street. At the corner of Ursulines I stopped him and asked, "What happened to Janelle's sister?"

"Died. A botched up abortion. She was a beauty."

"Was it your child?"

"It could have been Ducoeur's or even Renard's. All of us seduced her."

"Ducoeur wasn't like that."

"Really, Anabelle, or should I say, Belle?" He lilted his head, arching his brow. "He plied you with wine and chocolate and you spent the night on his ship, maybe more than once, even when you had promised to marry Renard."

"Rene was a hideous man, perversely sick. Of course I wanted another man, one who loved me."

Philippe set the Sazerac on the ledge of a gift shop window. There was a "Closed" sign on the door. It was dark inside the store but the gold and purple masks displayed on the ledges were back-lit, the eyes glowing eerily through the cut-outs. A shiver raced down my spine. The Mardi Gras masks grinned evilly as if possessed by spirits. I took a breath, gathered my confidence and continued coolly. "And the gris-gris?"

Philippe tugged out a small cloth bag from his pocket. "Ducoeur is a player. No substance."

"And Markus?"

"Nice guy with an agenda." Philippe pushed me close to the shop window and turned me about to face a row of purple and gold feathered masks. "Look at them, darlin'. Concentrate. Remember the party. Bring us to the past."

166

I felt myself go weak. A white haze clouded the air and with my vision we were transported to an immense ballroom with wine red walls, high ceilings held up by Grecian columns, crystal chandeliers and gold accented ivory doors. Dancers in formal attire, the men in black tuxedos and the women in flimsy silk gowns, faceless in colored masks, whirled effortlessly to the music from a six-piece brass and string band. The dusky lead singer, long wavy ink black hair to her waist, with a deep throaty voice—rough from too many smoke filled nights in tiny bars drinking cheap bourbon, sang a poignant song of a black woman's suffering at the hands of her white owners. It tore at my heart strings.

"You did it, darlin'. We're back in the nineteenth century. This is pre Mardi-Gras, almost like a Crewe gathering, by invitation only. Anyone who was someone in New Orleans society came to Delphine's parties." He pointed to the buffet table. "Do you see him?"

I glanced over at a handsome dark man, his hair shoulder-length, talking closely to another man, stroking his arm in an intimate fashion. "It's Robert, Renard's son." Something was strange here. Robert was a ladies' man yet here he was. "He's interested in that man?"

"It's an on and off relationship."

I stared at the ruggedly good-looking man. "He's gay?"

Lafitte grinned. "Swings both ways."

Robert's lover was desirable, tall and muscular with broad shoulders. What marred this man's physical beauty was a jagged scar in the shape of a lightning bolt down the length of his cheek. He shifted around in his chair and caught my glance. His jaw tightened. A nervous tic twitched his cheek.

My jaw dropped. "Omigod, that's Blade Ryan. He's the guy I found in the cabin. He would have killed me if Alain hadn't stepped in."

"Ducoeur decided to leave him with a rather painful reminder."

"A very precise scar," I said.

"When you confronted him there was a struggle. He pulled out a knife. Luckily, you knocked his arm away. Ducoeur jumped in and you see the rest. He told me the story over bourbon one stormy night." Lafitte slid his hand down my arm. "Enough unpleasantness. Come dance with me. I want you to remember how it feels to be with me."

"Tell me more about the consortium," I said, putting my hand up in a stop gesture.

Lafitte snatched up my hand and led me forward. "The goods came in and out of the restaurant with produce and meat. You supervised the organization." He brought his lips to my hand and kissed my fingertips. "You have the scent of a spicy orchid. Incredibly alluring." Lafitte tightened his hold on my waist and angled into a turn.

As we circled an image became clear. Blood poured from the cut on Ryan's face. I missed a step. "Was Alain really cruel?"

"I know it's hard to believe when he appears as the charming Alain Ducoeur. He's multifaceted like a hard-edged diamond but, I would have done the same, darlin', were I him. Anyone in the business would. Ryan was pilfering goods. That's against the code."

"He was searching for information on the whereabouts of Alain's treasure, or was it yours?" I asked.

Lafitte shrugged his shoulders. "Ryan wanted it all. Don't waste your pity on that piece of dung. Watch your back, darlin'. He's got his own gang of Irish and he holds a grudge for your interference."

"How do you remember all this?"

"You can if you force yourself. The pirates ruled the city with the consent of the governor."

"Tell me more."

"Jewels were sold in my shop or in Ducoeur's, but drugs were Renard's area."

"And me? What did I have to do with this?"

Lafitte laughed. "You were under contract to marry Renard."

"And Alain Ducoeur?"

Lafitte nodded. "When Renard lost at cards, Ducoeur egged him on to bet his lady. That lady was you, Belle. Ducoeur has the luck of the devil. He won. The jewelry I pledged to Delphine, Renard's restaurant and you, were all his. The arrogant rogue laughed in our faces. I was well-off financially but Renard lost the things that mattered to him most. Soon afterwards Ducoeur told you to move in with him on the boat."

I didn't like a man ordering me to do anything but in the case of Alain Ducoeur I was mesmerized. He was my pirate fantasy. When our energies joined it was like lighting a keg of dynamite.

Lafitte eyed me curiously. "Why did you go with Ducoeur?"

My eyes swept over the buffet table and stopped when I spotted Renard. "Mother Mary, Renard's here tonight." I let out an involuntary shiver. "We must go. If he sees me—I don't want a scene."

Lafitte laughed. "Really? The Belle I know thrives on trouble."

"Shut up, Lafitte. I mean it. Keep him away from me. I have the feeling he might force me to come with him and if he does I can't control what I'll do."

Lafitte twirled me around closer to the buffet table. "Look how he watches but doesn't dare come for you. Renard is finished. Breathe easy. He has to let you go."

"I hope you're right." The buffet table blurred as if the vision was fading. I had to hurry before we were back to the present. "Tell me about the drug trafficking."

"Trade, not trafficking. It's practically legal. Society folks of New O'leans, especially the women, needed the laudanum or marijuana to calm their nerves while the men liked a touch of the white stuff just for fun." He said dryly, "Scandals are stressful and New O'leans was boiling like a crayfish gumbo."

"Capturing ships and stealing merchandise." It didn't feel like me to be involved in illegal activities. I wasn't raised to be a criminal." I frowned. "It's acceptable here?"

"It definitely is, my darlin'. New O'leans is a city of sin like no other." He smirked. "Our citizens like the luxury of stolen goods as well as the opiates. The governor has no right to complain especially when he gets his share for looking the other way. I hear he indulges in the occasional pipe at Renard's."

A vision of a smoke-filled room appeared with Renard passing around a hookah to an obese balding bleary-eyed gentleman attired in a silk and lace shirt and tight pantaloons. "Renard sold drugs in that room upstairs in the restaurant."

Lafitte nodded. "And prostitutes."

The tempo of the waltz surged and Lafitte spun me around, his clear gray eyes dancing with mischief along with the rhythm. I was hardly surprised when he lightly kissed me but I was taken aback by the heat I felt in my cheeks. How fickle was I, flirting with one man and lusting after another? Wait a minute here. The body I was in was Belle, not me. I composed myself and asked, "The prostitutes weren't slaves."

"They were wives or daughters of the passengers on the Spanish or Portuguese merchant ships. White, black and brown, all of them in demand. Women and men to please any fancy."

"I get the feeling I had a powerful position."

Lafitte nodded. "Many were in your employ. There was the restaurant and the consortium which you ran for all of us. Even after Renard lost the card game, Ducoeur made sure you continued as the chef. He gave you the restaurant."

"Generous man."

"Ducoeur wanted to please you."

Alain Ducoeur certainly had the touch. Not many men could release that fire in me. "Tell me something, Lafitte. Who are my enemies? I mean there must be those who resented the change of ownership and my newly acquired power."

"True, but the women envied you."

"And Janelle?"

He snickered. "Loved you like a sister, that is, if you lived in redneck country. What energy do you sense in this room now?"

"Here?" I glanced at the black shadows which engulfed the ballroom and shuddered. "Dark."

"Dangerous too. Government spies are everywhere."

"Thank you for the warning." I stepped away. "This has been fun and most enlightening, Lafitte, but I really must return to the present."

Lafitte pulled me closer and kissed me on the lips.

"Stop!" I pushed him away. "Take me back to the present."

"Indulge me a bit longer. A short side trip. You have to see this." Lafitte snapped his fingers and we were in someone's back garden, a fountain in the center, enclosed by a high stone wall. It was crammed with masked blacks and whites gyrating to a drum beat much like a club grind.

"What's going on?" I said puzzled. I hadn't seen anything this crazy. "Are these people stoned?"

"More or less. Marie Laveau doles out drugs like candy."

"And we are here because?"

"See the redhead next to Marie Laveau?"

"Yes," I said slowly, recognizing Janelle, her hair in wild disarray spinning around like a dervish, a green elongated flotation device dangling from her neck. "What's is that thing she's wearing?"

"Zombie, the python. Marie Laveau's python brings fertility. Look!" His eyes flicked to a spindly giant wearing a tuxedo and top hat, black pit holes in a painted white face. "It's Baron Samedi," he whispered.

Drinking rum straight out of the bottle the skeletal giant twisted between the partiers, pouring liquor into their mouths as he passed. The bottle empty, Baron Samedi tossed it into the bushes. He turned. His white-gloved hand stretched out and pulled Janelle into his long boney arms.

I clutched Lafitte's hand in alarm. "Look at her. She's afraid. We need to help her."

"No, darlin', she wants this. He's the powerful Baron Samedi, the Haitan Loa of the dead. He will give her another baby."

"I hate this place. Let`s go. How can we re-enter the portal?"

"Chocolate." Lafitte grinned and pulled out two wrapped bonbons from his trouser pockets. "Exceptionally rich truffles inside a chocolate exterior."

As I popped mine inside my mouth I savored the rich cocoa, letting it melt slowly on my tongue.

Lafitte's breath felt warm on my ear. "Goodbye, Anabelle."

As I turned to him the vision dissipated and I was left standing alone on the doorstep of the Hotel Memoire. I shook my head disgusted with myself. What was I thinking wasting time with the notorious pirate Lafitte whose idea of fun was taking me to a sinister sex orgy in Marie Laveau's backyard.

I knew Belle wasn't an innocent young girl but it was the "Blade Ryan" story that rang false to me. From what Lafitte said Ducoeur was out of control, violent even.

Once inside the hotel I quickened my step through the door eager to see Markus.

"Yes, hurry, you selfish witch!" Logical hissed. "You should be ashamed of yourself. Partying while Markus lingers in a transitory state, slowly dying." Logical wagged her finger like a rebuking school teacher.

She was right. I had to hurry but I had to think about all this. What was I involved in? Could my ghostly lover, Ducoeur, be a vengeful man? Was cutting a souvenir scar into Ryan's face taking the "bad boy" image to an extreme?

"Ducoeur rescued you," Hormone said. "You like hero types and with him you hit the jackpot. Besides, that man is a pleasure machine, mouth-watering like rich decadent chocolate."

"Shut up," I said, under my breath to my brain. Ducoeur wasn't real. I had to remember that or they would commit me to the loony bin and throw away the key. I passed the glass door to the lobby so fast I didn't notice who was working the desk and frankly didn't care. That was the last thing on my mind. It was positively crucial to get this gris-gris cocktail to my boyfriend. I smiled, pleased with myself. Markus kind of was my boyfriend now—and a deliciously hot one at that.

Once inside the room a cell phone buzzed. Mine was in the side compartment of my tote, so where was this coming from? On the bed where Markus had thrown his clothes in our heated encounter, an iPhone peeked out of his shirt pocket.

My attention diverted to my lover. My handsome Romeo slept soundly, hopefully not permanently. Carefully edging my way over the duvet I reached out to touch his brow, slickly wet with a coat of perspiration. Concerned his system was shutting down, I picked up his hand and checked his wrist for a pulse. Satisfied by the steady beat, my glance flicked to his lean buff build and muscled six-pack. The thin sheet gathered around his waist allowed an eye-opening view of his broad chest, every inch worth stroking. In fact, he was as delicious as a marshmallow coated with rich, thick gooey chocolate waiting to be consumed.

A flicker of red light from the cell reflected on the surface of the brass bedpost. Attached to the bedpost there appeared to be a decoration constructed of brass and plastic in the shape of a massive beetle. Pretty, I thought at first, wondering if it was of Egyptian origin. I bent over to examine it and saw I could easily remove it—sticky double-side tape held it in place. Upon further examination it was apparent the device was more than a decoration. It was a miniature high-tech video camera. I was being watched.

Chapter 17: THE CHARIOT

"Cherie?" a voice whispered from behind.

I whipped around to face Raven and holding a finger to my lips to silence him, gestured to the balcony. He followed me outside, über stylish in a cream silk button-down shirt and black Calvin Klein jeans, a long, black umbrella in his hand. With his slender frame, he was runway perfect.

At the railing the wind heavy with humidity, fanned my face. Rain was rapidly moving in.

Covering the lens, I held up the video camera taken from the bedroom. On the top an indentation flicked open the beetle's shell, revealing a USB drive. Exploring the perimeters of the camera, I located a switch on the bottom of the beetle's body. My fingernail pushed the red plastic to the right. The device was now off.

"What took you so long?" I said.

Raven smirked. "Thought you wanted time alone with your man, Philippe. Oops, I forgot, you already have a man." He rubbed his chin thoughtfully. "Somewhat out of commission, however, hm-mm?"

"There is a problem, my blood-sucking friend."

"Something to do with that tiny enviable toy you are holding so gingerly?"

"I'll have you know this is a disabled video camera, not a sex toy."

Raven lifted a finely-arched eyebrow.

"Someone took it upon themselves to play spy."

"And your ardent lover? Why is he sleeping—tired from the workout, is he?"

"Unfortunately, Markus has been rendered inoperative but I don't think it was from any extraneous activity."

"You mean the Sazerac gris-gris combo didn't work?" He glanced at me speculatively. "You didn't use it, did you? Second thoughts?"

I shrugged.

"You can trust your sixth sense." He took the beetle and stroked it thoughtfully. "So this camera demonstrates the intricacies of your dalliance with Markus?" Raven smirked. "Must be something to view."

Rolling my eyes I said, "Hopefully not. I haven't seen it yet, but, Raven, you don't know the half of it. Intruders knocked me out, duct-taped my wrists and ankles and left me naked in the closet. I think they are after the diary."

"And they have it now?"

"You underestimate my capabilities, my blood-thirsty friend. Obviously, it was too well hidden."

"So the ruffians returned and installed a video camera." Raven stroked his chin thoughtfully. "To watch you, for whatever reason, besides of course to view your enticing body?"

"Hold that thought for later. I need to go back in." Under the cover of darkness I loaded up my tote, shrunk it to dime-size and scurried back out. "I'm ready. Let's make like bats. The vultures are gathering to pick at my bones."

***

Under the pavilion of the Cafe Du Monde we sat huddled over the diary, flipping page after page of Belle's flowery script in watery blue ink. It was starting to make sense.

"That was so cool how you transformed everything, including our totes when we switched into bat mode. You really are a talented witch," Raven whispered conspiratorially.

"Thanks, little bat buddy. I know you love your man bag. What do you keep in there, anyway?"

Raven's cheeks flushed. "Nothing you wouldn't have. Belle's wicked ways were always an inspiration. Bet your tote is full of sexy stuff."

"I wish. There is only so much I could carry on the flight to New Orleans." I flipped through a few more pages.

"Any idea where the treasure was buried?" Raven asked.

"As a matter of fact, I do," I said thoughtfully, looking out at Jackson Square. "Alain Ducoeur owned the same property Markus is claiming to be his family's estate."

"Which is where?" Raven asked.

"Ascension Parish."

"Coincidence?"

"No. Delphine says Markus has Ducoeur's soul residue." I leafed through the diary, making mental notes of spells and incantations. One of these might work to wake up my prince. I flipped to the last few pages of the diary.

"Markus is Ducoeur." Raven smiled flashing pointy ivory incisors. "And you get two for one."

"Not complaining," I muttered distractedly, wishing I had a replay button for our last sizzling encounter. I fanned my face with the menu. "I like him. Markus is real."

Raven snickered. "You mean real hot or just real instead of ghostly, like Ducoeur?"

"Markus is a hot item in the Quarter. I've made the neighborhood ladies a tad jealous."

Raven lifted an eyebrow.

"We were having a tarot card reading—" Something in the diary caught my eye. I smothered a squeal with my hand.

When I didn't continue, Raven said sharply, "What?"

"The treasure is buried on the property."

"Directions?"

"Yup." I flipped to the back pages. "Right here."

"Perhaps, Belle died because of the treasure." Raven said speculatively.

I shook my head. "Maybe, but what about Ducoeur?"

"Suicide or murdered?"

"A Romeo-Juliet death scenario," I said.

"One pretends to die and the other commits suicide?" Raven sipped his coffee and then set it down to add more sugar.

"Maybe, or one gets shot, for example, and the other kills himself or herself."

"Rather dramatic, Anabelle. So Ducoeur and Belle were in love?" Raven sat back in the wrought iron café chair and stared at me.

"You should know."

Raven stared reflectively at the coffee cup. "Belle was complex."

"I have no doubt about Alain's passion for Belle but that isn't love."

"Everyone had a thing about her. Even Janelle." Raven grinned. "She couldn't get enough of you."

"Maybe she was bi-curious."

"Naw, she was into you, chérie. And what about the crazy tale that nutbar spins?"

"The disappearing baby story? I know, right. Janelle's like a character out of a 'Days of Our Soap'."

"Renard had her hooked on opium. She made it up. She was a druggie." Raven's brow furrowed. "And what about the camera in your room?"

I felt heat rise to my cheeks thinking of what was recorded.

"Any idea who placed it? The hotel?"

I shook my head. "Not a ritzy place with a big budget but someone could be spying on me, from anywhere. On the bright side, a USB connection can be plugged into a computer to see the footage." I rubbed my temple reflectively. "There's a computer in the lobby."

"You are quite the techie, chérie. Could I see?"

"Definitely not! Now, if you will excuse me, I need to check Markus' cell." Snatching up the iPhone from the extra compartment of my leather purse I turned it on, glancing through the texts.

"Oh, Anabelle," Raven said.

I looked up.

"Getting back to your Voodoo ladies with the tarot cards. Who are they?"

"Sandie, Sue and Jacqui."

"Are any of them voyeurs? Maybe they wanted a closer peek at Markus' package so they installed a video camera." Raven giggled. "Or it could be the good doctor wanted to replay the naked Anabelle scenario on a boring rainy night? And let's not rule out Markus himself."

A jab into his ribs stopped his snicker. I leaned forward. "Listen to me. This is serious. There's no doubt in my mind the camera was not there to record the kinky things going on in my bedroom."

Raven glanced down at the cell I was scrolling through. "Find anything yet?"

"Just texts I'd sent to Markus. Wait. Let me switch to the other texts."

Raven slid his chair next to mine to get a better look at the screen. "What are you looking for, anyway?"

"The person who endangered Markus." Shoving the cell closer for Raven to see, I said, "Look at this. These are from Gen."

"Who?"

"Genevieve, the realtor. You know her?"

Raven nodded.

I glanced at the bar across the street as the blues band heated up. The lead singer with the deep gravelly voice was unexpectedly that of a blond. For a moment I thought that strange but New Orleans had a hodge-podge of immigrants intermarrying through the centuries. Nothing was strange here.

The singer sang a story about lost love. It was heart-wrenching. It made me think of all the bad relationships I'd ever had.

Raven squeezed my hand. "So tell me. Does Gen have designs on Markus?"

I shrugged my shoulders. "I was worried that she saw him all muddled and confused, so I dragged him to my hotel room." I put a finger on Raven's rosebud lips to stop him from laughing. "But what if she was the one who cast the spell and sent him through the portal to the 1800s in the first place?"

Raven frowned. "Genevieve wants to marry the prince and have his treasure."

"And there's a massive commission attached to it."

"Did he sign?"

"He didn't get the opportunity. But here's a thought. If Markus really is Ducoeur he knows where the treasure is. With the money from the treasure he could set up his studio and book project," I said.

"That is supposing you could force the information out of him. But don't you need to get him back to the present?"

I twisted my hands nervously. "Right."

"Don't forget the video camera recorded your movements and sounds."

"Which could help me," I said, placing Markus' cell on top of the diary. "Someone carelessly left a vital clue behind."

"Oh?"

"A huge green python. Sandie, the front desk girl, helped me put it in the hamper."

"And she was good with that?" Raven frowned. "Most women would be a smidgen apprehensive with a chore that daunting."

"I hoisted the thing in. Sandie took it away. I am supposing she knows enough Voodoo practitioners in the neighborhood to give it a new home."

Raven wiggled his brows. "Or bring it back to its owner?"

The tiny legs of a mosquito danced up my arm in a samba rhythm. Smacking the bejesus out of it interrupted the pest midbite and gave me a thought.

Raven could be right. Sandie was friendly, maybe too much so. And if the tarot reading was to be believed, she was about to dive into deadly waters.

Raven frowned. "This may sound all too Agatha Christie but could this girl be collaborating with the stealthy snake charmer?"

"Sandie is a stoner. She's harmless."

"Drugs and Voodoo? It fits! Now, think, why would Sandie break in?"

"Quick access to the diary to find the pirate treasure."

"But the thief came up empty handed." Raven flashed a white grin that made his lips appear a bright red, like fresh blood. "That's not to say the intruder gave up. Any suspects besides Sandie?"

With the back of my hand I wiped the sweat from my brow. "I was invited to a tarot card reading at Sandie's place across the street. She and the others were interested in the occult."

Raven tilted his head in an unspoken question. "I see. What are these Hoodoo ladies' names again?"

"Jacqui and Sue. Jacqui is a Voodoo, slash, Wicca trainee. Works for Doctor Philippe, who by the way, took me time travelling to the 1800s again. Turns out he was Jean Lafitte."

"Suspicious."

"Belle had a liaison with Lafitte and the diary confirmed it, but I'm more worried about Markus than finding the treasure right now."

"I thought you had that aspect covered."

"I'm not so sure. It occurred to me that a Sazerac would be wrong since it takes a person back in time. As for the gris-gris, I have no idea what's in that. I was only taking Philippe's word that it was from Marie Laveau."

"Greeks bearing gifts?"

"Exactly," I said, as my cell phone went off. My tote was hanging behind my chair. Grabbing it, I set it on the table, and pulled out the cell.

4 elements should restore Markus. I want to read your cards. Jacqui

I texted back: *Come c me. Hotel Memoire #400.*

Jacqueline sent a smiley face emoji.

I dropped my cell back in my tote and looked at Raven. A reading now wasn't the best timing but she could help me figure out how to work the spell.

"Good news?"

"Jacqui told me I need the four elements. I have a feeling I have to get soil from Indigo Oaks for Markus."

"I want to go with you."

"I'll handle it, Raven."

The vampire nodded imperceptibly. "What do you know about Indigo Oaks?"

"The place has been neglected for decades." I frowned. "Markus' father worked for Tyron Industries. He didn't know the plantation was his." My voice trailed off thinking of the predatory look in Gen's eyes whenever she glanced at Markus. Much like a cat with a claw in a mouse's tail—letting it go and then hooking it in again. "Raven, I don't trust Genevieve Severe. What do you know about her?"

Raven looked thoughtful. "She lives in the Quarter. Makes a lot of deals around here. She gets out in the parishes. Pulls in the big bucks. Does she seem a threat?"

"Women have instincts about other women."

Raven regarded me steadily. "She wants Markus?"

"I wouldn't be surprised. Why don't we have a peek at the diary? I need to find a spell for the four elements," I said, leafing through to the back where most of the spells were.

The first spell was something to be used to rid oneself of spirits. I filed it on my brain's hard drive to be retrieved when needed. Paging further under time-travel I found a reference to stagnating in time. "Here." I pointed with my finger. "*Reditum.* It says to repeat it three times."

"Let me show you something." Raven pulled out a small red book from his man bag.

"Strange," I said, slowly noting the gold edging on the tiny book. "It's identical to my diary—or rather Belle's diary."

"We bought them in a little shop in Paris. I have almost the same account of our voyage, the convent, and your affairs." He chortled.

"Can I see?"

He shook his head and picked up a pen. The vampire started scribbling something in the diary.

"Raven?"

A ping sounded.

His dark eyes narrowed. "Was that your cell phone?"

"Sounds like it. Excuse me. It might be important." I pulled the cell from my tote and scrolled down.

We need to talk. Where are u? "It's a text from Philippe."

"What did the Voodoo man say?"

I shoved the cell over to Raven.

Raven rolled his eyes when he saw the text. "Seriously? With Lafitte's soul inside him I doubt Philippe wants to *talk*. I imagine he wants to offer you his help in finding the treasure after he treats himself to your luscious body."

"Not going to happen."

"But you are attracted to him." Raven shook his head. "How strange—depriving yourself. You are as fickle as Belle."

Busy. I texted Philippe. *Sorry.*

Raven leaned over to see my text. "That's my girl. It's difficult to balance all those eggs in one basket and so Canadian of you," Raven said, patting my hand."

"What?"

The vampire flashed his pointy incisors, grinning widely. "The 'sorry' bit."

"And you are so French, my fashion forward friend." I glanced at the street beyond the canopied area, getting busier with tourists and locals. From the bar across the street the raspy blues singer sang about being the son of the seventh son. "Seven is a number that goes hand in hand with Voodoo just like three. Spells are done in threes or sevens."

"Say, did you wonder why the three local bitches, I mean

witches, invited you? Did you feel a tug at your hair?"

I frowned. I was buzzed but not really wasted when I met with the girls at Sandie's place. It would have been easy enough for someone to pull out a hair, I suppose. You're thinking a Voodoo doll spell with a hair fiber?"

Raven nodded. "Not unheard of. And the video camera? How do you see that connecting with the diary?"

"Someone's casting a spell on Markus."

"And the motive?"

"They set up the camera when they didn't find the diary." I pointed to Raven and then at my lip. "A crumb."

"Hm-mm?" Raven licked off the chocolate flake clinging to his lower lip. "Beignets are so good. Too bad you have that gluten allergy. Belle must have had some stomach pain for it to cling so aggressively to your tummy all the way to this life."

"I have to find out how she died once I cure Markus. But this treasure thing, you really think they're all after it?"

Raven shrugged "Money is the root of all evil. Witches like treasure but don't forget about your men."

I nodded. "Philippe and Markus."

"People are greedy."

"No denying that." I placed the cell back in my tote. "I have to break the spell. Markus needs to go back to the Indigo Oaks plantation. He may die if he doesn't get the last components of the spell."

"Indigo Oaks is on the river road, isn't it?"

"It's one of the plantations along the Mississippi."

"I recall it was the third after Sugar-Belle and Southwood. Beautiful mansions."

"Couldn't see anything from the road."

Raven bit into the remains of his beignet. "I really should go to protect you."

I shook my head. "No, I have this. You know, I think it's possible Lafitte is connected to all this."

Raven scratched his head thoughtfully. "So the nefarious Voodoo priest, Doctor Philippe, aka the infamous pirate Lafitte, comes to you with his troubles."

"His past life is calling out to him and another thing, Philippe picked up that I have possession of Belle's diary."

"You have the treasure clues. So TV residuals are paying peanuts and the Voodoo priest wants his pieces of eight."

"You think he's not interested in me? According to him, Lafitte and Belle were passionate lovers."

"Bah! Sex."

"And Markus, you think he's playing me too?"

Raven raised an eyebrow. "What do you think?'

"Markus' cell will enlighten us." I took the cell out and opened a text from Genevieve. *Sugar, let's get together.* My heart sank.

"Bad news?"

"Not sure." Over Raven's shoulder my gaze landed on a slender man in a close cut mauve T-shirt and pencil-cut jeans standing near the washroom. "Raven," I nudged the vampire. "Look, over there."

Raven's eyes widened. "Gabe's with a woman. She's tall and gorgeous. And look at the 'big' hair. You think she flipped that boy?"

The sour taste in my mouth didn't come from the coffee I was sipping.

Raven gestured to the couple as they glanced around the room checking for an empty table. "Over here, Gabe!"

"Hi, y'all!" Genevieve called out, as she approached.

"Please, join us." Raven said, rising to his feet.

"What a surprise," Gabe said, grabbing a chair and plopping in. He set his pink floral umbrella down against his chair. "Two Voodoos," he said to the dusky waiter wearing a crisp white shirt and black dress pants.

Gen's eyes narrowed unpleasantly. "You were with Markus at Indigo Oaks," she hissed, settling on the cushioned wrought iron chair.

She was a tall glass of bourbon, all right, I thought, giving her the once-over.

Looking down her nose at me, Gen said, "He's such a bad boy, my Markus. Didn't get back to me about those papers." Genevieve swiveled in her chair. "Where did you hide that cutie, Annette?"

"It's Anabelle, Gen," I said.

The realtor curled her lip back and hissed, "I prefer Genevieve."

"Oh, is that so?" I tipped back my cup. "Fabulous coffee. I'd forgotten how much I liked it."

"Talks about me a lot, does he?"

"Not really. He is happy he found the estate, though."

Genevieve didn't look pleased. "Yes, about that. It's best he sells it to the oil company. They've made a solid offer."

"Too bad for them. Markus likes the property."

Genevieve's cheek ticked nervously. "Sh-sh! Someone might hear," she warned, scanning the crowd across the street. The color drained from her face. She clutched my arm tightly like a person trying to stay afloat in a raging river. "It's important you do your best to persuade him to sell."

"Why?"

The realtor frowned.

"Is someone threatening you?"

Genevieve's glance flicked over to the bar on the other side of the street. Two massive men in vinyl suits ate pasta at a cafe table.

"Tyron Industries is a powerful company." She lit a cigarette, inhaling deeply before she slowly exhaled, regretfully allowing the smoke to escape her blood red lips.

"Your point is?"

"It's a dangerous city. It pays to be careful." She tapped her nails on the table nervously. "Where's Markus?"

I shrugged.

Her eyes shot daggers. "This is serious, Ana."

I pursed my lips thinking how I was so sick of this Amazon with the husky voice. "What's the urgency?"

"Did he tell you he's exclusive?" She flashed me the square-cut diamond on her right hand.

My jaw dropped. "You're engaged?"

She nodded.

Something was off. Snatching the diary and cell phones, I dropped them into my tote. "I've got to run."

"Wait," Raven said, hastily standing. Surveying the dark clouds above the spires of the cathedral facing Jackson Square, he gave me his black cane-length umbrella. "Take this. It comes in handy." He eyed Gabe, smiling surreptitiously. "I shan't need it."

Chapter 18: QUEEN OF SWORDS

Drops as big as beach pebbles hammered the umbrella as I weaved my way through the crowds on Decatur. Under the massive black shield, I was dry and seething. I had let down my guard and been betrayed.

At the corner I turned left and headed up Ursulines. A couple passed by leaving me alone in an empty street. The old buildings were dark on street level, but on the top floor the residences were occupied, the curtains filtering light to the sidewalk. At the cross street, the open windows of the Ursuline Convent, blazed like deacons in a storm.

When the rain petered off to a thin mist leaving the street shiny like a mirror, I closed Raven's sizable umbrella. Past the convent the street lights were dim and far apart, making the uneven and cracked sidewalk a precarious hike on high heels.

To be totally aware is a karate mantra. When a stone rolled on the sidewalk behind me, a reflex triggered. As giant black gloved hands tightened over my arms restraining my movements, I reverted to fight mode. I couldn't be sure if this punk had a weapon but when another guy in a black hoodie came at me flashing a knife, I screamed a kiai and stamped on the big man's foot with my heel. Wiggling my hip to the right, I struck a fist to his groin. His high pitched moan told me everything. I was on target. His arms dropped. I was free to deal with the Hoodie.

The point of Raven's umbrella pitched the knife out of Hoodie's hand. It clattered over the cement into the street. Twirling the umbrella about I smacked the wooden handle on the bridge of his nose, retracted it and poked into his solar plexus. Hoodie's screech was an octave too high for opera. I tried to see his face but a Baron Samedi mask hid everything except the glitter of his black eyes.

When I turned my head I saw the big goon was crouched over, head down, hands to his groin. A gold and purple Mardi Gras mask covered his face. Not eager for a rematch, I raced to the entrance of the hotel.

On the balcony of the second story apartment across the street, two men appeared. One called down, "You all right, honey?" I recognized him as the baker from the pastry shop across from the hotel.

My eyes swept back to the street. The thugs were gone. I sighed with relief. Not only was I alive but I had my tote. "Yes, thanks! They're gone."

With the hotel's outside door firmly shut I entered the hallway and caught my breath. I had to lose the small town mentality and realize I was in New Orleans, a city laced with crime.

My cross-strap bag was still firmly on my person. A quick examination of my tote revealed the cell phones and the diary. As for the umbrella, it was unbreakable. Raven had been right about it coming in handy. Without it, I'd be dead.

At the front desk Warren had his head down writing, intent on the hotel's ledger. I didn't stop to chit-chat. I wasn't in the mood. The safety of my room was more enticing.

When I pressed the "up" button the ancient elevator opened immediately. With a rattle it shook its way in the ascent. Inside the empty tapestry-lined elevator the air was heavy and stifling. A tarot card lay face-up on the floor. Tentatively, I picked it up.

A lady was resplendent in a majestic robe, a sword raised in one hand while the other was held up high. She was the Queen of Swords, signifying an intelligent, malicious woman. With the skirmish on the street I had almost forgotten about Jacqueline and the card reading. She must have dropped it on her way to my room. Tucking it into my purse I stepped out of the elevator thinking she would be waiting at my door, yet when the doors opened to the landing, it was empty.

Inside my suite it was cold enough to keep a corpse from decomposing. That reminded me I had a comatose cheater in my bed.

Markus tossed restlessly as if fighting off evil entities. He had played me for a fool. That image of the portrait at Renard's flying off the wall stuck in my mind. I should have taken that warning seriously. I didn't know him, not then, and not now.

To the touch he had a high temperature. Sweat spotted his brow. Still I was puzzled. Why would Genevieve want to harm Markus?

It wasn't logical but I couldn't let him suffer. On the night table there was a candle with a box of matches. Remembering I needed fire, air, water and earth, I lit the candle, held it over his head and repeated "*reditum*" three times wishing for Papa LaBas' help in bringing Markus back to the present.

As if in answer, the wind from outside pushed the balcony door ajar. Good, I thought. Now there was wind. Again, I repeated the spell.

Holding his head in my arms, I breathed in his fresh scent, lightly stroking his firm chin rough with a day's beard growth. Softly, I kissed his shapely mouth and felt his body respond. Markus opened his eyes and struggled to sit up resting his weight on his elbows.

"Wait." I shoved two pillows behind his back to prop him up. "You shouldn't rush this. Rest a while. I won't be long."

"Belle," he touched my hand, "someone was here during your absence. Be careful."

"Who?"

He shook his head. "I'm so tired, I can't think straight."

Cradling his head, I repeated, *"Reditum."*

A sudden flashback to a moment in my past life had me holding someone else in my arms. Janelle was sobbing uncontrollably.

"Now, now," I said soothingly, "they've only taken the baby to lay it down for a nap. Don't worry."

"No," she muttered, her fingers tearing frantically through her wavy red locks, "they've taken my baby away. He is heir to the Renard fortune."

Just as I was about to speak the vision faded and I was left alone with a sleeping Markus.

I repeated the spell twice and then thinking of the camera in my bag, I grabbed my tote and took the elevator down. When it thudded to a halt, I charged into the lobby. The front desk was deserted but a computer had been left on. The USB on the camera fit snugly into the computer port.

On replay, I saw my upstairs bedroom. I was not happy to see footage of Markus pressing me against the wall. I forwarded the recording but the room invasion revealed only shadowy figures. Just my luck, I thought.

"The camera must have been installed much later," Logical said.

Hormone snickered. "Could have been hot if Markus opened up that closet door and found Anabelle tied into submission earlier.

She's such a dominant girl, it would have been a break for her."

"She doesn't need to be bound to have a good time with Markus, Hormone. Anabelle is hardly bored with their sexual activities."

"Yeah," said Hormone, "but it might have been interesting."

Frustrated, I muttered, "Stop!"

Once again, I watched the video.

Another figure entered the room after the first two left. He searched the room and left abruptly. Fast-forwarding, a large python slithered under the table just before I sprang out of the closet. Then I recalled what Markus had said about seeing someone. At the end just before the video blacked-out, an obscure figure approached the bed, nudged Markus, and spoke, but the audio was too muffled to make out who the person was or what was said.

A shout from the hallway put all that research to an end. I dropped the video camera device into my tote and rushed out into the hallway to see what was going on. Warren, Sandie, and the bearded goon I had met when I first arrived, were all standing around a woman lying on the stairs. The unconscious female was blonde and slender.

Sandie swung around. "Anabelle, it's Jacqui. They said," she waved at the group, "she fell."

Warren raced down the hall to the front desk.

"He's getting an ambulance."

"That's Jacqui?" I said in confusion, staring at the slender pretty girl lying on the landing. "She's a blonde?"

Sandie nodded. "She wears a black wig to go with the Voodoo priestess gig. See her snake tat on her upper arm?" She stared at the prone figure. "Strange how she looks so much like you without that Voodoo getup and the Goth makeup."

"What happened?" I asked.

"Don't know."

I knelt down and touched a dark matted area. "Her head is bleeding."

Warren called out from the hall. "Ambulance is comin'."

"Jacqui was to do a reading for me but she wasn't there when I came."

Sandie leaned in closer, whispering, "She was pushed, I bet." She added hastily, "I don't mean by you. I think she met someone. People don't like being told a bad fortune."

"Why do you say that?"

"Some of her tarot cards fell out of her bag. I'm not sure if I should have touched them or not, but I know she loves those cards so I put them back in her purse. The police will be coming too."

The goon who had been standing by suddenly headed to the entrance.

"He sure was in a hurry to go. Is he a guest?"

"I don't think so."

"She looks so pale."

Sandie nodded. "I think she'll be okay. I saw her move just before you came."

"I feel bad. She was here to do a reading for me."

"Maybe when she didn't see you she thought she'd like to see Markus for herself. Then she got all excited to see him alone and helpless from the gris-gris spell. It's like a date drug so she could have tried to seduce him."

I rolled my eyes. "Seriously?" I stared at her. "How did you know about Markus?"

"I was with her when you texted." Sandie scratched her head. "You don't suppose in his messed up state he threw her down the stairs?"

"He's messed up all right." If he hadn't been so pale I would have had it out with him.

"You said he's caught between two lives, didn't you?" Sandie said. "That's why he's disoriented." She babbled excitedly, "He could have hit Jacqui with a lamp thinking she was a thief. We need to go up to your room."

Voices from the door signaled the arrival of the paramedics and two police officers.

"Come on!" Sandie grabbed my arm and tugged. "Hurry! Warren can deal with the police and give them details."

"I feel responsible, Sandie. She came to give me a reading."

"Never mind that. Let the police deal with it. No way do I want to spend the night at the police station."

We went by way of the courtyard and up the outside stairs to the fourth floor. Sandie squeezing her hands together every few seconds as she rattled on. "Poor girl doesn't have a family, ya know. But don't worry, I'll phone the hospital later to see how she's doin'."

When I opened the door to the suite, Sandie was right behind me.

Markus was shirtless, buckling up his belt, humming a bluesy tune. "Hey, cher. You've been a while." He glanced at Sandie. "You're Sue's friend. We met in the café, remember?"

"Yup, I'm Sandie. What's yat? Are you Markus or the pirate?"

"Hm-mm?" Markus forehead furrowed.

"Do you know who Alain Ducoeur is?" I asked.

"Of course. He's a Cadeaux. Bought Indigo Oaks Plantation from Jean Lafitte."

Sandie and I exchanged looks. The fire and air spell might have worked.

When he bent to pick up his leather case he wobbled unsteadily, scattering newspaper clippings from the case onto the floor. "I need those," he said uncertainly, trying unsuccessfully to retrieve them.

Sandie snatched up the fallen papers from the floor and glanced at them. "Lookee here, Anabelle." She handed me one of the papers. She stared at Markus. "I thought ya was a photographer. Look at this, Anabelle."

The name "Markus Cadeaux" under the article title "Oil Ravishes Louisiana" caught my eye. "You write for the Times-Picayne?"

"Freelance. Crime investigation mostly. It pays the bills." He sat down on the edge of the bed. "I'm so exhausted."

"These are about oil companies, in particular, Tyron Industries. Isn't that the company where your father worked?"

Markus held out his hand for the papers. "The company that wants to buy Indigo Oaks."

"Expansion at the environment's expense," I said, taking the papers from Sandie and tucking them into the leather case and placing it on the bed.

"My ex is involved with those crooks," Sandie said bitterly. "Don't trust any of them."

"Nobody should," Markus said, his jaw clenched. "They're big time polluters supported by crooked politicians. They bought land after Katrina. Insider contractors who got the big bucks rebuilding New O'leans based on lies." He placed his fingertips to his temples and closed his eyes.

"You should know about liars," I hissed. "Tell me about you and Genevieve. How long has this been going on?"

Markus groaned and slumped back on the bed. "I have this tremendous headache."

"Forget the headache. What about Gen?"

"What the hell is happening to me?"

"Convenient memory loss." I exchanged looks with Sandie. "Are you playing me?" I said softly. "You honestly don't remember?"

Markus lifted his head high like an excited stallion and shook his thick mane forcing wayward locks off his forehead. "Someone hexed me I'm sure. I had a Sazerac at the bar but it didn't taste right. Gris-gris."

"Or a drug like GHB." I sat down on the bed beside him and much like a doctor with a patient. "What exactly do you remember from Lafitte's Blacksmith Shop?"

"Well, now that you mention it, I was talking to Janelle." He face softened and his eyes looked far away. "I can't get you out of my mind, Belle."

Not Belle again.

Markus frowned. "I need to sleep this off. I am so fatigued."

I was ready to punch his lights out. "So when is the big day, stud-muffin?"

"Hm-mm?"

I was like Katrina blowing in strong, stoked with anger. "With Genevieve?"

"Who?" He wiped his forehead. "I swear I've got malaria. The fever keeps coming back. Get me a blanket, cher."

His eyes did look strangely distant and his face had the sheen of someone jogging top speed on a treadmill.

I shoved the duvet over him. "How's that?"

"Thanks. That was some night we had, Belle."

"It's Anabelle."

He smirked, his green eyes dancing. "Is that what you call yourself now, Belle? Still, a pretty name for a pretty girl. Come kiss me, cher." Markus threw off the duvet and glanced at Sandie.

"Now I feel too warm. Say goodbye to your friend, Belle. We have some catching up to do."

"Do you remember Genevieve bringing you the sale papers to sign at Lafitte's Blacksmith Shop?"

"No more talking, cher." He pulled me to him. "Time for you to leave," he said to Sandie. "Give us privacy. This can't wait."

"I bet it can't, dude." Sandie glanced down at the bulge straining Markus' jeans. "You were drunk?"

"I suppose."

"A guy like you?" Sandie's eyes swept up and down from Markus' athletic physique, wide chest and shoulders down to his six-pack. Her eyes glazed over. "You're a big man. Alcohol can't hit you that hard."

"Never happened before, but honestly it's a haze." Markus, rubbed the tendons of his neck distractedly. "I know I was at Lafitte's Blacksmith Shop. A redhead came in wanting to make a deal, but you dragged me here and then we—"his voice trailed off and he grinned. "I'm beginning to recall something." He waved his hand at Sandie. *"Au revoir,* Miss.*"*

"No way. I'm not leaving, so forget the goodbyes, handsome. This is gettin' too good for me to leave." Sandie bounced on the back of her heels. "I'd bet your memory had plenty of steamy bits."

I put my hand up to stop Sandie from continuing. "Listen to me, Markus. Someone put gris-gris in your Sazerac to open the portal into the 1800s. You went back to the time when you were Alain Ducoeur, the pirate. Do you remember?"

"I am Alain Ducoeur."

"Do you know who drugged you?"

Markus scratched his head.

"My guess is Gen. Do you remember her now?"

"Sorry, no. Can't think of why the wench would want to drug me unless," Alain said with a slow grin, "she was plannin' on seducin' me."

I wasn't about to mention that the gator girl already had her jaws firmly planted on his package, but since the cheater brought it up, my temper flared. "You don't need a Sazerac to be seduced. You don't mind giving it away."

"Oo-oo. I can just imagine." Sandie sighed, her eyes dreamy.

"I saw Gen at the Café du Monde. An hour ago she was eager for you to sign away your property. She told me you two are engaged."

"This is crazy talk, cher. Pirates don't marry."

Sandie's eyes widened and stared at Markus. "You're engaged to Gen Severe?"

Markus' brow furrowed. "I have no knowledge of said wench." He shrugged his shoulders. "I feel like I've consumed week-old fish food, ladies." He reached out for me. "Come here, cher."

Backing away, I said, "Don't touch me."

"Don't be angry. I really don't know this Gen of whom you speak."

"Okay, Markus," I muttered. "I believe you."

"My name is Alain Ducoeur. Who is Markus?"

"That's your name now. For you to understand any of this we need to get the spell reversed."

Sandie glanced from me to Markus. "You are Alain Ducoeur the pirate?"

Markus nodded solemnly.

Sandie giggled. "Why would he hook up with Gen Severe? I hear she eats nails crushed in grits for breakfast."

"All I know is Gen was frightened. At the Café du Monde she kept watching the bar across the street. My gut tells me it wasn't because she likes blues." I glanced at the purple bruises on my forearms. "On the way back, I was attacked."

Markus glanced at the bruises. "Thieves?"

"I have no idea. What worries me is I've had intruders before—right here in this room. I was knocked out, tied up, and stashed in the closet."

"Bastards! I'll find them," Markus growled.

"Never mind. You need to stay calm." I stared at Sandie thoughtfully. "What did you end up doing with the snake?"

"Warren found it a home. Pythons are good for virility and fertility."

Markus slumped back on the bed, smiling surreptitiously at me from heavy-lidded eyes. "I have plenty of that kind of strength, sexy little witch."

CHAPTER 19: JACK OF CUPS

Sandie was sitting behind the wheel of a red and white '57 Chevy Belair, parked in front of the Hotel Memoire. "Come on, y'all." She chuckled. "I have a hankerin' for a plateful of gumbo."

I opened the door and helped an unsteady Markus climb into the back before getting into the passenger's seat. "Know where to drive?" I asked Sandie.

"Markus filled me in. He's not up on the latest roads," she whispered, "being a pirate and all, so I looked it up on my app just in case the route changed in the last two hundred years." Sandie called out like a tour guide, "Headin' west, then south to the Mississippi. Ascension Parish comin' up."

"This is so vintage." I said, sinking into the cushy white leather seat. "How did you ever get a hold of this beauty?"

"Not mine. The owners are the caretakers of the Beauregard-Keyes house. With them jetting off to France they let me use it. Even when they're here, they stick to the Quarter and walk."

My rumbling stomach reminded me I needed a refill. "There's a little bar on the river road."

"I'm so in. This is exciting, guys." Sandie pulled out onto the dark road and turned on her headlights. She shot me a worried glance. "You have the treasure directions, don't you?"

"Yup. Just don't expect too much. Erosion could have destroyed all the landmarks, besides, don't forget the reason we're going is to bring Markus back to the present."

Sandie nodded. "I know, but a girl can hope." Shouting over her shoulder, she called out, "How are you doing back there?"

"*Mon dieu*, I feel as helpless as a baby. What a ridiculous pirate I am," Markus said mournfully, the usual swagger missing from his voice.

"A pirate, hm-mm." Sandie grinned like a monkey on drugs. "I like. Um-hmm, that big long sword. Oh, so hot."

My mind went straight to the steamy bathtub, Alain Ducoeur's eyes sizzling with passion and the water temperature just right to get my lady parts aroused. If some idiot hadn't knocked me out I would have floated right off to orgasmic heaven.

Yeah, in my dreams. Alain, the pirate, was a wonderful fantasy, but the other guy, Markus, the louse, was for real. My red hot lover had played me for a fool. Once I dabbed him with earth and water and he returned to normal, I would dig the truth out of him.

"You are so lucky, girlfriend," Sandie said her eyes on the road. "Food and sex. You get it all. Wish some of that mojo magic would rub off on me."

I grimaced at her words. "I wish."How did I always manage to choose the wrong guy? First my no-good ex who cheated me out of a small fortune and now the charming Markus, Genevieve's lover and husband to be.

Sandie gunned the pedal, putting New Orleans behind us. The Chevy raced past the other cars like a young filly let loose to pasture. On the I-10W, the traffic trickled off. Behind us, a burgundy pickup truck followed. When we veered left onto the road that took us to the river plantations, the truck tailgated, headlights glaring in the mirror.

Number eleven lines appeared on Sandie's forehead. "Damn that A-hole. Folks, this is stressful. I need a picker-upper."

"Over there." I pointed to a building ahead. Turn just past that live oak."

Sandie gunned it into the parking lot, the tires rumbling over the gravel. On a gray wooden building, a neon pink sign flashed "open" like a sleazy motel rental.

Narrowly missing us, two Harleys headlights glaring, flew out into the road followed by a cloud of dust, the bulky riders in helmets and black leather garb barely visible in the darkness.

"Holy crap! Those bozos can't drive worth a shit," Sandie said, parking between two white pickups.

Over the door the sign "Joleen's" was painted in yellow cursive above a spoon filled with a gigantic orange crayfish.

Sandie focused on the sign. "A place like this has good eats, guys."

"I'm on board," I said enthusiastically. I was on a full-blown high-carb diet—one which layers millions of fat cells on unsuspecting abs overnight.

Markus flashed his ivory-whites at me. "My hunger is excruciating, but it's all for you." He leaned over, his lips brushing my neck. "We need to test that bed at Indigo Oaks. Or have we already? Regrettably, this spell has made me forgetful. You must fill me in on our fervent trysts."

Pushing him away, I said, "I only know of the ghostly encounters. I'm not Belle, remember?" The man was incorrigible. I was not okay with this turn of conversation. I glared at him but he took no notice.

Markus' eyes shone as he spoke softly in my ear. "What I do know is we are explosive—like a lit match dropped on a dry forest, but unlike that woodland," he said, his lips turning up at the corners, "we are far from dry. I recall the sweat of our bodies entwined in an ardent embrace."

I could feel myself tingling with the mental image, he had such an effect on me, but a tiny fragment of brain matter realized I was being a fool.

Hormone started jumping up and down like a coke-head in need of a fix. "Don't lose Markus, lose Sandie. Drive that delicious man to Indigo Oaks and shake his bones or I will."

"Don't be ridiculous!" Logical snapped. "Can't you see she needs food? Anabelle can only function if she's had food—plenty of it."

From the car window the full moon, hanging low in the dark sky, shone red. Super moons are rare and rarer still are the ones they call a "blood moon", a phenomena where the moon squeezes between the sun and earth lending a red film on its surface. This one lit the parking lot brighter than the lantern strung on the rickety wooden porch. As I glanced up the road, a chill raced down my spine. I had a premonition of danger. That was the downside of being psychic, not knowing what—only when. It would happen soon.

Sandie pulled the key out and the Chevy settled in for a rest.

When I tried to help Markus out he got all macho and waved me away. "I can manage, cher. Let's get some sustenance," he said, suddenly sprinting to the pub door and holding it open for us. "I think the fever has passed, ladies." With a flourish of his hand and a bow, he motioned for us to go ahead.

From the corner of my eye I recognized the red pickup on our tail pulling in beside a white rusty Ford Focus. The passengers didn't get out.

"The pickup," I said.

"Never mind them. Let's go eat, girlfriend," Sandie urged, pulling on my arm.

The smoky room was appointed in prison gray, wood beams on the ceiling and uneven grubby plank flooring, but filled nevertheless with sweaty men, big and unshaven. On the far right a space was occupied by the band, where they were setting up speakers and a microphone. Not to be deprived of a solid meal, Sandie charged past the local guys in bib-overalls and baseball caps and plopped on one of the few remaining bar stools. I took a seat beside her and luckily one of the customers left, clearing a seat for Markus to slide into.

A fish hook hanging from one ear, a massive bald bartender with skin a pleasant shade of mocha, wearing a white T-shirt and jeans, was busy wiping the counter with a frayed rag. "What can I get y'all?"

"Three 'Ghost in the Machine'," Sandie piped up over the din. "That all right, folks?"

I had no idea what she ordered but I nodded. Long necked bottles with the whimsical label were promptly placed on the counter. The bartender opened each one and grinned. "Anythin' else?"

"You have gumbo?" Markus asked.

"Do one legged-ducks swim in circles?" The bartender's broad smile had a gap where his front tooth wasn't. "We've got a gumbo yer mama would be proud to call her own."

"Sounds good." Markus said, "Three?"

When Sandie bobbed her head, I said, "Yes, please." I would have liked the shrimp listed on the blackboard behind him but gumbo would be faster. The sooner we arrived at Indigo Oaks, the sooner I'd have Markus back to the strong man he was. Then he would answer to me about his fling with snake.

If this hottie was a cheating slimeball I needed to know. I was so riled up I felt like shaking the truth out of him but when I glanced over and saw those strangely mesmerizing eyes gazing back, I calmed down.

"Belle, you are so lovely. I'm so glad you came back." Markus took my hand and kissed my wrist. "Tell me you still have feelings for me."

This was not fair. He was enticing, yet I hardly knew the man.

"I have questions."

"I will gladly answer anything I can."

"You've killed people." I was thinking of the pirate Ducoeur, but as present-day Markus he had seen death, as well.

"I have. That's why I quit the game."

"And yet you carved up Ryan's face?"

Markus sighed. "You were in danger. He nearly killed you. It's what he deserved."

I held up my wrist. The lightning bolt scar was white on my tanned skin. "How did I get it?"

He showed me his wrist where a similar scar marred his arm. Markus shook his head. "I don't know how you got yours but I think because I have the same one, it's a sign of our connection."

"Tell me about the fire."

"Someone set the boat ablaze. I tried to save you."

I had to find out more before I would be free of the nightmares but I wanted to know this man better. "And the slavery? Did you do it for the money?"

"Lafitte captured the Spanish galleon. I swear I had nothing to do with selling slaves." Markus lifted my chin and looked into my eyes. "So I changed my life, kept my ship, the shop on the Mississippi, and part of the treasure. I was the new doctor in town."

I wanted to believe he was not a vengeful man capable of psychopathic violence. "All right, after I reverse the spell we will talk again."

Delicious cooking odors wafting through the open door of the kitchen made me salivate in anticipation. My stomach was gunning for a treat.

Soon enough I was the lucky recipient of the grand gumbo prize—gator, shrimp, chicken, and sausage smothered in okra, peppers and tomatoes drowning in a thick brown roux surrounding a neat pile of cooked rice centered in the bowl.

"Dang this is good!" Sandie spooned the gumbo enthusiastically, licking her lips with her tongue and fingertips, not bothering with the serviette. "Isn't it, Anabelle?"

"Um-mm." She wasn't the only one gobbling it down. Markus was digging in like this was his last supper.

I bit my lip. Maybe it was. Nothing was guaranteed when it came to magic.

Around us, men tossed back shots, the noise level increasing as the liquor flowed. The beer washed down the last smidgen of gumbo scraped from the bowl, and I began to feel rejuvenated, ready to tackle Voodoo and bad gris-gris.

The place was loud but the noise level became deafening when the band started up with toe-tapping Zydeco. The lead singer a slender girl, straight black hair to her waist, had a voice as sweet as sugar. A brawny, bearded auburn-haired man played the accordion, the rifts melodically in sync to the spoons tapping.

I felt Markus' big hand cover mine and I smiled on the inside. From this angle I could admire his manly profile, a significant chin balancing out his strong nose.

Bubba, the bartender, sauntered up, spread his arms out on the rim of the counter and lifted an eyebrow. "Well, folks?"

"This is pure heaven," I said. "My compliments to the chef. He wouldn't be willing to share the recipe, would he?"

Bubba shook his head. "The chef is a she. Joleen doesn't know what she puts in there from day to day. A pinch of this, a taste of that. I ax her but she don't tell me."

I nodded. "I understand completely. I'm a chef too, from Canada."

"Colder than a witch's tit, ain't it?"

"Can be."

"Where you headin'?"

"The Indigo-Oaks place," Sandie chimed in. "You know it?"

"Just down the road some. Used to be a high-falutin place. Funny thing, no one's been there for a coon's age until today," he said, scratching his head

"How so?" Markus asked.

"Just before y'all came in there was bikers—" Bubba's head shot to the far end of the bar where a man signaled for drinks. He set down our bill and took up a couple of beers from the bin.

"Bikers?" Markus repeated, frowning.

The term puzzled him. Cars, trucks and motorcycles hadn't existed back then. From my tote I took out some bills, and tossed the money on the counter. "Two bikers?" I asked, remembering some drove out when we entered the parking area.

The bartender picked up the cash, counting it before depositing the pile into the cash register. "Uh-huh. They sure was in a hurry. Knew where Indigo was and all." His jaw twisted as he added, "Kind of strange that. Been abandoned for years. Heard the place has an owner."

"Hey, Bubba!" A tall black man called out from the end of the bar. "You comin' here with them beers or what?"

"Gotta go back to work. Enjoy yer visit." He smiled a toothless gap in a mouthful of yellow teeth.

I was about to reach over to help Markus off his stool but he shook my hand off.

"None of that, woman. I'm a hexed man not an invalid."

Soon enough we climbed back into the Chevy and headed west on the river road. Live oaks cloaked with cypress moss, dark and shadowy, bordered the road obscuring the sky in places yet the moon managed to creep through the undergrowth gleaming stop-light red through web-like branches.

"We're being followed by that thing you called a pickup," Markus said softly.

I swung around to the glare of headlights.

Sandie's lip curled. "Dang! They've got to be after the treasure."

"I'm more concerned about a carjacking."

Sandie scowled. "They'll have to fight for my money."

"I hope not," I said. I'd had enough for one night. My forearms felt sore and bruised from the goons' attack earlier. I was lucky then, but not so much now.

Sandie was a small plump female, hardly a physical type. She wouldn't be able to handle punks, and Markus, for all his bravado, was weak as a kitten. The last thing I needed was to deal with scumbags when my sidekicks had no kick.

"Wait, they're turning off," Markus said.

"Good," I said. "Ours is the next road to the left."

There was a particularly large live oak at the driveway entrance.

"That thing is humongous!" Sandie shrieked.

"Two hundred years old, at least," I said. "Take it easy down this road, Sandie. There are potholes."

At that, the car bounced, jerking the Chevy hard to the left causing us to swerve towards a tree. Springing into action, I straightened the wheel as Sandie stiffened in shock.

"Dang! You're quick. I hardly blinked before you took control. I'm impressed. Isn't she somethin', hun?"

"She moves fast," Markus said slowly, his voice husky, "and look at those sleek lines, like a fine ship."

"Good thing I am fast or you'd be lying dead on the floor at Lafitte's Blacksmith Shop," I said dryly. "I dragged you away from Genevieve in the nick of time." Then recalling he was engaged to the snake, I added, "but I should have left you in the dirt. We are so over!"

In the backseat Markus was silent. It enraged me he wouldn't explain and that I was stupid enough to want to cure him.

Up ahead, I glimpsed Indigo Oaks through the trees. Sandie eased slowly down the road, allowing the headlights to scan for potholes.

"Pardon me for being curious but are you breaking up?" Sandie asked. "Personally, I thought you made a great couple."

"We were over the minute he took up with that skank." I waited, expecting some sort of sarcastic remark but when I heard nothing, I glanced back.

Markus' closed eyes and his ghostly pallor demonstrated the powerful effect the gris-gris was having on him. I needed to find the antidote or I would lose Markus permanently and all my anger at his betrayal would be wasted on a dead guy.

Stately Indigo Oaks, appointed with Grecian columns, a roomy veranda and a balcony fronting the two-storey building shone ivory under the light of the moon. The day's humidity was now a glowing mist rising up from the grass.

Sandie stopped the car in front of the veranda. She glanced over her shoulder. "Anabelle, I think he's dead."

Sprawled on the back seat, Markus lay limp on the plush leather seat. I leaned over and slapped Markus' face. He muttered something indiscernible.

"Wow, that's lucky. Girlfriend, I know yar mad, but maybe you should put aside that negative energy." Sandie grabbed the shovel from the back seat, and got out of the car.

"I'll think about that." I glanced up at the veranda and spotted the wicker chairs. "Give me a hand. We have to take him up there."

Even with Sandie's help it was a struggle. Luckily, Markus roused himself enough for us to drag him up to the porch.

"Get him into this one," I said, pulling Markus to the nearest chair while Sandie pushed his back.

When we had settled Markus in, I let a sigh of relief.

Sandie straightened up and rolled her shoulders. "Helpless like a baby." She smirked. "A hunk of burning love, eh, Anabelle?"

"That's enough, Sandie. You don't know what I'm dealing with."

"I'm listening."

"In my past life I was Belle and he was Alain Ducoeur, the pirate. They died a violent death. I have to find out how they were killed even if he is a cheater."

Sandie tilted her head and scratched under her chin. "You think he cheated on Belle like he cheated on ya?"

"Ducoeur could have been with other women just like Markus was with Gen. Some men are bottom feeders."

Suddenly, Markus became agitated, his body shaking. "Get off the boat!" he shouted, sitting upright, his eyes staring at the tree near the river. "Smoke's comin' in," Markus slurred in a heavy French accent as the spell took him deeper.

"What happened?" I urged, hoping to get the story out of him.

Markus shook his head. "I need to get those off. Hold still." Markus made some motions as if he were untying a rope. "Damn Renard. He did this."

"Set the fire?"

Markus' eyes took on a confused look.

I shook his shoulder. "Tell me!"

He leaned back on the chair and shook his head. "The wine was drugged." He grabbed my wrists. "Stay low. I'll knock the door down."

Markus was closing in on his last living moments. He would die if I didn't reverse the spell soon. My boyfriend was in danger of slipping away. Boyfriend? Hardly, I reminded myself, yet he was the fuel that lit my fire in a way no man had before. I glanced over at Markus now slumped back in the chair, his arresting face pale and expressionless, eyes closed. Even in repose Markus was killer-gorgeous.

Soon it wouldn't matter if he cheated on me or not. If I didn't cleanse his energy he would die in that chair. "We need to hurry," I said. "I have to fill the vials at the river."

"Wait!" Sandie ran off the porch to the Chevy, and grabbed the shovel leaning against the car door. "We need this for the treasure hunt."

I nodded. "Fine, but you will be searching on your own. I have to find the right ingredients to help Markus. Don't expect anything.

The Mississippi has changed through the years and this is a long shot."

Sandie sighed. "I know it's not a done deal, but Anabelle, you are a witch."

"You think I can sense the exact spot to confirm the location?"

"I'm counting on it."

I dug up the diary from my bag and opened it to the page with directions to the treasure.

Sandie handed me the flashlight. "Take hold of this for a minute while I memorize the instructions."

When she was done, I led the way down a trail through the bushes. The air smelled like wet trees and night-blooming flowers. Someone had maintained a garden at one time but only the scents gave an indication that the now abandoned plantation house had been lived in. The narrow yellow beam aimed down between the oaks cutting a path through the darkness.

My eyes shot ahead. Under the light of the blood-red moon, patches of the Mississippi sparkled through the foliage. I felt my stomach somersault as my heels sunk into the soft grass.

At this point I was at an all time low imagining how pitiful the heels of my favorite pair of Italian sandals looked dirtied with fresh Louisiana mud. I had packed for the city streets of New Orleans never thinking I'd be trekking through the countryside on guard for rattlesnakes at every turn of the path but that's exactly what was happening.

***

"Ya think the pickup is hid? They won't see it, will they?" When the skinny druggie didn't answer Chuckie tugged on the boney man's arm. "What ya lookin' at?"

"The woman. It's her, Shuckster. I swear it is."

Chuckie was feeling good, closing in on the jackpot. "Course it is, Doobs," he said patiently, as if he were talking to a half-wit. "The woman has a map to the treasure."

"No, dude. Meant the other one."

Chuckie peered through the branches of the mangrove tree. "She does look familiar." He scratched his bald head. "Ah-huh. Yer right. That's the sharpshooting lesbian from the Beauregard-Keyes house."

"Huh? She a dyke?"

"No Southern straight lady would try to shoot prime meat."

"What meat?"

In the darkness Chuckie could see the whites of Doobs' eyes staring back at him.

"Me, dummy."

Doobs chortled. "Good one, Chuckie. The gals love ya, right? Get serious. That girlie's carrying a shovel to go treasure huntin', ah-ha." His head bobbed as if confirming this concept. The money be there alright.

Doobs shivered uncontrollably like a leaf in a gale. Man, he was colder than a polar bear's tush even though the temperature was ninety plus by the river. It had been twenty-four hours since his last fix. He had to get to the Meth clinic or he'd be crazier than Shuckster.

Meanwhile, Chuckie was watching Sandie trot over to a massive live oak near the river. He watched her take two giant steps, turned left, and take two more. At that point she stood still and yelled. The pretty girl came back, nodded her approval and rushed back to the river, leaving the round woman to dig.

Chuckie watched in awe. The chubby girl was powerful, breaking ground quicker than a possum rooting for turtle eggs. His lips curled into a frown. It still pissed him off how she'd made them dance a two-step before chasing them off the property. No one makes a fool out of him. The bitch needed to be taught a lesson, he thought, his eyes squinting at the plump female through the branches of the mangrove tree.

A good-sized hole appeared within minutes as Sandie dug in with the spade, tossing the mud out in a steady rhythm. Every few minutes she would rest her forearms on the handle and take a few deep breaths before getting back at it. Suddenly, she screeched, "Found something, Anabelle!"

"Good work, woman." Doobs' tweaker eyes blinked faster than his trembling fingers. "Ya sure there's money?"

"Let me have a looksee." Chuckie pulled on Doobs' thin rainbow-colored sleeve.

"Lay off, Shuckster." Doobs was about to push Chuckie away when he heard a noise. An addict is highly sensitive to sounds even when he's high. It's survival of the fittest out in the streets. "Hey, listen." Seconds later two motorcycles appeared on the road headed towards the Indigo Oaks plantation house. "Fuck me," Doobs said softly.

***

"I don't understand, Anabelle." Sandie said, as they hurried up the path. "This box I dug up is tiny and all that's in it is a bag. How could it be Ducoeur's treasure from Lafitte?" she said, jiggling the bag. "It's way too tiny."

I took the bag and tucked it into my tote, handing the box back to her. "Hold on to that. Maybe you can get something for it."

"Can't we stop and see what's in the bag?" Sandie whined.

"Not now," I said, breaking into a slow jog. "Time is running out. I have to try and save Markus."

On the grassy trail a few yards behind, Sandie panted to keep the pace. "Listen, girlie, a dead Markus is a loss to womankind," she squeaked, her voice fainter as she fell further behind, "but once they cheat they'll do it over and over."

"You think that because of your husband," I said, over my shoulder. "What happened to letting go of the negative?"

"Too new-age for me." Her voice grew raspy. "I'm beat, Anabelle. You go ahead."

I handed the flashlight to Sandie, and started running to the mansion. In the sky shedding an eerie glow, the blood red moon sat low over the live oaks. Using its light I was able to follow the path to the Indigo Oaks manor.

Belle's code was designed for good deeds—helping alleviate suffering. Marie Laveau taught her to make healing gris-gris. No matter what kind of a man Markus was, I had to help rid him of the dream-state he was in. My own repetitive nightmare of Rene's suicide convinced me. Rene had been devastated by the card game where he'd lost everything to Ducoeur. Belle's affairs broke him and maybe even caused her death. I had to try and make it right.

The veranda was shadowed by the magnolia tree, heavy boughs laden with blooms, a sweet scent perfuming the air. Markus was where I'd left him, motionless in the wicker chair. Setting my tote on the table, I tugged out the vial filled with Louisiana soil, and poured the contents into Markus' dark waves, massaging the soil into his scalp. He moaned softly as I whispered, "*Reditum,*

reditum, reditum in his ear. From the corner of my eye a movement drew my attention.

A burly bearded man stepping out from behind the Romanesque pillar, the business end of a Glock pointed at my chest. "Howdy, ma'am. Hate to interrupt your spa treatment."

"I know you," I said, staring daggers. "You were at my hotel, threatening me. What are you doing here?"

From out of the shadows Shotgun Sue appeared, wearing a black motorcycle helmet, jacket and jeans. Nudging the end of her shotgun into a trembling Genevieve Severe's back she corralled the realtor into a patio chair next to Markus. "Took you long enough, Anabelle. Your hottie kept asking about you, that is, until he passed out."

The bearded man shot a look at Markus. "He's as wasted as Cooter Brown."

"Sue?" I was blown away. Gen had given Markus the gris-gris, I decided, but why would Sue be here?"

"Guess I'm the last one you expected."

"Why the guns?" I asked, stepping away.

"Stay where you are," growled the goon.

I was puzzled. "What do you want with us?"

"Your boyfriend has what we want," Sue said, her eyes narrowed.

"His land?"

"Smart." Sue glanced at Ben. "See?"

"How did you find us?"

"GPS device. Clever, hm-mm? This guy put it in your bag." Sue waved over at the bearded man. "Meet my associate, Ben."

"We've met. You hit me on the head and left me in the closet?' Ben grinned.

"Why?"

"Left a camera to see what you and Cadeaux had goin' on."

"But why leave the python?"

"Wasn't me. That was the other boyfriend, Doctor Philippe." Ben squinted at my chest. "He was snoopin' in your room. Maybe wanted to steal some hair for his Voodoo doll or more likely a pair of panties." The henchman poked Markus' shoulder. "He don't look too good, Sue."

"To be expected, Ben." Sue pursed her lips. "Our mistake was letting Gen give him the whole dose. The alcohol combo did him in."

"Markus was pushed through the portal into the past. He thinks he's Alain Ducoeur!" I hissed the words through my teeth I was so livid. Sue was a back-stabber. My instincts had been so wrong. "How could you?"

"Becoming your friend was the first step in helping myself to billions. Philippe said you would be coming into the neighborhood and you might be trouble. Of course he had his own agenda. I already knew Markus was the owner of this property but he was holding his cards close, so I introduced you thinking you'd tell me what he's up to."

"So why sic your dog Benji on me?"

"Eh!" Ben thrust his forearm out in the famous Italian umbrella gesture.

"Back at you," I said. "What did I do to you, Sue?"

"Like I said, at first I wanted to keep an eye on you. Word was out that there was a witch in the neighborhood. Philippe was freaked. He thought you had something to do with his past life and was out to destroy him. Turns out he wasn't the only one. You had visitors in your room coming and going as fast as costume changes at a transvestite show."

"Ya know, Shotgun, this plan sucks. Why don't I shoot him and be done with it?" Ben interrupted. "We can fake his signature."

"No!" I edged in past Sue's sidekick. "See this?" I held a vial of Mississippi water up. "I can revive him. Look." Forcing a few drops between Markus' parted lips caused a reaction. He groaned and opened his eyes. I ran my fingers over Markus' forehead. "He has a fever." Then leaning close to his ear, I whispered: *Redde praesenti, redde praesenti, redde praesenti.* Almost immediately, Markus became alert. "He'll do anything you ask. You don't need to kill him."

"Well look at that, Shotgun Sue," Ben said in awe.

"Keep Anabelle away from him. You can't trust a witch, boy." Sue held out a roll of duct tape. "Bind her hands so we can deal with Markus."

The big man grabbed my shoulder and whipped me around. "Hands out, darlin'."

I held my hands compliantly in position as he taped my wrists together. "What are you planning on doing to us?" I figured I needed to keep them talking to gain time. I didn't think they'd let us ride off into the sunset.

Markus' eyes darted to Sue. "What are you doing here?"

"What do you think, hun?" Sue purred. "Give him the papers and a pen, Gen. We need signatures and then we're done."

"Wait a minute, Sue," Gen said, placing papers on the table. "Let him sign the marriage papers first. I promise I will sell the land to you."

Sue laughed raucously. "What a joke you are. You had your chance and looked what happened. The boy was tripping in a K-hole. Alcohol and drugs. He's lucky to be alive."

Shotgun Sue licked her lips, staring at Markus. "I shouldn't have introduced you to Gen or Anabelle," she said softly. "We could have been great together if you had given me half the attention you gave those two. And rich beyond your dreams. Unfortunately, that's no longer the plan. There are hungry gators out here by the river, you know. A person has to watch his step."

Markus' eyes riveted to Genevieve. "I thought we were friends."

"More than that. Lovers, remember? And more recently," she flashed her diamond, "engaged. Sue said if I didn't get you to sell the property, I'd be in Lake Pontchatrain, a cement block chained to my leg." She smiled surreptitiously. "I came up with a plan B that would benefit us."

"Married, you get half my estate," Markus said thoughtfully.

Gen smiled wistfully. "Yes, darlin'. Plan B works. The property is worth a pretty penny even if we split it—two ways."

Sue plopped down on a chair. "Your plan B is cancelled, Gen."

"Why do you need my property, Sue?" Markus said.

"Simple, my innocent hunk," Sue said. "I am Tyron Industries. I'll be livin' in high cotton with a new refinery located on this land. Now, hand him those papers to sign, Gen."

Markus flashed a smile. "What's my incentive, Suzy Q?"

"I'd love to take you up to the third floor and try out the Sealy but I think we need to finish up here." She flicked her chin to the big man. "Ben has an itch to eliminate problems, don't you, darlin'?" She handed the pen to Markus. "Sign where the stickies are."

Markus stared at Sue a moment and said, "I'll let you buy the estate for five and a half million."

Ben laughed. "What a hoot. Your pretty boy wants to make a deal. I say we off him now. We forge the signatures and dump these airheads in the Mississippi."

"Don't you think the police would find our bodies suspicious? Markus sells you the land and then he's dead?" I gazed at him pointedly.

Ben guffawed. "So Canadian. Reality check. Bodies turn up in the river out here twenty-four seven. And girl, in Louisiana we mind our own business. I've seen curious police end up as a gator snacks."

"See? Makes perfect sense, Anabelle," Sue added.

"Wait! The sale has to be completely aboveboard," Genevieve said. "Markus has to read the papers first," She snatched up the papers, holding them close to her chest. "I don't want to lose my license."

"You hear her, Sue? That gal's two sandwiches short of a picnic." Ben shook his head. "I say we let her live. She can witness these two lovebirds sitting by the river drinking champagne, celebrating the sale. When a gator drags one in, the other one tries to help, and bingo!"

"Makes sense, Ben. She'll do what I say or bye-bye Gen." Sue took off her helmet and ran her fingers through her curls. "Helmets are so bad on the hair, aren't they?" She poked a finger into Genevieve's thick long auburn waves. "Bet you had extensions sewn in at that wig shop on Decatur, didn't you? I hear they've made specialty wigs for Dolly Parton." She snarled, "Now, wise up and hand over the papers, Genevieve, or I'll kill you and put you in the river with them."

Markus held his hand. "Take it easy, ladies. I'll sign." He started to write and then stopped. Tossing the pen on the patio table, he said, "Pen doesn't work."

This was my chance. I needed to keep these scumbags distracted to turn the tables on them.

I glared at Ben. "It was you who threw Jacqui down the stairs at the Hotel Memoire, wasn't it? I recognize you from the elevator. What did you hope to gain from killing Jacqui?"

Sue laughed derisively. "Absolutely nothing, girl. Ben's a fool." She shook her head. "This big idiot thought Jacqui was you,

Anabelle. You see, she left her Goth makeup and black wig at home when she came to read your cards. Ben can't tell one blonde from the next. Sees tatas and gets his head up his ass."

Ben scuffled his feet and regarded his Glock. "Weren't that way at all."

Sue rolled her eyes. "It was, but here's a slice of irony for you. Jacqui told me she had a feeling about Tyron Industries being the cause of Markus' problem. That little gal actually had the sight."

"See, Sue, offin' little Jacqui was a good idea." Ben snickered. "This way she didn't have time to connect you to Tyron Industries."

I couldn't believe what I was hearing. These two were cold as ice. "Jacqui died?"

"Hospital says her brain is swollen," Sue said, smiling contentedly. "I was worried she'd give away our gig but she didn't know how much power I had at Tyron. Time was running out. Markus ditched Gen and was looking forward to a future with you. I had to put a stop to that."

"So you sent those tools to work me over."

"Work you over?" Shotgun Sue grinned widely. "You were meant to die."

"And now?"

"Why do ya think we's here for, bubble brain?" Ben clicked his metal lighter and lit a cigarette. He drew in deeply and let the smoke out slowly.

I was fuming mad. First chance I got, I'd punch that punk in the throat.

Fingers tapping on the armrest, Gen hissed, "Put that cig out, Ben." When he didn't move, she snarled, "Now!"

Sue chortled. She patted Genevieve's bouncy curls as she would a dog. "Can you believe this gal?"

The duct tape escape trick would work. I pushed my wrists into position. "Wait a minute, Sue. Why the video camera?"

Sue curled her lips downwards. "It's always a pleasure to see Markus so perfectly ripped, but no, Anabelle, what I saw confirmed Markus was a dirty paparazzi working on a smear campaign against Tyron Industries. His story was going to the Times-Picayune." Sue turned to Markus. "You wanted to destroy my company's reputation."

Markus' jaw clenched. "Toxic chemicals killed my father and others. He might have been scum but he was the only father I had."

Gen gazed at Markus, a dreamy look in her dark eyes. "Bet Markus sizzles on that video."

Sue slapped Gen across the cheek. "Shut up!"

"How dare you!" Gen grabbed her purse and stood. "I've had just about enough. I'm leaving."

"Sit down." Sue jerked her chin at Ben who shoved the realtor back in the chair with one huge hand. "We need a pen."

"No worries." Markus tugged out a silver pen from his jean pocket. Swiveling around to the bearded man, he aimed the tip of the pen at Ben. Gray spray hit Ben's face. As the chemical ate into his eyes he lurched forward, groaning.

Thrusting myself forward, in magician's escape mode, I tore open the duct tape and swung into action. A two-handed-heal strike brought Gen into Sue. Both women fell on the floor in a messy heap of arms and legs. Genevieve yelped, but even with her in my path, I managed an awkward kick to Sue's hand. The shotgun trigger released a deafening blast. A scream sounded from within the bushes.

Sue's jaw dropped. She struggled to regain control of her weapon. With another kick I knocked the shotgun away.

Out of the corner of my eye I saw Markus give Ben a right cross to the chest and a left to the jaw.

In a crouch Sue stepped towards the shotgun. Lunging forward, I grabbed a handful of red hair, brought her in close, and kicked out at her knee. She yelped, but was hell-bent on retrieving the shotgun. A big woman like Sue has a weight advantage. Luckily, she was hurting.

Sue stumbled a moment trying to regain her balance before barreling forward. I managed to grab her arm, placed my leg between hers, and brought her down like a sack of potatoes.

"Damn you, Anabelle!" Sue shouted from the wooden floor of the veranda. "Ben, get the gun!"

But Ben was out of commission.

I didn't feel any remorse as I stabbed the heel of my Valentino into Shotgun Sue's temple. Slumping down, eyes rolling back, she joined Ben in a slumberfest. I breathed a sigh of relief and surveyed the scene.

What the heck? Gen had grabbed her cell from her bag and was texting as Sandie came up the path carrying a shovel and the wooden treasure box.

"Hey, guys!" Sandie's platinum blonde hair shone angelically in the moonlight. She looked puzzled when she saw Sue unconscious on the veranda. "What's up? Why are they all here?"

Before I could reply, a burly guy charged out from behind the trees and grabbed Sandie. Pulling her close to his chest, his arm around her waist, he shoved her forward. "This is what's up, fat ass. You feel my Smith and Wesson?"

Sandie glanced over her shoulder. "You're one to talk, nigga' Santa."

It suddenly dawned on me who the café au lait guy was. He was the potato man from the Hotel Belfoire on Bourbon. I'd pegged him then as a man with a mean streak. Holding my palm out in a stop gesture, I said steadily, "Chuckie, what do you want?"

"You have to ask?" He shook his head. "Simple. I want the Lafitte treasure this cracker dug up."

"Hey, finders keepers," Sandie said smoothly, and then added hastily, "Of course you get first dibs, Anabelle, being as the directions came from your diary."

Chuckie growled, "Shaddup! The treasure is mine, bitch. My great great great granddaddy was Jean Lafitte."

Sandie let loose a snort. "That guy was white, you dickhead."

Sue rolled over on the veranda floor. I kicked her head. She flopped back, face down.

"Where did that duct tape go?" Markus asked, ignoring Chuckie. "Gen?"

Sitting motionless as a defunct robot, Genevieve Severe jump-started with the smooth cadence of Markus' voice. "It dropped off the deck, but as a matter of fact, I have a roll in my bag. Never know when it might be needed." She reached into the taupe leather Michael Kors satchel on the table. "Are we bindin' Shotgun and her goon?"

"Wait a minute!" Chuckie shouted. "I'm the one with the gun. I decide what to do."

Gen stared up from winding the duct tape around Sue's wrist. "Can I finish this?"

Chuckie frowned and spoke to Markus. "That gal on the deck

dangerous?"

"She sure is." Markus grinned. "And her associate."

"Okay, go ahead, ma'am. Tape them tight."

Chuckie poked Sandie in the back with the gun. "Open the treasure box."

"It's too awkward to get a good grip." Sandie moved forward. "Can't hold everything at once." She jerked about and shoved the box at Chuckie's chest. "You do it."

While he struggled to hold the gun and the box, Sandie swung her shovel down on the bartender's shoulder.

As Chuckie tried to regain his balance, the treasure box fell on the grass. Before he could snatch it up, Sandie brought the shovel down on Chuckie's back. He grunted and sank to the ground still holding onto the revolver.

A police siren sounded and a black and white tore up the driveway in a cloud of dust. Deputy Malone stepped out the driver's side waving a gun in the air. Another cop in uniform got out of the passenger side.

The Deputy caught sight of Chuckie. "Drop yer weapon, boy! What's goin' on here? You all right, Miss Gen?"

Before anyone could answer we heard a load groan and a skinny man staggered out from the bushes, took a few steps, and dropped in his tracks.

"It's Doobs," Chuckie sputtered, dropping his revolver. "He's hurt. Call an ambulance! He's bleedin' bad."

Genevieve got on her iPhone and started speed-dialing.

"Give me your shirt," I said to the bartender.

"What for?"

I glared at him. "He'll bleed out if I don't wrap it."

Chuckie reluctantly shook himself out of the denim shirt he wore over his black muscle shirt. After I rolled it up, I tied it around Doobs' injured leg and tightened the material.

"He'll be okay, won't he?" He looked at the deputy. "I didn't do nothing wrong. Only came to get my treasure. My great great grand-pappy was Lafitte's baby." Chuckie picked up the box from the ground. "This here is mine."

"No, it's not," Gen said. "Lafitte sold his part of the property to a pirate named Ducoeur. This man's descendents married into the Cadeaux family and now it's Markus Cadeaux's estate,"

Genevieve explained to Deputy Malone. "He owns the land and any treasure buried here." She waved her hand in a queenly manner at Sue and Ben stirring on the veranda. "That woman and her goon threatened Markus and me. They were about to kill us." Genvieve's mouth curled with displeasure. "Arrest them."

***

Sunlight streamed in through the balcony doors filling the master bedroom with a golden hue. I wasn't really sure if I could pull this off. I repeated the spell and said, "I summon you."

Abruptly, the balcony door flew open and a warm balmy breeze ruffled the curtains.

His hair tousled, devastatingly handsome Alain Ducoeur stepped into the room. He was one delicious pirate in an open white shirt, breeches and high black boots. "Cher," he said, his voice husky. His arms enveloped me and he stooped to kiss me but I put my hand out to stop him.

"It's not me you love, Alain. You love Belle."

"She doesn't want me."

"You tried to save her, didn't you?"

"When the fire started I untied her but I was drowsy from the drugs in the wine and the smoke—" Alain Ducoeur frowned.

"Belle was tied up? Who did that, Rene?"

"No. I did."

"Huh?"

He grinned. "Well, she liked it sometimes."

"Oh-hh."

"Belle was very amorous when I tied her up. I didn't hurt her, Anabelle. Believe me."

I felt bad for him. "I don't blame you. Rene sent me the dream to come back and set things right."

"I was cruel to that stupid old man."

"Rene hated you."

Alain Ducoeur laughed. "Can't help it if I won the game, can I? Rene treated Belle like dirt. She was way too precious for a degenerate like Rene. It wasn't difficult to seduce her."

"You did that?" I frowned. "I guess I should have known. Men had no respect for women then, did they?"

"Wish I could contradict you, but yes, men were men." Alain

214

Ducoeur nodded reflectively. "But I loved Belle. I should have stolen her away. We were good as lovers."

"And you'd have married her?"

"I'm a pirate, remember?"

"Rene wanted justice."

"Don't feel bad for him. He made his own bed. Besides he had Robert, who despite his attraction to Blade, managed to have a son of his own to continue the Renard lineage."

And here I'd thought the guy was gay. "Really? With whom?"

"The missing baby Janelle ranted about was Robert's. He took the child away at birth. He didn't trust a drug addict to raise the heir."

"Then why did Robert want Belle dead?"

"He thought that Belle's baby was Rene's. He didn't want another heir to what was left of Rene's investments."

"And Belle's baby was?"

"Ours." Alain Ducoeur put his arms around me. "Can't we be together?" His gaze held such a depth of passion I wanted to say yes.

I shook my head. "I'm not the one for you."

His eyes looked so sad, I added, "Don't you see? You need to go to the otherside to be with her. That's one of the reasons I came here. Belle waits for you. There is no reason for you to stay here any longer."

"But there is. I must warn you now that you've found it." His eyes flicked to the velvet bag on the bedside table.

"The necklace was in the box."

He nodded. "There's a reason it was buried. Belle found out its history after she wore it, but by then it was too late. The necklace is cursed. It once belonged to a Moroccan prince who died horribly before it became a Lalaurie heirloom. The Lalaurie family perished in a fire set by the slaves in Santo Domingo. Only the daughter escaped. When she arrived in New O'leans hatred consumed her— the house servants were killed and tortured. Lafitte won it in a card game and gave it to Delpine but when he lost he paid me with the necklace. It was apparent that we all suffered from contact with its negative energy. Be careful not to touch it or you will be cursed and end up in limbo like the rest of us."

I looked down at the bag and when I gazed up Alain Ducoeur

appeared to have disappeared. "Alain?" I said quietly.

"Ss-hh!" he whispered. "She's coming."

A rush of frigid air filled the room. From a white haze, Delphine, clad in a long black gown, stepped forward, her eyes flashing dangerously. In her hand she held a knife. She closed in on me, the knife pointing at my chest. "The pirates taught us how to kill, remember? Hand over the necklace."

Conscious of Alain's warning, I hesitated.

"Get it!" Delphine hissed, bringing the knife to my neck.

"Drop it, wench!" Alain Ducoeur said. Stepping out from behind the closet door he pulled Delphine's arm behind her back, locking it in.

Delphine flinched, as Ducoeur tightened his arm hold. "You're hurting me!"

"Now," Ducoeur growled dangerously.

When the knife clanged to the floor, Ducoeur released Delphine.

"Why do you want the necklace so badly?" I asked her.

"Have you not seen it? It's magnificent, a sapphire pendant surrounded by diamonds. Lafitte took the necklace from me and gambled it in another round of bourré, losing it to Ducoeur. He gave it to Belle. That stupid girl refused to wear it so he buried it in the treasure box hoping she would change her mind one day. She knew it was precious to me but she wouldn't return it."

My eyes flicked to the bag on the table. Delphine caught the tell and snatched up the bag.

"Ah-ha! It's the necklace, isn't it? " She held it away as if daring me to take it back.

"Let her have it." Ducoeur said quietly. "It's perfect for her. Put it on, Delphine."

Delphine beamed with delight when she saw the sparkling jewelry. "Difficult to do up. Won't you help me?" she asked me, fumbling with the clasp.

Alain Ducoeur put out a warning hand as I stepped closer. "I will help her. I'm dead, remember? I'm safe." he said, fastening the clasp.

Delphine held her head high, the sapphire necklace surrounded by diamonds resting in the hollow of her neck. "A perfect piece."

"It is yours now. Take it and go," I said, repelled by the darkness of the jewelry.

"Funny how Belle didn't want my jewels either, but she took Ducoeur. He was mine once, Anabelle." Delphine stroked the sapphire sensuously, eyeing Ducoeur all the while. "He is fine but Lafitte was my soulmate."

"You can look for him. Perhaps, he will welcome you," I shrugged, "or not."

"Belle was just like you. Full of herself. At least I had a son with my lover."

"And that son had a descendent who was arrested for attempted murder."

Delphine chuckled. "I guess you didn't hear what happened?"

"What?"

"They dropped the charges. Apparently some gris-gris turned up on the deputy's desk."

"He's your blood relative, alright. Takes after you, Delphine. Plain evil," I said. "I wouldn't be surprised if he attacked that pretty bartender. Once she recovers he will be arrested."

Delphine laughed. "You mean, if she recovers."

Ducoeur took Delphine by the shoulders. "Tell me what drug you put in the wine. You owe me that much," he said, his jaw clenched.

"I don't owe you anything after you left me for Belle. But believe me, I did not poison your wine." Delphine stroked Alain Ducoeur's cheek. "And it was Blade Ryan who burned your ship."

Ducoeur clenched his jaw. "I will kill him for what he did to us."

Delphine held up her hand. "No need. Your boys did it for you. Blade broke the pirate code when he set your ship aflame."

"Worthless coward. Couldn't fight like a man," Ducoeur growled. "I ache for Belle and what we had."

"Will you try to find her?" I asked.

"You know the answer to that, cher." Smiling slightly, Ducoeur took my hand and kissed my wrist.

I felt sad seeing Alain Ducoeur's image slowly fade to orange. As a bright light appeared, the orange vapor streamed into a white tunnel. He was gone. Out of my life forever.

When I heard a knock on the outside door, I raced to open it. Markus entered with Philippe on his heels.

Delphine pointed an accusing finger at the men. "To the end these two betrayed me for Belle."

"My bet is *you* killed Belle," Markus growled.

"No." Delphine shook her head. "It was Blade Ryan. He did whatever Robert wanted. Enraged that his pappy gambled and lost the restaurant he told Ryan to set the boat on fire."

"And you're innocent?" I asked. "You hated Belle for taking Ducoeur and Lafitte as lovers. Perhaps you locked the door on the outside?"

"I didn't cause their death. I only served the drinks. That's all." Delphine's eyes flicked to the Voodoo priest. "Tell her the truth."

Philippe stared into the distance. "Lafitte wanted to take Belle to his ship. If she was drugged she couldn't resist."

"Why didn't he help Belle when the boat was on fire?" I said sharply, wondering what sort of sicko would drug a woman to have her.

Philippe sighed. "The fire spread rapidly. He couldn't get to Belle in time to save her."

"Forget Belle." Delphine's eyes shot daggers. "She had everything. I was Lafitte's abused plaything. Lafitte never wanted me or his child."

"Your boy went on to marry, have children and so forth, before everything went sideways with that scumbag, Chuckie," Markus said.

"The poor boy is misguided."

"That's putting it lightly," I said. "What happened to Lafitte?"

"When he gambled away my necklace," she said, fingering the chain, "I betrayed him to the authorities. He escaped New O'leans with his new mistress." She shot a look of disgust at Philippe and at me. "For that, y'all had the nightmares. Belle had no right to the necklace or my man." Her dark eyes flicked to me. "Did you keep the treasure?"

"There was nothing inside except the necklace. I gave the box to Sandie. She should be able to get something for an antique box, but be content, you have what you wanted, after all. Now you can go to the otherside."

"I will go but not because of your say-so. I didn't like you then, and I don't like you now, but it is getting to be a bore living in this hotel." She stroked the sapphires gently.

I raised my arms. "Enter the light, Delphine."

A radiant glowing beam, bright as the sun, appeared behind the spirit woman. She turned, her face intense. With two long strides she floated up towards the light where her hazy figure slowly vanished into a haze.

"The sapphires are cursed," I said to the men. "She got what she deserved."

"And will I get what I deserve?" Markus said in a husky voice.

"Depends," I said, asking a question with my eyes.

"I was never engaged to Gen. I did have a few nights with her but," he shrugged, "it meant nothing."

"What about the ring?"

Markus shrugged. "It was a scam to get you away from me. The only woman in my life is you," he said, his green eyes looking deep into my being until I felt heat surge straight to my core.

I smiled slowly and took his hand. "Mm-mm," I purred.

"And what about me, Anabelle?" Philippe interrupted abruptly.

"You tried to con me with that gris-gris and Sazerac. If I had listened to you, Markus would have gotten worse, not better.

"I thought I'd have a better chance with you if," he gestured at Markus, "he was gone. Sorry, man."

"Was the gris-gris really from Madame Laveau?"

Philippe shook his head. "It's mine, always in my pocket, just in case. But, none the less, I have genuine feelings for you. I would like a chance to treat you like a queen."

His full lips curled up at the corners. "Tell me, darlin', what do I deserve?"

"Why Doctor, you deserve," I winked, "the best I have to offer— a bowl of my very own authentic New O'leans oyster gumbo, guaranteed to recharge your mojo."

AnastasiaAmor.com

Anastasia.Amor@hotmail.com

http://anastasiaamor1.blogspot.ca

ACKNOWLEDGEMENTS

Thank you to the people of New Orleans who shared their stories in the writing of this book. I am also grateful to Jane for her input and Kristen for her portrait photo. Special thanks to Bruce for his edits.